4 + 9/

THE RAKE

Elizabeth was comfortable with Somers now. She was sure she had tamed his passion to possess her. So sure that she felt free to joke with him.

"I really do not believe your reputation," she declared. "Here I am with the premier rake in the realm, and he has not made an improper advance toward me."

"Elizabeth," he breathed softly, edging closer to her.

The touch of his lips was hesitant at first and she did not flinch, as she had before. She knew him now, trusted him. And truly, she was curious how a man reputed to be a hardened rake would kiss.

Elizabeth was about to find out—more than she cared to know . . .

MELINDA McRAE holds a master's degree in European history and takes great delight in researching obscure details of the Regency period. She lives in Seattle, Washington with her husband and daughter.

SIGNET REGENCY ROMANCE
COMING IN MAY 1991

Sandra Heath
Lord Buckingham's Bride

Irene Saunders
The Dowager's Dilemma

Dawn Lindsey
Devil's Lady

THE DUKE'S DAUGHTER

Melinda McRae

A SIGNET BOOK

SIGNET
Published by the Penguin Group
Penguin Books USA Inc., 375 Hudson Street,
New York, New York 100014, U.S.A.
Penguin Books Ltd, 27 Wrights Lane,
London W8 5TZ, England
Penguin Books Australia Ltd, Ringwood,
Victoria, Australia
Penguin Books Canada Ltd, 2801 John Street,
Markham, Ontario, Canada L3R 1B4
Penguin Books (N.Z.) Ltd, 182-190 Wairau Road,
Auckland 10, New Zealand

Penguin Books Ltd, Registered Offices:
Harmondsworth, Middlesex, England

First published by Signet, an imprint of New American Library, a division of
Penguin Books USA Inc.

First Printing, April, 1991
10 9 8 7 6 5 4 3 2 1

To Megan, Liz, Linda, Jena,
Sharon and Elizabeth . . .
for all those Thursday nights

1

"Hell and blast."

Somerset Graham could be forgiven his angry outburst, for even his thick, many-caped greatcoat proved ineffectual against the deepening cold of the late March afternoon. The tall beaver hat, crammed low over his ears in a most unfashionable manner, did little to keep the wind-whipped snow out of his face. And the elegant kid driving gloves, their leather stained dark with moisture, provided no comfort at all to his numbed fingers.

Damp and chilled to the marrow, Somers railed at the folly of having set out on this trip, against all advice, in order to merely avoid one more night at what was now looking more and more like one of the most pleasant inns he had ever graced.

It had been an even more stupid folly to send his groom on ahead with the traveling coach and luggage. Somers cursed himself seven times over for insisting on this mad plan of tooling his own curricle down to Knowlton's estate. And he cursed Knowlton for the damned fool idea of holding a house party in the middle of the worst winter storm of the season.

Of course, it had not looked so dismal when Somers had started out in the morning. The sky was gray and leaden, but with no imminent sign of snow. In fact, if the lead horse had not cast a shoe all those miles back, Somers would have been well past this spot when that blasted white stuff began drifting out of the sky. But by the time he had gingerly walked his team to the nearest town, hunted out the blacksmith, and had the horse reshod, several precious hours were lost. He was only a few miles out of town when the first flakes came floating down.

Somers, in his confidence, decided it was only a minor flurry that would ease up after the next bend in the road. But bends came and went and the snow had not ceased. Now it was fast coming on to dark and he was out here in the middle of some lonely country lane that was rapidly disappearing from sight. Thank God for the local practice of fencing and hedging, for if it was not for those dark barriers on either side of the road, he would long since have lost his way. As it was, with his impatient team held to a snail's pace, he prayed he was nearing the next quaint hamlet.

Judging he had traveled the prescribed miles to the upcoming village and looking forward to any form of dry shelter, Somers allowed his restive team to set a livelier pace. Cold, wet, and miserable, he wanted nothing more than to sit in front of a roaring fire with a good glass of brandy. He snorted derisively, thinking of the foul brew he would probably be offered at whatever inn served this godforsaken village of Chedford.

With the snow limiting his vision on a dark and unknown road, Somers should have known he invited trouble. But when he finally realized just how sharply the road curved and at what pace the team was taking it, the curricle was already sliding sideways on the slippery surface.

"Damn!" He braced himself for the inevitable jolt of the curricle crashing against the roadside hedge.

But the drifting snow had hidden the ditch running alongside the hedge. The carriage tilted wildly as it tipped into the trench, and the sickening loud crack told Somers he had met disaster.

In words that would have made a grizzled sailor proud, he clambered from the drunkenly leaning vehicle and walked around to survey the damage. As he had thought, the wheel was broken. He was in a fine spot now: carriage damaged, snow coming down as if it intended to obliterate the earth, and his only companions were two horses that looked about as pleased as he at the situation.

He extricated his light portmanteau from the boot, examining it doubtfully as he tried to imagine how to manage it and two restive carriage horses for a journey of indeterminate length. At last Somers admitted defeat. He hastily pulled a shirt from the bag, cramming it into his coat pocket in a manner that would make his valet cringe, and replaced the bag in the boot.

Certainly some  rieve the carriage in the mo rom that blasted village, bu too far to suit him. With lengthy process of unharne ces. He clumsily mounted the other by the rein, and headed once again in the direction of Chedford. Knowlton better have planned one hell of a house party to make up for this.

Elizabeth Granford set down her book with a sigh of disgust. She had been reading the same page for an interminable time. Shivering involuntarily as a gust of wind whistled about the eaves, she drew her warm woolen shawl closer. She cast a grateful glance at the roaring fire that bathed the small parlor in its welcome heat, and sought to curb her sense of restlessness and disquiet. It is only another winter storm, she chided herself. Even the most ferocious wind remained ineffectual against the cottage's thick walls of Cotswold stone. There was nothing to fear from the elements.

She briefly looked to the other occupants of the room. Emily Camberly sat across from her, ensconced in a comfortable chair, her fingers busy as her knitting needles clattered away in a rhythmical pattern. Sally fidgeted at a table near the fading light from the window, laboriously copying a passage from the book before her. Her stained and blotted paper bespoke of the arduousness of the task. Neither woman seemed bothered by the storm that raged outside.

Elizabeth sighed and put a marker in her book. There was no point in continuing that struggle. When there was little else to do but read, that once-longed-for pleasure began to take on the boring sameness of all the other everyday aspects of life. She rose from her chair and paced to the window, peeking out into the gray light. She uttered a small expression of dismay at the sight.

"The weather has turned on us again."

The other two women raised their hands, as if this remark was a signal to abandon their labors. Each looked out the window at the swirling white flakes.

"I said it would snow afore the day was out," Emily announced, pleased that her prophecy had been correct.

"Shall I get some more wood, Miss Lizzie?" the girl at the table asked eagerly. It was clear she found the chilling cold an infinitely more pleasing prospect than the paper before her.

Elizabeth peered over Sally's shoulder, examining her work with a critical eye.

"I do see some improvement, Sally," she said, choosing to ignore the large black blots that resembled some hideous bugs marching across the paper. "However, I should like you to finish this passage. I shall gather wood this time."

So deciding, Elizabeth left the cozy parlor for the cooler air of the entry hall. There she stepped out of her fashionable house slippers and pulled on a more serviceable pair of wool socks and heavy country boots. Wrapping herself in a thick, warm cloak, she donned a floppy but practical hat and gloves before venturing out into the cold.

Several trips later, the precious armloads of wood deposited in the box near the kitchen stove, Elizabeth hung her damp garments carefully on the wall hooks beside the door. Stamping the last bit of clinging snow from her boots, she untied the laces and gingerly stepped out of them, seeking to avoid any damp puddles on the floor. She donned her house shoes and reentered the warmth of the front parlor and gratefully took her place before the fire.

"I think we are in for a long one this time," she commented, holding her cold-reddened hands out of the fire's warmth. "If it does not let up within the hour, I think we should not plan on seeing Tommy Baker this evening. We can manage with the horses and a few more loads of wood will see us safely through the night."

Sally presented her handiwork with a self-conscious air to Elizabeth, who praised her greatly for her skill, tactfully pointed out a few minor errors, and said nothing at all about the buggy inkblots. Then she sent Sally into the kitchen to prepare tea.

As the afternoon wore on, the snow continued to fall in a determined fashion. The footsteps left by Elizabeth were long obliterated when the darkening gray shadows outside warned of night's imminent arrival.

"I do not like the looks of this," Emily clucked as she peered out into the growing darkness. "Snowing now for four hours without a sign of slackening. Mark my words, we are in for a lengthy storm. This is not the time to be stuck out here in the country, Elizabeth. We should be snug in town on a night like this."

"Oh, piffle," said Elizabeth. "Nothing could possibly be worse than that cold two years ago, and we survived it with nary a problem, did we not? This will probably be gone in the morning. These late-spring snows never last."

Her light words belied her concern, and with her memory firmly resting on that miserable winter of 1814, she and Sally carried out the necessary precautions in case that situation arose again. Countless loads of wood were brought into the house, to cut down on the number of trips that surely would have to be made on the morrow. The horses were fed and watered, their stalls heaped with straw for comfort and warmth, and the barn doors tightly latched to keep out the cold.

And with foresight gained during the last blizzard, Elizabeth strung a rope, purchased for this particular purpose, between the barn and the corner of the cottage, to guide the next person—probably herself—who would be checking on the animals in the morning. It was quite clear that Tommy Baker would not be here this day, or even the next, if the weather did not miraculously improve during the night. They would be on their own for a day or so.

Elizabeth took a last look around her at the darkening world before she stepped back into the house. She could barely make out the black line of the stone fence alongside the road. She remembered, briefly, how she had so loved winter days as a child, when there was sledding on the big hill, and ice skating on the pond when it was cold enough to freeze. And when the cold finally became too great, there was hot cocoa in the nursery, with baked apples and cinnamon sauce for a special treat. Elizabeth sighed softly, willing that brief memory to vanish. This was now, she reminded herself, and childhood was so very long ago.

Somers almost missed the cottage as he strained to discern the path of the road in the ever-darkening night. Glancing up to gather his bearings, he caught the faint glimmer of light peeping out from amid the cracks in the window shutters. This was not Chedford yet, he was certain, but it was habitation and at this moment he wanted nothing more than to be warm and dry. Just the thought of a roaring fire caused a deep shiver.

He guided his mounts toward the light, nearly crashing into the low stone fence that stood undistinguishable from the surrounding ground by its blanket of white. Cursing under his breath, Somers dismounted and floundered in the roadside drifts until he found the entry gate. Carefully tying his two animals, he wallowed along what he hoped was the correct path toward the door of the cottage, cringing for the finish on his boots with every step.

The three women looked up with a start at the loud and persistent summons coming from the front door.

"Who could that possibly be at this hour? And in this storm?" Emily gave a suspicious sniff.

Sally looked at Elizabeth for directions. She nodded and the girl moved to answer the door, returning a few moments later, a glint of excitement in her eyes.

"It's a gentleman, Miss Lizzie. Says his carriage smashed a wheel in the ditch. He's got his horses with him and wants to know if there is an inn nearby."

"He can find room at the Bull in town, I am sure," Emily offered.

"Nonsense! No one would ever find their way to town on a night like this. We could be sending the poor soul to his death. How does he appear, Sally?"

"Quite the swell. One of those fancy caped coats like Squire John's, and a big tall hat. Looks mighty respectable to me."

Elizabeth looked pensive for a moment, then nodded her head. "Show him in."

Somers was grateful to be ushered in out of the snow, where he had been impatiently waiting under the nonexistent protection of the eaves. The biting wind sliced through his heavy coat as if it were stitched of the finest lawn, and his fingers, encased in the thin driving gloves, felt like leaden lumps. He looked about him in grateful curiosity, wondering what manner of country rustics inhabited this isolated dwelling.

Three pairs of inquisitive eyes were all turned upon him as he stepped into the parlor, still garbed in his snow-covered coat.

The girl who had taken his hat was obviously the maid, but the other two women he could not place. He would have guessed mother and daughter, but the elder lady was not yet of an age for that.

"Excuse me, ladies. My carriage met with an accident down the road. Is there an inn nearby? I need stabling for my horses and a bed for myself. I was told this was the way to Chedford. Is it far?"

"Much too far on a night like this," Elizabeth said, brushing back her brief flicker of dismay. This was no common traveler. His arrogant stance, the haughty expression in his cool blue eyes as he surveyed the room, told much of his place in society. Why, of all cottages, had he found hers?

"We can accommodate your horses in our stable, if they do not mind close quarters," she offered. "I am afraid we cannot provide you with much more, but you shall at least be warm and dry."

At this moment, Somers would readily have agreed to sleep in the barn. But how much more pleasant to stay in the house with this exquisite creature dressed in green. Perhaps this storm was not such a disaster, after all. With an appraising look, he surveyed her shapely form with frank admiration. He ignored the severe lines of her plainly arranged hair and concentrated instead on her liquid brown eyes, framed in thick, dark lashes. "I am most grateful for your offer."

"Sally, would you show Mr. ah . . . ?"

"Wentworth," he hastily interjected, noting how the flickering firelight brought out the red-gold highlights in her dark hair.

"Mr. Wentworth to the stables. There is the extra stall and one of our horses can be placed in the aisle if his will do better enclosed. Mind you, keep near the rope."

Sally bobbed a little curtsy, exhibiting an eagerness to show off her best manners to this elegant man.

Emily turned to Elizabeth when the others had stepped out into the storm. "Have you lost your wits? What maggot has gotten into your brain?"

Elizabeth smiled pensively. "I am convinced one lone man, half-frozen with cold, cannot bring harm to three women, Emily. Do not be silly. We shall shelter him here for the night, and he can make his way to town in the morning. Surely, in the name of Christian charity, we cannot do else.''

Her companion scowled. ''What makes you so sure he is safe?''

''Emily, do not tell me you think he is a highwayman?'' Elizabeth's laugh was light and musical. ''I highly doubt he is even a mister, if you must know. With that polite arrogance? That air of gentle condescension? The unfortunate lord is reduced to staying with some poor country family and he will endure the indignity, for it is a matter of survival. But such a dreadful comedown for a man who is used to fine linen sheets, I am certain.''

''Do you know him?''

''No. But I knew many like him.''

Sally and Somers returned to the house in a short time. While the girl prepared him a repast from the remainders of that evening's dinner, he tried to ascertain how long he would be marooned in this spot.

''I shall need to get my wheel fixed first thing in the morning,'' he began hopefully.

''I shall need to get my wheel fixed first thing in the morning,'' he began hopefully.

''Chedford is less than two miles off,'' Elizabeth replied. ''We have a farm lad who comes in the morning who can make the arrangements—if he is here at all. The snow is rather deep, I fear, if it is drifting across the road as you say. It may be a day or so before the roads are clear.''

Somers forced his lips into a weak smile. He did not relish the thought of his new curricle sitting for untold days under a damaging mantle of snow. Perhaps these ladies were a trifle fainthearted; things would be better in the morning. These spring snows did not linger long.

''Excuse me,'' Somers said, his face a bland mask. ''You have not introduced yourselves. Am I privileged to know who my hostesses are?''

''My pardon.'' Elizabeth hesitated for a fraction of a second. ''You have met Sally. This is Miss Camberly and you may call me Miss Elizabeth.''

She noted the quick gleam of interest in his blue eyes and

berated herself for making such a foolish mistake. No lady gave her first name to a total stranger.

While he ate the simple meal Sally set before him, Somers carefully scanned the room. There were no signs of a male presence; he guessed the three women were the sum total of the occupants. And it was very obvious who ran the household—"Miss Lizzie" was mistress here. Even the elder woman looked to her for guidance. Why did she insist on just plain Elizabeth? Highly unusual.

There was an awkward silence in the room while all parties endeavored not to stare at one another. As Somers mused about the ladies, Emily made a semblance of returning attention to her knitting while Elizabeth stared blankly at the same page in her book.

Elizabeth remained wary about her unexpected guest. He looked to be a man who was comfortably at home in the drawing rooms of the *beau monde*. Dismay and curiosity warred within her. She held no high opinion of the male species of aristocrat, but the opportunity for examining a well-to-pass London male intrigued her. His skillfully tailored chocolate-colored coat fit snugly across his broad shoulders, and his snow splattered Hessians had once been polished to a high gloss, but there was little sign of the dandy in him. The dark blond hair and side whiskers were cut along conservative lines, neither too long nor too short. Subdued elegance, she thought. Monied elegance.

Yet his very presence made her uneasy. He represented a world that she viewed with alternating hatred and longing. She had enjoyed the isolation of the Cotswolds precisely because this type of man did not often make an appearance. So, why, when one did, had it been on her doorstep?

"That was a very nice meal, Sally," Somers said politely as she cleared his dishes away. He was amused to see how his casual compliment set her all atwitter.

"I am afraid we do not keep town hours here in the country," Elizabeth announced, setting aside her unread book. "You may stay awake, if you wish, but the rest of the household will be retiring."

"Where am I to sleep?" he asked with a trace of suspicion.

"Unfortunately, there is only the sofa here in the parlor."

"You intend for me to sleep on the sofa?" He could not hide the tone of incredulity in his voice.

"Would you have me turn Sally out of her bed?" Elizabeth did not hide the faint scorn in her voice. "I am afraid it is either the sofa or the stable, sir. There are extra rooms upstairs, but they are neither warmed nor furnished. On such a cold night, I think the fire would be most welcome. Surely you can endure the hardship for an evening?"

There was a veiled challenge in her words that he did not miss.

"I shall find the sofa quite acceptable," he retorted.

She gave him a cool smile. "Excellent. Sally will gather up enough blankets to make it a tolerable bed, and the fire will certainly keep you warm. Until morning, then."

As if on cue, she and Emily rose and crossed the room.

The two women exited into the hall and he could hear their gentle treds on the stairs. Somers was disappointed there would be no opportunity of furthering his acquaintance with Miss Lizzie this evening. He had half-envisoned a cozy chat in front of the fireplace, with senses warmed and lulled by brandy or wine. A little light flirtation . . . and perhaps something more. With a regretful sigh, he turned to the pile of blankets on the sofa. It was all a piece of this disastrous trip. Knowlton owed him.

Somers entertained even less charitable thoughts in the morning, when the noises of Sally stoking the fire and the kitchen stove woke him from his slumber. His muscles were stiff and sore from the exertions of the previous day and from lying on the blasted sofa. He had discovered, to his dismay, that the sofa was not of a length to accommodate his stretched-out frame, and his cramped position had made sleep difficult. Rubbing the annoying crick in his neck, he swore he hadn't slept more than five minutes during the night.

"There is some water in the kitchen if you would like to make yourself presentable before the ladies come down," Sally told him as he began to roll up his makeshift bed.

That would be a monumental task, Somers thought as he surveyed his rumpled clothing with undisguised dismay. He did have the change of shirt he had stuffed in his coat pocket, but it might be wise to hold that garment in reserve until he knew how long he would be separated from his baggage. He followed Sally into the kitchen.

A hot cup of tea slightly restored his spirits. But they sank to an even lower level once he looked out the window. The snow had continued through the night and still gave no sign of easing. He was well and truly stranded.

2

Elizabeth surveyed the white scene outside her window with dismay. She had not turned Mr. Wentworth away last night, when he could easily have become lost and died in the storm. It was equally apparent he would not be able to continue his journey today, and she resented the strain of hosting a stranger—a stranger who was obviously part of the *beau monde*.

She had feared, one day, she would meet such a one as Wentworth again. But after six long years, Elizabeth began to believe Chedford was so far removed from that world to make her apprehensions groundless. Now an unexpected spring snow had blown in, bringing with it an equally unexpected Mr. Wentworth. Elizabeth frowned. That was a bouncer if there ever was one. The man had been born to a title, she was certain. It was obvious in his every utterance.

Turning away from her window, Elizabeth shrugged. Even if he were a titled nobleman, he did not pose a threat to her. She did not know him, and he could have no idea of her identity. The snow would melt soon and he would be gone, never to return. She must keep that firmly in mind.

The man occupying her thoughts was already in the dining room when Elizabeth entered. "I trust you slept well?" she inquired when she stepped into the small room across the hall from the parlor.

"I think that would be a slight exaggeration," he replied in a deliberately offhand manner. She knew very well he had spent a wretched night on that miserably short sofa.

Elizabeth ignored his sarcasm and took her place at the table.

18

He had already eaten, she noticed, his cutlery placed neatly across his crumb-strewn plate. She watched as he noiselessly swirled a spoon in his tea, concentrating as if it were the most important task in the world.

"The storm did not abate during the night." An inane remark, but Elizabeth thought anything was better than this awkward silence.

"No, it did not." Here, in the brighter, harsher light of morning, she was even lovelier than she had appeared by the softer glow of the candles last evening. She was not in the first blush of youth—mid-twenties, he judged. And an obviously unattached female. Perhaps he could yet turn the day to his advantage.

"Sally makes such excellent muffins," Somers remarked with a pleasant smile as he watched Elizabeth reach toward the plate.

"Indeed, she does."

"She is rather young for a cook."

"Cooking is only one of her jobs," Elizabeth explained, smiling fondly as the girl walked in with a heaping platter of steaming ham. "And she is very good at it."

Sally dipped an appreciative curtsy, then nearly collided with the entering Emily.

"Good morning, Mr. Wentworth. I see you are still with us." Her tone was dismal, as if she were disappointed he had not disappeared like a bad dream during the night.

"Unfortunately, I seem to be at the mercy of your hospitality for another day, Miss Camberly," he retorted in a drawling tone.

"I am sure you will find our company decidedly flat," she continued. "We lead a very simple life, I assure you, and I fear you will become hopelessly bored."

"I could never be bored in the presence of three charming ladies," he replied, offering Elizabeth a flirtatious smile. The look she returned wiped the grin from his face.

The slight tremble in her hand distressed Elizabeth as she poured tea for herself and Emily. Why did this man disconcert her so? She had long ago perfected the art of masking her inner turmoil behind a serene exterior. That skill dared not fail her now.

Nibbling halfheartedly at her breakfast, Elizabeth stole

surreptitious glances at her guest, who was engaging Emily in desultory conversation. He looked much less the superior aristrocrat this morning, with the faint shadow of beard across his cheeks and chin. The poor man's valet would be horrified to see his master in such disorder, and she smothered a giggle at the thought.

Somers was well aware of Elizabeth's perusal but deliberately ignored her. He knew women found him attractive, and he had discovered that his feigned disinterest only sparked their attention. With the snow preventing his imminent departure, he could afford to wait.

Unnerved by her wayward thoughts, Elizabeth stood up quickly and made to move into the parlor. "We commonly have prayers after breakfast, Mr. Wentworth. Should you care to join us?" That would certainly erase those leering smiles from his face, she thought.

As Somers rose to his feet, he was filled with a momentary flash of apprehension. Had he fallen in with some Methodists? Or were they part of an even more radical sect? But in an instant he relaxed. This house showed no signs of the austerity common to those practitioners. They looked to be no more pious than his own mama, and he had survived that situation. He once again offered Elizabeth a lazy smile. "Why not?"

That, he decided later, was an easy question to answer. He had been correct in his estimation of the ladies' religious philosophies, for the short session was much like the ones he had reluctantly participated in all his life at his parents' home. But they had been markedly different in one respect, for the lessons at home were never read in a halting style by a young farm girl who was obviously still mastering the skill of reading.

It was a deucedly odd situation here, Somers realized when the Bible had been put away and Sally skittered off to perform her assigned chores. As he took more time to inventory the furnishings of the house, he was struck at once by the quality. This was no genteel impoverished household—there was money here. The china was not Sevres, but it was not country-store-bought either. The carpets were Belgian or Aubusson, he would wager, and the furniture could easily have come from Gillow.

He made attempts to engage the two women in polite conversation, but neither seemed inclined to talk. They were courteous, of course, but he received the distinct impression they wished him elsewhere. Somers could not blame them, for he had the same desire himself. However, there was little any of them could do to accomplish that at the present, so all parties were doomed to disappointment. Particularly since there looked to be little promise of a diverting flirtation with the lovely Elizabeth.

Miss Camberly drew out her knitting again, and as her concentration increased, her participation in the conversation decreased in kind, so soon only Elizabeth was a party to Somers' halfhearted attempts at conviviality.

"I fear you are sadly bored," she said at last when the gaps in their small talk grew louder and longer. "I am afraid there is little we can offer you in the way of entertainment, unless you would care to read."

He leapt at the opportunity. Anything at this point would be welcome, even some horrible Minerva Press drivel. But he somehow thought he would not find that here.

Somers followed Elizabeth into the hall and toward the back of the house, where she opened the door into a small room. He instantly recognized it as her office, for in addition to the book-lined walls, there was a small writing desk and an orderly pile of accounts. He tried to glance surreptitiously at the papers as she led him to the far shelf, but he could not discern anything without a more careful examination.

"I hope you shall be able to find something to your tastes," she offered, her warm breath leaving wispy smokelike tendrils in the unheated room.

He turned his attention to the shelves she indicated and he was, indeed, gratified to discover there were several volumes that met his tastes.

"One would almost think you a bluestocking," Somers remarked lightly as he ran his finger under the titles.

She laughed, for the first time since he arrived. He thought the sound enchanting and wondered if her looks were equally so. Before he could catch a glimpse of her mirthful face, her guarded expression had returned.

"That is hardly the case. But one can read only so many gothic romances before one becomes thoroughly inured to diabolical dukes and hen-witted young ladies. I find I much prefer weightier novels."

"And history? And political theory?" He arched one brow.

"There is much to be said for variety as well," she replied.

Somers turned his attention back to the shelves and selected a volume. He had not read Fielding in an age, and his rollicking fun might be just the thing to pass what Somers judged was to be an interminable wait until the roads cleared.

As she turned to leave the room, he put out a staying hand. "Yes?"

It had been on the tip of his tongue to ask about her odd situation, the expensively furnished cottage a sharp contrast to her apparently simple life. But he saw in her eyes a fleeting look of apprehension and wariness that caused him to pause. He decided against speaking for the moment. Perhaps he could unearth some explanation from the others.

"Thank you for having such a well-stocked library," he dissembled.

The morning passed in an eerie silence, broken only by the occasional strains of a softly hummed country air from Sally as she bustled about, performing her housemaid's tasks. After two hours of enforced inactivity, Somers was nearly ready to scream from frustration, Mr. Fielding notwithstanding.

"I think I shall bring in another load of wood," he announced, standing and stretching his still-stiffened muscles. "And see to the horses."

"An admirable idea," Elizabeth murmured, only briefly lifting her eyes from the book cradled in her lap. "I am sure the fresh air will do you good."

Somers spent a lengthy time in the barn. His horses were fine, of course. The building was snug and warm despite the cold outside, its thick stone walls effectively retaining the heat of four coddled beasts. Taking a long, critical look at the other horses stabled within, he noted they compared favorably with his own. There was money here as well.

He accepted the mystery of this household as a challenge to unravel during his enforced stay. It was as good a way as any to while away the time. And he might have an interesting story to tell when he finally reached Knowlton's.

"That is a snug little stable you have," he said to Elizabeth when he regained the front parlor. "And those bays of yours look like sweet goers. Rather prime bits for the countryside, aren't they?"

Elizabeth frowned, as if contemplating his criticism. "No, I think not. They serve a very admirable purpose here. Quality horseflesh is an asset whether one uses it for transportation or display."

He winced at the thinly veiled rebuke. Did she think he was a Hyde Park dandy? He tried another tack. "Did you buy them locally? I would not mind picking up some new cattle if they are in the neighborhood."

"I cannot tell you who bred them," she replied. "They were purchased for me by my business agent, and I did not question him so thoroughly."

"Do you drive yourself? I noticed the tilbury."

"Yes, Mr. Wentworth, I drive myself."

"What else does one do for amusement in this area?" Somers' chin had a stubborn set to it. He would get a revealing answer out of her if it took all afternoon.

"Very little that would appeal to you, I am certain."

"On the contrary, I often forsake the pleasures of London for the delights of the country. It is a much more peaceful existence. But since I imagine you do not hunt, or shoot, you must have some other occupation during the long winter months."

Elizabeth gave an exasperated sigh. She had half a mind to tell the man to go away, but a small part of her almost enjoyed this deliberate fencing. Neither the vicar nor the squire was noted for their wit.

"Very well. Three mornings a week I teach at the school for girls we have established in Chedford. The other two mornings I usually visit the parish poor. On pleasant days we sometimes drive to Carmody, for the change of scenery. I dine out one or two nights a week, usually at the vicar's or the squire's. I teach Sally her household tasks, her reading and writing, and needle arts."

"Sounds dreadfully dull," he blurted out.

She gave him a quelling glance. "I do not doubt you would find it so, but I do not."

"Do you not ever go to country dances or county assemblies? Visit friends? Make the journey to London? Surely you must have acquaintances or relatives outside the neighborhood."

"I do not go out in society."

"Why?"

"That, Mr. Wentworth, is none of your concern." Elizabeth rose from her chair, clearly indicating she was no longer willing to continue their discussion. "It is time to prepare dinner," she directed Sally, turning away from Somers.

After her rebuke, he made no further attempt to question Elizabeth. Following the midday meal, Somers announced he wished to improve the path to the barn, and set to work with a shovel he had unearthed from the far reaches of that building.

He liked the monotonous and repetitious labor. Bend, scoop, lift, and toss. Somers knew his muscles would regret this in the morning, after another night on that blasted sofa, but for now he reveled in the activity. And he could ponder the very strange situation of Elizabeth. Why in blazes was such a lovely lady living in this out-of-the-way cottage?

He had almost determined she was a widow. She wore no rings, but many women removed them after their official mourning was over. But her obvious reluctance to be in society puzzled him. She was certainly no antidote, needing to hide herself away. In fact, she was one of the most beguiling women he had met in an age, with her wide brown eyes and thick chestnut hair. And she had made no attempt to throw out lures to him. That, more than anything else, piqued his curiosity. He was not accustomed to being ignored by women.

Was she someone's cast-off mistress? She certainly had the looks for one. If she was, she had done well in her former profession, for she supported herself in a style many women still in the business could barely afford.

Yet there was her deep involvement in parish work. It would seem an odd occupation for a former cyprian, although it might be her way to atone for past sins and put on a respectable front. But it was also the logical activity for a lady of quality. Many lords maintained village schools where their wives and daughters played an active role.

It was odd there was only one serving girl about the house. There were certainly signs Elizabeth had ample funds to employ several more retainers. There had been some mention of a farm boy who came in daily; perhaps there were other day helpers as well who could not come because of the snow.

The most puzzling matter of all was her refusal to use her last name. In society, only the closest intimates called each other by their Christian names. Yet she had pointedly introduced herself with hers, making him suspect he would recognize her surname if he heard it. What scandal was attached to that unknown name?

He was filled with a sudden desire to make his way to Chedford. There, he might find someone who would answer the questions Elizabeth would not. Everyone knew everyone else's business in these small towns. He would likely have to pass a day in town anyway while his wheel was being repaired; he could take the opportunity to probe a little deeper.

So involved was he in his shoveling and thinking, he did not notice the dark-colored figure in front of him until he nearly bumped into her.

"You have been out far too long in this cold, Mr. Wentworth," Elizabeth chastised. "Come inside and warm yourself. I do not wish you to acquire a nasty case of frostbite."

He looked at the short distance remaining to the house. "Allow me to finish the path," he said, giving her a warm smile for her show of concern. The resultant faint flush in her cheeks widened his grin.

"As you wish. The tea is hot and Sally has a fresh batch of muffins out of the oven, so you may wish to work with speed." She returned to the house as silently as she had come.

The thought of the hot brew and buttered delights spurred him on, and he finished his track in short time. Knocking the snow from his boots on the front step, he resolved to try a different method of probing the mystery of Elizabeth.

He nodded a greeting when he entered the parlor and took his place at the window table, where Sally once again worked at her letters. Miss Camberly brought him tea and a buttered muffin, which he gratefully accepted. Somers made a long show of enjoying the repast, until the other women had settled back into their reading and knitting.

He looked with feigned interest at Sally's handiwork.

"You are doing a nice job, Sally."

She beamed at his approval. "Miss Lizzie is teaching me the ways of a lady's maid. When I learn to read and write well, and dress hair and sew a perfect seam, she is going to find me a job in London."

"An admirable aspiration. Are you from Chedford?"

She nodded. "My dad's farm is on the other side of the churchyard," she explained. "I went to Miss Lizzie's school and I was the girl she picked for training this time."

"This time?"

"Miss Lizzie trains the promising girls as maids. I was her best pupil last year." Her eyes glowed with pride at her achievement.

"She teaches you how to take care of a lady's things?"

"Oh, yes. She gets all the fashion magazines—even those funny ones in that foreign tongue—and we go over them for weeks, learning all the right names and keeping up on changes. She says it's funny how so many things are different from her day. But she pays attention, even though she isn't in town, for she says it would not do any good to send up a maid who was not up to the mark."

This earnest tale amused Somers. He had never met a girl whose aspiration was to become the slave of some addle-pated lioness of the *ton*, but to hear this girl, it was a dream come true.

"That is very good, Sally. I am sure you shall make a capable lady's maid."

The girl was a wealth of information, but he did not want to arouse suspicion. He would talk more with Sally later. "I should let you return to your letters. I do not want Miss Elizabeth to read me a scold for disturbing your work."

Sally giggled at this thought and reluctantly picked up her quill.

Somers opened his book, but could not keep his attention on the page before him. The situation grew more curious by the minute. "Miss Lizzie" was certainly no stranger to the *ton*. She must be a widow, he decided, who was determined to wear the willow for her late husband for the remainder of her life. Rather odd, but not unheard of. Yet if that were the case, why was there no obvious symbol of her devotion? She was not garbed in black. He had seen no portraits in the rooms he had entered; the pictures on the wall in her private office were floral prints. Perhaps she kept all the cherished mementos in her bedroom. And that was one place he was certain never to see, he admitted reluctantly.

He once again tried to rally conversation at the dinner table, but achieved little success. With so little activity, there was no news of the day to report, and the residents, with the exception of Sally, seemed disinterested in any of his stories of London life.

Resigned to another dull and quiet evening, Somers slipped out to check the horses for the night.

3

"It has been an uncommonly long time since Mr. Wentworth went to the barn." Emily looked up from her knitting, a slight frown marring her face.

Elizabeth glanced at the ormolu clock on the mantel. "I did not notice when he stepped out, I fear. Has it been that long?"

"I've read three whole pages, Miss Lizzie," Sally piped up. "And you know how slow I read. Shall I fetch him?"

"We can give him a few more minutes," Elizabeth declared. "He may have decided to stretch his legs. I am sure the lack of activity is frustrating for him."

Upon hearing the front door crash open a few minutes later, Elizabeth nodded in triumph to Emily. Neither woman was prepared for the ashen-faced countenance appearing in the parlor doorway.

"I think I've wrenched my ankle," Somers gasped, his whitened complexion and thin-lipped mouth reflecting his all-too-obvious pain.

In an instant Elizabeth and Emily were at his side, carefully assisting him to the sofa. They helped him out of his greatcoat, and he sat down with obvious relief.

"Which ankle?" Elizabeth asked, attempting to mask her concern with a calm demeanor.

"The right. I stepped in some sort of hole coming back from the barn and twisted the blasted thing."

Elizabeth felt a twinge of guilt. "I feel dreadful. Emily thought you had been gone for a length of time, and I assumed you were taking the opportunity for a few moments' exercise. I should have gone out at once."

28

"Not necessary." Somers winced as she pulled off his left boot.

"I assume you do not wish me to cut the other boot off," she said as she apprehensively eyed his right Hessian.

"Damn right," he replied. "Excuse me. But it is the only pair I have with me, and I do not want to walk around in my stocking feet for days."

"I am afraid you are not going to be doing any walking for some time," she warned. "I shall try to be careful, but I must get the boot off before your ankle swells. There is no question of sending for the doctor in this weather, but I daresay I can deal with a sprain."

He nodded his assent and clenched the arm of the couch in preparation for the pain he knew would come.

Elizabeth thought he handled himself well. She had twisted her ankle once as a child, and though she was certain it had not been this severe, she remembered how painful it was. After Mr. Wentworth's grumbling about his makeshift bed of the previous evening, she half-expected him to be a fainthearted soul. Yet he made no noise other than a sharp intake of breath when she pulled the tightest part of the boot over the ankle.

"There," she announced, holding the footwear in her hand. After carefully stripping off his stocking, she examined the injury with competence.

Somers watched as she gently touched and probed, his involuntary reactions telling her where the ankle pained him. If the sight of his bared lower limb distressed her, she gave no sign. She had beautiful hands, he thought, with long slim fingers. No one had yet indicated any interest in the pianoforte standing in one corner of the room, but Somers would bet a monkey it was hers. She had the perfect hands for it.

He suddenly drew in his breath when her fingers probed a particularly sensitive spot. Her eyes flashed to his face and the anxiety he saw there surprised him.

" 'Tis only a trifle sore." He forced a faint smile to his lips.

"Sally, run to the kitchen and fetch a pan of cold water and some linen." Elizabeth looked again at Somers. "I should like to wrap it in cold cloths, to keep the swelling down, before I bandage it. I do not think you have broken it. I doubt you would have made it back to the house else. I have dealt with a few sprained ankles in my time and do not think you will suffer from my handiwork.''

He nodded his assent. The blasted thing hurt like hell and anything she did to reduce the pain would be welcome.

''Do you have any brandy?'' he asked hopefully.

''I am afraid not. You are in some pain, poor man. We do have some laudanum—''

''I will be fine,'' he said hastily. He was not some weak-livered dandy, to need to dose himself over a simple sprained ankle.

''I shall have Emily fetch it, in case you change your mind.''

While Elizabeth carefully wrapped the cold, wet strips of cloth around the rapidly puffing ankle, Emily hovered nearby, concern etched on her face as well.

''I feel like a blasted fool,'' Somers complained. ''I've never had more than a minor bump or lump in my life.''

''You should be glad this is such a mild injury,'' Elizabeth responded tartly, then instantly regretted her snappy answer. He was being a tolerable patient; anyone would be frustrated at having injured himself. She gave him a conciliatory smile. ''I know you are vexed, for this will delay your departure. I am sure one day of our tranquil existence has been ample for you.''

''True enough.'' He gave a rueful smile. ''I do not wish to seem ungrateful, for had you not taken me in last night, I doubt I would have arrived in Chedford. But this is not quite the jovial hunting party I was on my way to attend.''

''Since I feel partially responsible for this unfortunate occurrence, I shall try to make amends tomorrow. We will do our best to be amiable companions. It is one thing to be forced under our roof by the weather, but quite another to be injured while helping us.''

''I was checking on my horses as much as yours,'' he pointed out.

''Nevertheless, we shall maintain it is our fault, and then we will all feel more charitable toward you,'' she insisted. Only the faint glimmer of a smile in her dark eyes betrayed the teasing quality of her words.

In a short while, Somers had to admit he felt much better. The soothing coolness checked the persistent throbbing in his ankle, and once he was stretched out on the sofa with his foot raised upon a pillow, he thought it was not such a bad situation, after all.

"I shall move Sally from her room and you may sleep there tonight," Elizabeth told him while she began the delicate task of wrapping his ankle.

"That will not be necessary."

"Of course it will. Certainly, if you are able to sleep on the sofa, Sally is equal to the task."

"I do not need to be bedridden," he protested.

"I do not intend to imprison you there," she explained, her eyes dancing. "I only thought you would be more comfortable and less likely to disturb your ankle in a soft bed."

He nodded at the wisdom of her words.

"There," said Elizabeth, sitting back to admire her work. "That should hold you until we can get the doctor here. I think if Emily assists, we can get you to your room without too much difficulty. Sally, get your nightclothes. You can sleep in the parlor tonight."

He was glad there was no one of consequence to see him this night, for he must look foolish in the extreme, hopping across the parlor with his arms draped about two ladies. Negotiating the doorway was a bit of a problem, but the old-fashioned hall was wide enough for three. There was again a tight fit at the door to Sally's chamber, which lay off the kitchen, but finally Somers found himself sitting upon the first servant's bed he had ever graced.

"I trust you can prepare yourself for bed?" Elizabeth asked. Somers glanced at her sharply. Was she roasting him?

"I am not certain if I can manage," he said, allowing a lazy smile—one of his most successful weapons—to steal across his face. "I don't suppose you . . ."

The quelling look Elizabeth gave him would have dampened even Casanova's ardor.

"You are correct, Mr. Wentworth. You do not suppose." She turned and left the room, shutting the door behind her.

Somers lay back on the bed, a broad grin on his face. My point, he thought.

He found he was not so eager to grin later that night. Awaking at some unknown hour of darkness, his ankle throbbing to beat the devil, Somers cursed his earlier rejection of the proffered laudanum. He dimly recalled Miss Camberly setting it upon the parlor table; surely he could find it without too much difficulty.

Tossing back the covers, he sat up on the bed. That had not been too difficult. Swinging his legs over the side, he carefully planted his one stockinged foot upon the floor. Easy now, he warned himself as he cautiously rose to a standing position. Gingerly, he placed the tiniest bit of weight on his injured foot, and was rewarded with a shooting pain in his ankle. Swearing, for the action had only made the need for laudanum more critical, Somers slid along the edge of the bed until he was able to reach the candle on the nightstand.

Not that its flickering light would do him much good, he discovered, for he could not quite picture himself hopping across the floor, candlestick in hand. At least he would be able to find his way to the hall. Shaking his head at his folly, cursing the blasted snowstorm that had landed him here in the first place, he began hopping across the floor in a thoroughly undignified manner.

Even that action hurt. Every time he landed on the floor, the jarring motion radiated throughout his tender ankle. Why had he been such a stupid fool earlier, refusing the laudanum? Reaching the door, Somers jerked it open and hopped out into the hall. Halfway there.

By leaning onto the wall, he was able to hop with slightly less force. The candle in Sally's room provided the barest light as he made his way slowly down the hall to the front parlor. He paused before the door and tried to recreate a mental picture of the room and just where he might find the relief he sought. He thought wistfully of his house in London, where the halls were illuminated with gaslights that burned all night. No one needed to stumble around in the dark there.

He stood in the doorway for a long time, willing his eyes to adjust to the dark. But the room yawned before him like a pitchblack cavern. Shrugging, he cautiously hopped forward. The table was somewhere to his left, he knew. Maybe five hops forward, then turn and two hops . . .

"Bloody hell," he muttered as his toe made forceful contact with some solid object. Reaching out to steady himself, he grabbed what he quickly realized was the back of a chair as it teetered precariously before crashing to the floor. Somers jumped back in alarm.

"Ow," Somers cried in real pain as he touched his other foot to the floor.

"What?" a sleepy voice asked.

Sally. He had forgotten she slept on that couch.

"It is only I, Sally," he called out. "Do you possibly have a candle you can light?"

There was a brief noise in the dark and the room suddenly flared into brightness. Somers hopped over to the nearest chair and sank into it wearily. He saw the sleepy wariness in Sally's eyes.

"Thank you," he said. "I was attempting to find the laudanum."

"Oh," she said, jumping out of bed without a moment's hesitation.

"I heard a crash." Emily stood at the door. "Sally? Mr. Wentworth?"

"Is it your habit, Mr. Wentworth, to visit young ladies while they sleep?" Elizabeth's voice was cold.

"She is getting me the laudanum that I so foolishly turned down earlier," Somers explained in irritation. How could they think he had designs on Sally? My God, a country serving maid? What did they think he was, some elderly lecher with a fondness for young girls? Why, his ladies were either the cream of the *beau monde* or the most expensive money could buy. To accuse him of wanting to tumble a serving wench!

Emily sniffed.

"My ankle hurts," he said between clenched teeth. "Particularly after your blasted chair fell against it. If I was going to attempt Sally's virtue, I would have done it last night, when I could walk." He glared at the shadowed figures in the doorway.

Sally handed him the bottle.

"Two drops," Elizabeth said. "Sally, take your candle and see that Mr. Wentworth makes it back safely to his room. I would not like him to have another accident tonight."

"Thank you," Somers retorted acidly.

Safely back in bed at last, Somers lay against the pillows and waited for the throbbing in his ankle to cease. How long did it take for this stuff to take effect? And how could a lowly sprained ankle hurt so damn much?

When he awoke it was near morning, for he could make out the shadowy outlines of the few pieces of furniture in the darkened room. His ankle felt as if tiny men were beating on it with hammers. Reaching again for the soothing liquid, Somers settled back against the pillows, listening for signs of activity in the house. These prim and proper ladies awoke with the dawn, he knew, so surely they must be up and at their duties.

Duties. He uttered a short laugh. They had no duties. They were women of leisure, although their manner of living was very different from the town ladies. Miss Camberly reminded him of several maiden aunts he knew, involved with her knitting and conversation. But Elizabeth . . . she was the one who would live a very different life in town.

In London, she would not stir from her bed until ten at the earliest, and more often it would be closer to noon. With a maid or a friend in tow, she would pay her morning calls, perhaps visit a modiste to fit a new gown, or explore the shops to find a new pair of gloves. Somewhere during her hectic day there would be a small meal, and then she would dress for an evening at the theater or an elegant rout. She would awake the next morning to begin the process all over again.

When laid out so simply, it did not sound particularly exciting. But Somers knew his mother thrived on such days and never seemed bored or weary with the process. And his mother was not a frivolous woman. Yet he could not picture her living here in the country, with only charity work to amuse her. Surely Elizabeth had once lived a life much like his mother's. Why was she now so content to live her current placid existence?

A tentative knock on his door disturbed his musings. "Yes?"

Sally peeked around the edge of the door. "Miss Elizabeth said to see if you were awake yet. I can bring you hot water for washing and then your breakfast."

"I will not have breakfast in bed like some invalid," he grumbled. "Bring me the water, and I will eat in the breakfast parlor."

When Sally returned, she set the pitcher on the bed table,

so he was able to wash without getting onto his feet. He appreciated her sense.

It would be pleasant to have a bath, Somers mused as he carefully washed himself. He was not overly fastidious, but one never really felt clean bathing out of a bowl. Particularly when one's dirty clothes had to be put on again. Hopefully, when the weather eased, he could send someone to fetch his portmanteau from the carriage. Perhaps Sally could wash out his other shirt today and he would have fresh linen on the morrow. He smiled to himself when he imagined the look of horror that would cross his valet's face if he could see his master now, in a shirt crumpled from sleeping, no cravat, and one sockless foot. He would probably resign in horror on the spot . . . Somers grinned, then winced as he foolishly attempted to stand.

"What?" he growled at another knock at his chamber door.

"Are you ready to come to breakfast? I thought you would appreciate some assistance in moving about the house," Elizabeth suggested.

She was right, he conceded reluctantly. He was not yet prepared to move about on his own. "Come in."

"How is your ankle today?" she asked.

"Sore."

"I hope the laudanum helped."

"It did. I apologize for waking the entire house."

"Your actions could have been performed with more grace, I believe."

Somers appraised Elizabeth carefully, hearing the teasing tone to her voice. "I hope you are satisfactorily convinced I was not up to mischief with Sally."

Her smile instantly disappeared, to be replaced with her usual cool demeanor. "I believe you adequately explained your actions," Elizabeth said, moving toward the bed to give him her arm for support.

Muttering a curse against changeable women, Somers rose to his good foot and with Elizabeth's help hopped his way into the breakfast parlor.

With his hunger assuaged, Somers allowed Elizabeth and Miss Camberly to settle him comfortably upon the couch in the parlor.

With a blanket around his shoulders and his ankle propped up on a pillow, he was more inclined to judge his situation with toleration. Particularly since all three women hovered about him with solicitous concern.

That circumstance was not unusual. Women always hovered about him. But usually their attentions stemmed from different motivations, and with quite different ends in mind. These women concerned themselves with his comfort out of a politeness to a guest in their home, and out of a slight guilt that he had been injured while assisting them. Most women were attentive because they wanted something from him: his money, his name, or his body. But Elizabeth and her companion would act the same to whatever poor devil had appeared on their doorstep during a raging snowstorm, and he appreciated the fact they offered him kindness without knowing who he was. He could be absolutely certain their motivations were sincere.

The remainder of the morning passed by quicker than he anticipated. The laudanum fogged his brain to a point where he was more asleep than awake. He enjoyed lying there peacefully on the sofa, letting the conversation in the room drift about his head. The words were not clear, but he listened with pleasure to Miss Camberly's low-pitched tones and Elizabeth's elegantly modulated timbre.

Somers must have dozed off, for he awoke with a start. He looked about him in confusion, and it was a moment before he recognized where he was. The parlor was empty. He shut his eyes and listened carefully. He could just make out the low hum of voices coming from nearby; they were probably in the dining room. He carefully twisted about to look at the mantel clock. It was past one. He had been asleep for hours. And his ankle hurt again.

"Sally," he called out. "Sally!"

Elizabeth peered into the parlor. "I am not Sally," she said, "but will I do?"

"It was easier to yell 'Sally' than 'Miss Elizabeth,'" he explained peevishly. "It is now after noon and I want my laudanum."

"Would you like a light luncheon first?"

"No!"

Elizabeth smiled. "Very well, Mr. Wentworth. You were an admirable patient this morning, so you may have your medicine."

"Thank you," he growled.

However, soon the laudanum and food restored his spirits and he was able to look upon his situation with more charity. He had planned to pry deeper into the mystery of Elizabeth's life, but found the peaceful haze induced by the drug incompatible with clear thinking.

"Is that your piano?" he asked. At her nod, he requested, "Play for me."

"You are a brave man," she responded. "How do you know I am not an atrocious pianist? I could be tone-deaf and pound the keys with the skill of a blacksmith."

"But you don't, do you?" he countered. "Play for me, Elizabeth. This laudanum may make my ankle feel better, but it turns my head to fuzzy wool. Music would suit."

It pleased Elizabeth that he wanted music. Music had always held a special meaning for her. As a child, she never dreaded her lessons; the endless hours of practice were a joy. The piano brought her comfort when her mother died, and gave her a companion when her elder brothers and sisters had all left home. And here . . . here it was her sanity.

Somers lay back against the cushions and let his mind drift away on the clear, ringing notes that filled the room. She was far more than adequate, he thought. From elegant Bach fugues to Beethoven sonatas, from Mozart to English country tunes, she played with skill and enthusiasm. Half-coherent as he was, he knew a talented pianist when he heard one.

He almost vocalized the pang of regret he felt when she at last rose from the keyboard.

"That was marvelous," he said when she rejoined his corner. "You play wonderfully." He saw her obvious pleasure in his compliment.

"Thank you, Mr. Wentworth. It is always nice to play for such an appreciative audience."

"Call me Somers," he insisted. "I feel a trifle awkward as Mr. Wentworth when I am draped all over your sofa with my bare toes hanging out."

"Somers?"

"Somerset." He grinned ruefully. "Dreadful name, isn't it? Been in the family for generations."

"It must be vexatious going through life not knowing whether you are a person or a county," Elizabeth teased.

He smiled warmly. "Exactly. Where did you ever learn to play so well? You must have studied for years."

Her smiling face turned serious again. "My father loved music very much," she said by way of explanation. She stood up. "Now, I must let you rest before dinner. Do not hesitate to call Sally if there is anything you need." With a rustle of skirts she was gone from the room.

Somers stored away that new piece of information, too tired and woozy to mull it all over now. Later, when his head was clearer . . .

4

"Miss Lizzie, Miss Lizzie, 'ere comes Tommy. Right after breakfast, just like you said." Sally ran in from the kitchen.

"Gracious, how did he ever manage to get here?" Emily rose from her chair and walked to the front door, opening it just as the young boy raised his hand to knock.

"I came as soon as my dad let me," he said, quickly slipping into the warm house. His nose and cheeks were red from the cold. Emily herded him into the parlor without ceremony.

"Goodness, we did not expect you even today," Elizabeth said as she pushed him down onto a chair near the fire. "We have been managing adequately in your absence. Now have a cup of tea and warm up before you turn to ice."

The boy readily complied and sat sipping his tea in silence for some moments. Then, with a clatter, he returned the cup to the saucer. "I thought I would bring in more wood and then tend to the horses," he said, looking to Elizabeth for approval. "Did you shovel out that path to the barn?"

She shook her head. "We have a guest staying here who was so kind as to do that for us. I am afraid I need you to accomplish a large number of things today, Tommy. The man's carriage crashed in the storm. His horses are in the barn and you must look to them for him. But I also want you to fetch the doctor, for the man hurt his ankle. And we need someone from town to get his carriage out of the lane. Do you think you can accomplish all that in this snow?"

He nodded. "I rode over on old Ben. He don't mind a little snow under his feet."

Elizabeth suppressed a smile. Old Ben was an ancient but monstrously huge plow horse that only a stone wall would stop.

"Tend to the horses quickly, then find Doctor Moore. Tell him I do not feel the injury is severe, but I should like him to examine it all the same."

Tommy nodded and headed out to do her bidding.

It was scant moments later when Sally announced that their guest was ready to join the company in the parlor for the day. Elizabeth followed her to the bedroom and they both helped Somers hop into the front room. He settled again on the sofa, looking not at all like the arrogant aristocrat he had seemed at first. To Elizabeth's eye, the wrinkled shirt, absent cravat, and three day's growth of beard painted a much more relaxed picture.

"What shall we do to entertain you today, sir?" Elizabeth asked him with a mischievous grin.

Somers' head throbbed from the laudanum he had consumed during the night. It matched the throbbing in his ankle and he was decidedly out of sorts.

"Nothing," he said petulantly.

"Oh, come now, surely we are not so terribly dull as to cause you to prefer nothing over our best efforts at amiability? If you do not wish to converse, I will not pressure you. Perhaps you would like me to read?"

He nodded his head wearily.

"Did you finish Mr. Fielding yet?"

He looked at her with surprise. It was one thing to have the book on her shelf; it was quite another to read it aloud to him.

Elizabeth chuckled. "You look so surprised, Mr. We— Somers. Perhaps you do not think it a proper book for a lady? Or is it not a proper book for yourself?"

He smiled weakly. "Read, if you wish."

She went to Sally's room and fetched his book. "I do remember how wicked I felt when I read this the first time," she said, settling herself into a chair. "But it was so marvelously funny."

Somers lay back against the pillows and gradually relaxed as she launched into Mr. Jones's adventures.

To Elizabeth's surprise, the morning flew by. She and Emily

often read aloud; it was something they enjoyed. But she had not thought her guest would respond as favorably.

While Elizabeth's pleasant voice washed over him, Somers' headache receded. She read well, reminding him of what he had not thought about in years, his mother reading him nursery tales before sending him to bed. The experience was equally pleasurable now that he was an adult. One could almost imagine *Tom Jones* as a fairy tale for grown-ups.

Elizabeth did not pause in her reading until the midday meal, which Sally served with her usual aplomb.

"Would you like to return to your room to rest?" Elizabeth asked Somers when the dishes had been cleared away.

He grimaced. "I much prefer being in the parlor," he declared.

"Rest is important for a healing ankle."

"What do you think I have been doing all morning?" he retorted in an exasperated tone. "Lying on the sofa is not the height of activity. I have been off my feet for two full days now, and that is rest enough. Do not think to banish me to some sickroom, for I am not sick."

Elizabeth suppressed a smile. All this inactivity wore on him, she was certain, for his trim, muscular form hinted at his athletic pursuits. She sympathized with him, knowing he found the dull company of his hostesses and the enforced rest dreadfully boring.

"I fear I cannot read more today, or I shall be too hoarse to speak," she apologized.

"I will read to you, then," he said reluctantly.

Elizabeth eyed him with surprise.

"Why do you look at me so? I assure you, I do know how to read."

"I did not doubt that," she replied. "It is kind of you to offer."

"Well, then," he said, as if her curiosity made him self-conscious. He cleared his throat and began to read.

It had been such a long time since she'd listened to a male voice reading, Elizabeth thought. Her papa had often read aloud to the family when she was growing up. That had been one of the special times of the day, after dinner, when they all gathered in the small drawing room. Her father read, her elder sisters and her mother sewed, and Elizabeth, who usually had sewing of her own, ignored it and sat with her hands folded in her lap, listening entranced as her father spun out the magic of Shakespeare, Milton, Spenser, and Swift. Unknowingly, she let out a deep sigh of regret for times long past.

Somers heard her sigh and peered at her over the top of the volume he held. Her eyes were closed, her long, thick lashes lying against her cheek. It was certainly not his reading that had caused her to utter such a mournful sound, for Fielding was more of an inspirer of grins than sighs. Something else caused that soft outburst. There was an indefinable air about Elizabeth, a vague sadness that seemed to shroud her like a cloak when she was not directing her attention to some matter.

"Is something wrong?" Elizabeth asked, her hazel eyes blinking open when she noticed his pause.

Somers flushed, realizing he had stopped in his reading while he mused about his hostess. He thought of making a flippant, flirtatious remark, as was often his wont with attractive women, but he resisted. It was becoming clear that Elizabeth was not a woman who sought a casual flirtation.

"I am sorry," he apologized. "Something distracted me." He returned to his book and picked up his spot smoothly.

The next interruption came with a loud banging on the door. Sally glanced out the window. " 'Tis Doctor Moore, I think," she said as she responded to the summons.

"Doctor?" Somers asked suspiciously.

"Doctor," Elizabeth replied. "I think I did an adequate job wrapping your ankle, but it does no harm to have him look."

Somers hated doctors. The few he had seen in his relatively healthy childhood had not been friendly sorts, only interested in poking and prodding and forcing vile brews down his throat. No, he did not like doctors.

But this man was a surprise. He looked to be no older than Somers himself, and although he was loathe to admit it, the doctor was a rather handsome man, with wavy dark hair and a pleasant face.

"So, you are our patient," Doctor Moore said in a cheery voice as he walked across the room to Somers. The two men shook hands. "Elizabeth sent word that you twisted your ankle in the snow two days ago. How is it feeling now?"

"The discomfort comes and goes," Somers said. "It ached abominably this morning, but it feels better now. Took laudanum yesterday, so I can't rightly say how it was then."

"Take any today?" the doctor asked as he unwrapped the offending ankle.

Somers shook his head. "Gave me a deuce of a headache," he explained. "I would rather have the hurt than that. I don't suppose you have any brandy in your medical bag? I think that would work much better."

The doctor laughed. "I do not, as a regular habit, carry any with me. But I think I can arrange for a medicinal supply to be sent over from the Bull Inn." While he talked, he examined Somers' ankle, feeling the swelling, gently moving it.

At last he seemed satisfied with the examination. "Elizabeth was right, this is only a nasty sprain. There seems to be no evidence of broken bones. I'll rewrap it. If you stay off it for another week or so, I think it should heal nicely. Keep it elevated, and you should soon be back to rights."

Somers scowled at the prescription. Another week of lying upon the sofa? He would go mad.

The doctor retreated across the parlor to where Elizabeth sat at the window table, pouring tea. The doctor helped himself to a cup and then engaged her in a low conversation.

Somers strained his ears to hear their words, for he shrewdly guessed he was the topic of conversation. He saw Elizabeth laugh initially, then her face grew troubled as the doctor persisted in his talk. Her voice began to rise in an angry tone and Somers made out one sentence, "It is far too late for that concern." He saw the bitterness in her face.

The doctor continued to speak with her for some minutes, but then tossed up his hands in a gesture of defeat and returned to his patient.

"How soon could I undertake a carriage journey?" Somers asked.

Doctor Moore considered while he rewrapped the ankle. "Assuming the snow melts, I think the roads will be passable in a few more days. I would not recommend traveling for another week, myself, but if you are determined to leave, it would not cause too much harm. That does not mean driving yourself, by any means. If you wish to be free of these parts, you will either have to hire a vehicle or have someone drive you.''

Somers frowned.

"There," the doctor announced, rising. ''I shall try to look in on you again in about a week, if you are still here.''

Somers considered that a broad hint to be gone by then.

''Thank you for your concern. Miss Elizabeth, if you will bring me my purse, I should like to settle the bill now.''

''Nonsense, nonsense. Elizabeth has helped me numerous times with my patients. She is certainly entitled to free medical care for her guests.'' He cast her a warm look that brought a faint pink to her cheeks.

Was the doctor courting her? Somers wondered. That might explain the man's aversion to a male presence in the house. He sensed the low conversation at the window table had centered on that topic.

There was a subtle change in the room's temperature after the doctor left. Elizabeth appeared distracted and aloof. She declined Somers' offer to continue reading and disappeared, he guessed, into her chilly rear office. Somers made a valiant stab at reading, but his heart was no longer in it. Indeed, his eyes seemed reluctant to remain in an open position and he slipped into a light doze.

Elizabeth, seated at her dainty tambour writing desk, looked out the window at the white world outside. Doctor Moore's words had caused her more distress than she was willing to acknowledge. It was improper for a man to reside so long in her house, but a man with an injured ankle posed no danger to three healthy women. As long as her personal safety was not in question, Elizabeth did not care a fig for what society would say. That was one of the lessons she had never taken to heart.

And it was also the reason she bordered on anger. To think that the local people, who knew her, who admired her work in her school and with the poor, would cast aspersions on her simply because she had extended a courtesy to a traveler in a storm! Even Dr. Moore, who knew very well why she cared so little about what others thought, voiced his concern at her nonchalant attitude about Somers' presence.

Yet perhaps that was for the best. The doctor had not been forward in his attentions to her, but she was aware of his regard. It would take little encouragement from her to cause him to come courting. And that was something she did not want. She valued the doctor as a friend, but she wanted nothing stronger than friendship from any male. She had never found them to be a trustworthy sex.

With resignation, she turned her attention to the account books, which she had neglected out of disdain for their tedious sense of order. But her mind refused to do as it was bidden and her thoughts drifted constantly. The bill for fabric brought to mind the elegant modistes of London and the fabulous splendor of the drapers. Shaking her head over the price of hay and oats for the winter, she thought to the two extra horses in the barn, and of their owner.

He was not, as she had first thought, a London dandy. She was pleasantly surprised at how well he had adjusted to his misfortune. There had been a few peevish outbursts, of course, since he had injured his ankle, but that was to be expected from even the most patient man. Despite his boredom, he remained polite and composed, when lesser men would have ranted and raved at the vagaries of fate. She wondered again who he was. He was certainly of aristocratic birth. He had that air about him, the knowledge that he was superior to lesser mortals and therefore treated them with a condescending politeness. Had she also had that arrogance? If so, she had long ago lost it.

And he was attractive. There was no denying that, or the fact that he was well aware of it as well. He knew how to use those azure-hued eyes for maximum impact. If ever a man had been a born flirt, she was sure Mr. Wentworth fit that description. An incorrigible flirt. Seven years ago, she would have taken delight in exchanging knowing glances and teasing smiles with such a man. Now, it was the farthest thing from her mind.

As the chill of the room crept beneath her warm shawl and flannel petticoats, she set her pen aside, recapped the inkwell, and shut the barely touched account book with a sigh. She would tackle this another day, when her mind was more obedient.

The weather continued cold, but thankfully, no more snow

fell. As one day tumbled into the next, the cozy house settled into a new routine, absorbing Somers into it as if he had always been a part of the household. He breakfasted with the ladies in the morning at an hour he never saw in London unless he was headed to his bed, listened to Sally's stumbling reading of the Bible, then ensconced himself on the sofa in the parlor for another day of peaceful but surprisingly nonboring rest.

They read aloud to each other, he and Elizabeth, while Miss Camberly's knitting needles clacked away softly. She had surprised him the previous evening when she hesitantly presented him with a gift.

"I know these are not in the height of fashion," she said, pale roses creeping into her cheeks. "But I thought they would be more practical than your present pair, seeing how you cannot wear your boot."

"Warm socks." He eyed the thick, gray articles with real enthuisasm. "These are wonderful. Just the thing I need, Miss Camberly. Why, I do believe these are the handsomest pair of socks I have ever owned."

"That is a royal bouncer," she replied, but her eyes were smiling.

"Well, they are certainly the warmest, then," he acknowledged. He was able to pull a sock over his injured foot and for the first time in days he knew his toes would be truly warm. The socks were gloriously unstylish but ever so practical for a man who could only wear one boot. In fact, they were so practical that he gave up on his left boot and limped about in his stocking feet. Tommy Baker's dad had fashioned Somers a rude crutch and he could now go from the parlor to the breakfast room and his bed without assistance.

The most important change was the reappearance of his portmanteau, liberated from the carriage the same afternoon the doctor arrived. Not only was he now able to clothe himself in fresh linen, but Somers had his shaving kit and no longer needed to endure the scratchy itch of an unshaven face.

His only frustration came from being confined to the house. No more new snow had fallen since his second day here, but that which remained on the ground melted slowly. Sally, Elizabeth, and even Miss Camberly went outside daily for fresh air and some exercise, while he was forced to remain on his sofa in frustration.

He took to sitting by the front window when they went out, for he could catch an occasional glimpse of them as they tromped about the yard. Miss Camberly stepped gingerly from one spot to the next, but Elizabeth romped merrily like a child through the snow.

Today, his attention had wandered from the scene outside until the sound of a loud feminine shriek recaptured it. He turned in alarm to the window, then nearly fell out of his chair as he started laughing. He saw Miss Camberly near the fence, a large white splotch marring her dark cloak.

"Duck, Emily," Elizabeth called as she let loose with another missile of white.

Somers grinned when her call went unheeded and the perfectly aimed snowball hit the mark. He watched as Elizabeth bent nearly double, convulsed with laughter at her actions. Somers held his breath, then chortled in glee as she remained oblivious to the return attack until the snow hit her shoulder. Elizabeth looked up in surprise, then laughed even harder as she dodged to escape the next onslaught.

He watched her for several minutes while the two ladies cavorted about the front lawn like silly schoolgirls, their aim growing worse by the minute as their laughter-shaken frames made careful targeting impossible.

Somers was struck by the look on Elizabeth's face. The cold had brought high color to her winter-paled cheeks. Her eyes were bright with glee and her face filled with laughter. Lord, how he would have loved to have known her when she was like this all the time, full of laughter and mirth. Before whatever tragedy befell her, the one that forced her into her lonely and isolated existence. For he was certain she was not here of her own volition.

He had thought her an attractive woman from the moment he first laid eyes on her, but seeing her now, full of life and animated, he found her utterly beautiful.

His injury and the relaxing atmosphere in the cottage had lulled Somers into inaction, but he determined to renew his efforts to discover the reasons for Elizabeth's presence in this out of the way corner of England. He had gained all he could from Sally, and he doubted Miss Camberly would be more forthcoming. He would have to pry the story loose from Elizabeth herself.

"Tell me about your school," he began, after luncheon, before she could open her book.

"I hardly think the details would interest you, Somers. Or are you truly so bored?"

"Expiring from it, ma'am. I will listen to any tale that promises to be new."

She gave him a skeptical glance, but proceeded. "It was actually Emily's idea. It started as a Sunday school, teaching the children their letters and Bible lessons. Enough parents expressed an interest, so we expanded it to several days a week, then hired a full-time teacher."

"There are enough pupils to sustain a teacher?"

"Most of the payments are in the form of goods or services. I pay her salary. Even if people were able to pay, attendance is so spotty, depending on the season, that it would never support a teacher. Most of the students are from the farms, and they come when they can, but their work at home comes first."

"What do you teach them?"

"Many do not go beyond learning the alphabet and how to spell their names. We teach them sums, and those with the time or inclination learn how to read. We have the girls longer, since the boys are needed more at home, and we teach them sewing and cooking as well."

"What do you teach?"

"I do the sewing, and help with the little ones."

"The little ones?"

"Some of our students are as young as three. For many mothers it is a great relief to get the small children out of the house for a short while, particularly if there is a baby at home. We sing, play games, and start on their letters."

"It sounds like a marvelous program." His eyes filled with admiration. Few women of his acquaintance gave more than a passing thought to charity work. Elizabeth's avocation set her apart. "Now, where does Sally fit into this?"

"Most of the girls will grow up and become farmers' wives, like their mothers. But some have other dreams. I know to you the idea of becoming a lady's maid sounds silly, but to a country girl it is an exciting life. And a sight less work than living on a farm. If they are bright and willing to work, I train them."

"Sally is not your first maid-in-training?"

"She is the third girl."

"It is a lot of work, turning a rough farm girl into a skilled maid."

"That is why they must be bright."

"But it has to be unsettling when you bring a new girl in. Your house must be at sixes and sevens until they learn their way about. And how do you know they will ever find jobs?"

"I write to friends and . . ." Elizabeth's voice trailed off, as if realizing she revealed too much. "A skilled maid is always in demand."

"An admirable project, Elizabeth," Somers hastened to add. He did not want her suspicious. "My mother would be very interested in your school. Have you thought of establishing others?"

"I do not have the funds for more than one," she replied.

"I did not mean finance them, but find a patron willing to take on the expense while you hire the teachers and set up the program."

She looked wistful for a moment. "It is a thought. But I fear I am busy enough here. And I do not wish to leave Chedford."

"Why not? Would it not be a nice break to see other parts of the country? Dorset, where my mother lives, is particularly beautiful in the spring."

"So is Chedford. No, one school is enough for me."

Somers did not press her. Recognizing her reluctance to leave this isolated village, he wondered anew what had driven her here . . . and what forced her to stay.

5

No matter which way he lay, Somers could not find a comfortable position on Sally's bed. He did not need the painful throbbing in his ankle to tell him he had overstrained himself that day. It was past foolishness for him to have taken that walk about the yard, but he would have gone mad if he'd stayed in the house another hour longer. For a brief moment he wished he had availed himself of the laudanum, but then shook his head. He could certainly endure some minor discomfort without drugging himself into a stupor. Lying back against the pillows, Somers willed his aching body to sleep.

A noise in the kitchen told him his efforts would be unsuccessful. The sound carried clearly into his adjoining room. Sensing the impossibility of sleep, Somers decided to assuage his curiosity and discover the identity of the nocturnal rambler. Was Miss Camberly raiding the larder? Or did Sally enjoy an early hours' snack? Somers pulled on his heavy wool socks and his breeches and limped into the kitchen.

Elizabeth did not hear him enter, engrossed as she was in measuring out the precious brown cocoa powder and stirring the pot of milk so it would not scorch.

He leaned against the door frame, watching her. Even at night she avoided caps, he thought, as he admired her chestnut hair streaming in wild disarray down her back. He had no idea it was so long, for Elizabeth normally confined it in the elegant chignon she favored. Unbound, it hung nearly to her waist in soft, curling waves. Even wrapped as she was in a thick dressing gown of some indeterminate cloth, she looked less formidable than in the day, and much more desirable. He suddenly wished it was summer, for a thinner wrapper would reveal more of the curves lying underneath.

"Here I hoped to catch a sneaking thief, and who do I encounter but the mistress of the house on a midnight mission."

Elizabeth jumped at the sound of his voice, the spoon falling in the pot with a splash.

"You startled me," she said as she whirled to face him.

He limped across the room and sat down on one of the chairs flanking the square kitchen table.

"I hate to be ill-mannered and sit in your presence, but my ankle is kicking up a deuce of a dust tonight." He flashed her a lazy smile. "Of course, I cannot complain, for if it had not, I would have been sleeping soundly and never heard you in here."

"I could not sleep either. Would you like a cup of cocoa?"

He nodded. They both remained silent while she finished preparing the brew, filled two mugs, and placed them on the table.

"Do you do this often?" he asked. "In the middle of the night, I mean."

Elizabeth nodded. "It is an old habit. I used to love to wake up at night. It was the only time the house was ever completely quiet. I'd wander through the rooms, carry on imaginary conversations with my numerous guests, serve them tea, and have a marvelous time."

"Most young ladies of my acquaintance would not dare to set foot outside their beds during the dark of the night."

"Fainthearted creatures," she scoffed. "I enjoyed the night. I never found it frightening, but magical. The moon cast the most amusing shadows on the pictures in the gallery. I loved to dance in the moonbeams. The light was so soft and shadowy compared to the sun. You could almost imagine all those ancient faces coming alive again. I cannot tell you how many minuets I enjoyed with my dashing great-grandfather."

Somers relaxed in his chair, envisioning a younger Elizabeth dancing amid the portraits of her ancestors. She would have been a charming little girl, he thought. Nearly as charming as the woman she had become.

"You must have led an exhausting life. Or did you sleep the day away after dancing all night?"

She laughed, a light trilling sound he found enticing.

"I did not scramble from my bed every night. It was far too cold to wander through the house during the winter months. The schoolroom stove always remained lit, so I would fix myself a cup of cocoa and dash back to the warmth of the covers."

Somers leaned forward eagerly. This was the first time she had ever been so open, the first strong clue she had given to her background. She obviously grew up in a aristocratic household. And she had been happy then. He saw that in the wistful expression on her face.

"Where did you live?" he asked in feigned casualness.

He saw the light go out of her eyes, and cursed himself for causing the wariness that replaced it.

"One house is much the same as another, is it not?"

Somers nodded. Do not push her, he warned himself. Let her grow comfortable again. He needed to lull her into further revelations. Perhaps if he talked about his past, she would be more forthcoming with her own.

"I never ran about in the moonlight, at least inside. But my cousins and I enjoyed more than one midnight swimming expedition on those bright nights. We had a small pond not too far from the house—"

"So did we," Elizabeth broke in. "Did you ever ice-skate in the winter? I did so enjoy that, despite all the times I fell."

He shook his head regretfully. "That is one adventure I missed, I am afraid. Even during the coldest spells, it never froze thick enough. Our pond was our summer play spot, for swimming, fishing, and boating."

"Have you ever sailed?" she asked.

"I went to Cowes last year with some friends. I did not participate in the racing, but watched from the sideline boats. It is a sport I think I would enjoy."

"We went to the seashore every summer, when I was growing up. I had a small dinghy and my father and I would . . ."

Her voice trailed off and Somers noticed the stricken expression on her face.

"What is it, Elizabeth?" he asked gently. "Why does it hurt you to think of your father?"

She did not respond.

"My father died when I was sixteen," he continued quickly, trying to put her at ease again. "I was away at school when it happened—a stupid accident on the hunting field—and he was gone before I even knew. I was so angry at the time, thinking how unfair it was to both him and my mother. And to me. I was woefully ill-prepared to step into his shoes. Do you know what it is like to become an earl at sixteen years of age?"

Her dark eyes widened for a moment and then she flashed him a knowing smile.

"I did not think you were Mr. Wentworth."

"Any more than I think you are Miss Elizabeth," he returned.

"What is your title?" Elizabeth did not wish him to question her too closely.

"I only lied a little," he explained. "Wentworth is the title."

"And Somerset?" She glanced at him skeptically.

He held up his hands in a gesture of surrender. "It's really my name. Somerset Edward Graham, Sixth Earl of Wentworth, Viscount Kempton, and Baron Kempton of Dorset. In its entirety."

"I remember, you said your home was in Dorset. But surely, one of your ancestors must have come from Somerset?"

"Some cross-border raid in ancient days, no doubt," he said dryly.

"Was it very difficult, losing your father when you were so young?"

"It was not easy, being forced into that role before I had even gone up to Oxford. I was fortunate in that my mother quickly realized the difficulties I faced, coming into the title so young, and did all she could to steer me in the right direction." He grinned ruefully. "She is not precisely happy with the way I have turned out, but I have not disgraced her."

"My mother died when I was twelve," Elizabeth said in a quiet voice. "It seemed so unbelievable at the time. I was the only child still at home, and suddenly there was this huge void where she had been. We were not particularly close, and I felt guilty about that for the longest time. I was always Papa's favorite, and her death drew us even closer together."

Seeing the pain in her face, he reached out and took her hand in his. Her long, tapering fingers were cold as ice.

"Why are you here, Elizabeth, living alone like this?"

"I hate to think what Emily would think of her hasty disappearance." She gave a faint smile.

"You know what I mean."

"Does it matter so very much?"

He nodded. "I do not want to pressure you. But I shall be willing to listen, if you would care to tell the tale."

Taking a long sip of her cooling cocoa, Elizabeth considered his offer. She liked Somers. He was not the top-lofty, arrogant aristocrat she had labeled him at first, even if he was an earl. And she thought he would not condemn her for what she would tell him. And even if he did, she would never see him again after his ankle healed enough for him to continue his journey. Earls did not often come to Chedford. With a deep sigh, she placed her cup on the table.

"It is a simple story, and a very old one, I am afraid. I was in London for the Season—my come-out, with all the assemblies, balls, Almack's and the rest. I was popular; I came from a good family. I had looks and money. I found it all immensely fun. Then my heart overruled my head."

She stopped for a moment and gave him a long searching look.

He met her eyes openly, not a hint of emotion displayed on his face as he silently urged her to continue. He squeezed her hand in encouragement.

"Among my admirers was a man of 'questionable' reputation. Oh, I had heard all about him. In fact, I told him very early that I knew he was an unprincipled fortune-hunter, and I would not be swayed by his honeyed words. He just laughed and kept coming 'round. It did not help, of course, that he was handsome and charming and every young girl's dream of love."

Somers tensed in his chair. He could sense what was coming and felt a growing anger. Why had no one protected Elizabeth better?

"I fear I read too many Minerva Press novels in those days, about the despicable rake saved by the love of a good woman. He gradually drew me into his web until I was trapped like a fly by the spider."

She was caught up now in her tale and Somers knew she would tell it through to the end. Elizabeth seemed unaware of his presence, all her attention focused on the story she told as she relived the agony.

"Up until the very last I truly believed I would win." She gave a short, harsh laugh. "But the victory was his. He ruined me totally, my father disowned me . . . Oh, he pays all my expenses, not that it comes close to what my dowry was, but he and the rest of my family have not spoken or written a word to me since."

"I am so sorry, Elizabeth," murmured Somers, feeling the inadequacy of his words as he uttered them.

She did not tell him of the miserable eight months that followed her abortive elopement, or the babe who had fortunately died at birth. It all seemed so unreal to her now, as if it had happened to another person and she had been there only watching, those six long years ago.

"Elizabeth?"

Her whispered name drew her mind back into the kitchen. Somers reached out and lightly stroked her cheek.

"I am sorry life has treated you so unfairly. You deserve to be happy."

"Oh, I am," she said with resignation. "I have come to realize that nothing happens to us without a purpose. My life is not what I, or my parents, had envisioned it would be. But I am able to give Emily—she is a cousin—a decent life, and she is not reduced to being an unpaid slave to a demanding relative. Sally is only a farm girl, but will soon be able to take her place as an upper servant in a house where she could only have hoped to become a scullery maid. I like to think my school is a modest success. Perhaps it is all for the best."

Somers did not know what to say. He loathed society's rule that an unmarried miss accept all the responsibility for any impropriety in her behavior. It was particularly foul when applied to an eighteen-year-old girl seduced by an experienced older man. Lord knew, he avoided young misses for that very reason, relying on paid companions or willing married ladies for his pleasures. Unmarried young ladies brought too many complications.

Her composure rapidly crumbled after her brave confession, and he drew her into his arms. Not because she was a beautiful woman, who would be a pleasing armful in any circumstance, but because she was a human being in pain who needed comforting. He hated to see her hurting.

"Oh, Elizabeth," Somers murmured, stroking her hair and rocking her like a child while she trembled in his arms. Her tears dampened his shirt. He wished he had not encouraged her to talk, never realizing the pain it would bring. Damn his impetuous curiosity!

Gradually, Elizabeth quieted, only light sniffs betraying her momentary loss of composure. He could tell the exact moment when her control returned, for she stiffened, as if at last realizing where she was and who held her. She pulled away from his chest, her red-rimmed eyes wide with suspicion. Releasing her instantly, Somers gently set her back on her chair.

"Not all men are scoundrels," he said when he saw the new wariness in her eyes. He reached over and wiped away a last trickling tear. "You extended a great kindness to me, Elizabeth, when I was a total stranger. I only wish to return the favor."

Elizabeth nodded, too overcome with emotion to speak yet. A part of her regretted her revelation, yet she was glad as well. She rarely thought about it anymore, but the past was always there, hovering in the back of her mind. It somehow felt better to talk it all through once again, particularly with someone who listened with such open sympathy. Still, it was foolish of her to burden Somers with her problems. And she felt the veriest widgeon for having cried like that.

Swirling the dregs of cocoa in the white china mug, Elizabeth was suddenly shy with this man who now knew so much about her. She glanced up and found him watching her, his brilliant blue eyes filled with concern. She gave him a woebegone smile.

"I am sorry to be such a watering pot. I do not wish you to think I go about feeling sorry for myself, for I do not. It all happened long ago, and I do not dwell on the subject."

"I hope I did not upset you by urging you to talk. I only thought you might feel better if you shared your story."

"Surprisingly, I think I do feel better. You are a good listener, my lord."

The teasing tone in her voice pleased him. She was not horribly overset, then. In fact, she looked much calmer than he felt. His mind whirled as it tried to absorb the implications of her tale. How could any father have been so heartless?

Somers gingerly patted his damp shirt. "I only regret I did not come armed with a handkerchief." He smiled ruefully. "I see I must be better prepared on my nocturnal rambles."

"Is your ankle feeling better? Shall you be able to sleep now?" Elizabeth brushed back a lock of hair. "I am rather tired. I think it is time to seek my bed."

He nodded, having totally forgotten that once-aching portion of his body.

Despite his no-longer-painful ankle, sleep eluded Somers for some time. Lying upon his bed, hands clasped behind his head, he looked out into the darkened room. God, what an awful fate for poor Elizabeth. He had half a mind to go to her father and demand he take his daughter back. She might never have much of a place in society—for society's memory could be terribly long when it came to sins real or imagined—but Elizabeth could at least be reconciled with her family.

But why should he care? He was forced to admit he liked Elizabeth. If he had met her in London or at a country party, he would have been attracted to her. A stab of desire raced through him as he envisioned her in her nighttime disarray again. Yet, in addition to her remarkable beauty, which struck him anew every time he looked at her, she was quiet, composed, and a very elegant lady. Her manner was reserved, but that was understandable after all she had endured. And she had spirit, mixed with bravery, else she would not have survived.

Yet she still maintained a sense of humor and fun. He recalled her smiling face during the snowball fight. He could picture Elizabeth as a happy, laughing child, the pampered and slightly spoiled daughter of a nobleman, racing down the long halls of the family portrait gallery in the moonlight. She must have been an incredible woman in her carefree days.

He wondered if he had ever seen her during that disastrous Season. It must have been many years ago, for he reckoned she had lived in Chedford for at least five. He rarely attended the *ton* parties for the eligible misses and had not set foot inside Almack's in nearly ten years. The patronesses probably wouldn't even extend him a voucher. He might have given Elizabeth a casual, admiring glance if he noticed her at a party, but he doubted he would have spoken a word to her. He studiously avoided each new crop of marriageable misses as they came up to London each Season.

Somers was filled with a burning curiosity to know who she was. She still was reticent about her identity; despite all her candor, there had never been any names mentioned during her tale of betrayal. Who was she?

He wondered, briefly, at the fate of her seducer. Banishment was too good for the lout, pistols too quick. Anger flared within him and Somers felt an inordinate desire to smash his fist into the unknown man's face. He hoped Elizabeth's father was powerful enough to have made the man's life miserable. He had ruined Elizabeth's life; he certainly deserved the same fate.

How complete had her seduction been? "Ruined me totally," could mean several things, but Elizabeth did not have the virginal mien of Miss Camberly. The lout probably talked her into fleeing to Gretna, bedded her the first night out, and ran off when her father caught them. Why her father had not insisted on marriage was a puzzle, for Somers thought any connection would have been better than none at all, under the circumstances. The fellow must have been truly ramshackle if he was not acceptable as her husband. Somers racked his brain to think who had been raking his way through the *ton* five years ago— besides himself, of course. Someone who suddenly vanished from the scene.

As he mentally went down the list of every male he knew, his eyelids grew heavier and heavier, and before he had decided upon a likely candidate, he was asleep again.

6

Elizabeth did not notice the early-morning chill as she sat at her dressing table, staring absently at her reflection in the mirror. Regretting her candor of the previous evening, she now dreaded seeing Somers again. What must he think of her? He might feel sorry for her, which in itself she would detest, but he also would not view her as favorably as he had before, she was certain. For gentlemen of his stamp did not regard with admiration women who broke society's rules. Despite his sympathetic listening last night, he now knew her for what she was, a disgraced and fallen creature. No man would ever look the same upon a woman in that state, no matter how much he empathized with her situation.

Yet she would be forced to face Somers across the table this morning and pretend that nothing had changed. She must act as if she had not lain weeping in his arms last night, act as if he did not know a word of her hateful story. She slapped her palm against the surface of the dresser.

It was not fair, she raged silently. For the first time since his arrival, she truly wished Somers had never come into her life. His presence brought back too many emotions and feelings that were long buried. He was from the world she had left far behind: the world of smiling, handsome gentlemen who flirted and laughed with pretty ladies. He was a painful reminder of all that she never thought to see again.

She looked—really looked—at the face staring back at her from the mirror. Poor, silly Elizabeth, she chided herself, wallowing in self-pity because a near stranger knew her tale.

She was worrying herself into a frazzle over someone she would never see again, who did not know her name or her family. It might be slightly embarrassing for them both during the remainder of his stay, but he would soon be gone from her cottage and life forever and she could forget they had ever shared this time together.

But could she forget him? Elizabeth reluctantly admitted she liked Somers. Was attracted to him. He had a remarkable sense of the absurd, a ready wit, and a sharp mind. He was not a Bond Street dandy, all flash with no substance. He enjoyed music and literature, as she did. He knew just the right teasing tone to use with Emily to get even that sobersided soul to laugh.

Somers was a man who was accustomed to women and knew how to deal with them. She suspected he was quite a favorite with the ladies in town. No man with his trim physique, handsome face, and easy manner could be anything less. And there was no doubt he was aware of his attractiveness. He knew the effect those azure eyes had on the opposite sex. Even if he flirted to tease her, she sensed his actions would turn more serious if she encouraged him. And for a moment, she wondered what that would be like.

Shaking her head at the absurdity of her thoughts, she twisted her hair into a chignon more severe than usual, and proceeded down the stairs to breakfast.

Despite his fitful sleep, Somers woke early the next morning. He was eager to speak with Elizabeth again, to propose he aid her in repairing the breach with her family. It was one way he could repay her kindness toward him. He sat impatiently at the breakfast table, toying with the cutlery while he waited for her to appear.

To his frustration, Miss Camberly reached the table first. It would not do to talk to Elizabeth in the presence of others; he had to catch her alone. He sighed. From what he knew of the household, that would be a difficult task.

Somers looked up briefly when Elizabeth entered the room. Her face betrayed no hint of what was in her mind after last night. She wore her same unruffled expression.

"Good morning." She put on a cheerful face to hide her apprehension. Thank God Emily was here.

"Good morning, Elizabeth." His own greeting was equally polite. "You are fortunate to have arrived when you did, for I was preparing to devour that last muffin. But now, alas, I must forgo that pleasure."

"Perhaps if you are very good Sally will bake us another batch this afternoon," she said, glad to have Somers set a light tone.

"I am always very good," he said with such a leering glance that both Elizabeth and Miss Camberly laughed.

"Of course, if you are so fond of muffins, perhaps you should learn how to make them. Then you could have them whenever you wished." Elizabeth flashed him a teasing smile.

"Now, surely, you are funning. My exalted position allows me a certain amount of leeway regarding eccentric habits, but I do not feel that baking muffins falls under the list of acceptable oddities. I could dress all in green from head to toe or allow obnoxious lap dogs to overrun my house, but to be up to my elbows in flour would simply not do."

"We have been laboring under a misapprehension regarding Mr. Wentworth," Elizabeth explained in a stage whisper to Emily. "The poor man is actually an earl."

Emily's eyes widened as she directed a piercing stare at Somers. He met her gaze without flinching and returned it with a slightly apologetic smile.

"I find then I must agree with the man," Emily finally stated. "Baking muffins would not do."

"Exactly." He nodded. "So I shall be forced to rely on Sally's good nature to keep me supplied with my favorite treats."

Somers thought he would never find the opportunity to talk privately with Elizabeth. If Sally was not asking her about some household question, Miss Camberly was there at her side. He almost thought there was a conspiracy to keep them apart, but then dismissed that idea as ridiculous.

When the moment came, he almost missed it. He had been gazing out the window, watching the yellow-brown patch of lawn grow larger and larger as the warming rays of the sun melted the overlying snow. He could hear Elizabeth and Miss Camberly chatting quietly across the room, and it took him several minutes to realize that he no longer heard both voices. He turned and saw that Elizabeth was gone.

With a sprained ankle and a crutch it was impossible to be surreptitious in his departure, but he did not care. Hopefully, she had not gone upstairs, for he would feel the veriest fool tromping up there in search of her. He glanced into the breakfast room when he gained the hall, but she was not inside. A quick peek into the kitchen revealed—oh, joy—Sally preparing another batch of muffins, but no Elizabeth. With determination, he followed down the hall to her office.

She sat at her desk, a ledger lying open in front of her, with pen poised above the page.

"May I come in?"

Elizabeth looked up, startled. He was learning how to move quickly and quietly. She had done her best to avoid him all morning, but trapped now, she nodded her acquiescence.

His maneuverings in the small room were less impressive, she noted with a quick smile. But he soon managed to ease himself into the other chair. She was very certain she did not want to have a private chat with him, for she knew he was going to bring up last evening. Yet to her surprise, she did not want him to leave either.

"I have thought a great deal about what you told me last night," he began. "I wanted to—"

"There is no need to discuss it further," she said hastily. "I appreciate your listening to my silly tale, but it need not concern you further."

"I must do something to repay you for your kindness to me," he protested. "I thought that if perhaps I acted as an intermediary, you might be able to effect a reconciliation with your father."

Elizabeth froze at his words. This was beyond her worst fears. She had expected cloying sympathy and soothing words, but not patronizing interference in her life.

"I thank you for your concern, Somers, but I do not wish you to do any such thing." She deliberately avoided meeting his eyes.

"But you cannot go on living here like this," he protested.

"And why not? I told you I am content with my life here. I have a school that provides a service to the community. I offer Sally and other girls a way to better themselves."

"You belong to another world, Elizabeth. Don't gammon me; you are as aristocratic as I. You should be in London, paying morning calls, shopping all day, and attending parties till the small hours of the morning."

"I do not wish to cut a dash in town," she explained in a tone she often used for obstinate children at school. "Why cannot you accept that? I am happy here. Why would you wish me to go to town, where I would be miserable?"

Somers sighed. He had not thought she would be instantly amenable to his suggestion, but he had not expected her to reject it with such vehemence. His mouth was set in a determined line.

"Wouldn't you like to once—just once—socialize again with your equals? Can you honestly say you would not trade an evening in the company of the vicar and his wife for one rout at Lady Jersey's?"

"I doubt she would let me across the threshold of her home," Elizabeth said dryly.

"All right, then, you can attend a rout at my mother's."

"And watch her other guests politely leave?" Elizabeth shook her head in exasperation. "Somers, I do not wish for a life in society. I spent one year living in that manner. After living six as I do now, I find I infinitely prefer this life. It may appear dull and uninspiring to you, but it is fulfilling for me. You are kind to be concerned, but you are offering me something I do not want."

"But you are wasted here," he blurted out.

"Wasted? How, precisely, am I being wasted?" His persistence began to irritate her.

He sensed her growing anger and decided to lighten the mood. "It is unfair that you hide your beauty here in the country. You were born to grace an elegant drawing room, where you could flirt from behind your fan with all the men and trade gossip with all the ladies. And I am sure you dance divinely. You do not know how provoking it is to constantly have my toes stepped on by clumsy ladies."

Elizabeth was forced to smile at his teasing. "I appreciate your concern, Somers. But truly, I do not desire to change my life. And I have been known to tread on a toe or two, so my presence will not be missed."

He knew there was no point in continuing this today, but he was not ready to give up entirely. His mother had often told him he could be as tenacious as a terrier when he set his mind on a thing. He would try again, when the memory of last night's emotional scene had faded in her mind.

Elizabeth breathed a sigh of relief when Somers finally left her alone again. She longed for the day he could leave her house. For now, each time she looked at him, she would be reminded of his pity. She could deal with scorn, or derision, or indifference for what she had done, but pity was another thing. She had tried hard to make a new life for herself in Chedford and thought she had achieved a modest success. His insistence that she should have more grated on her mind.

Who was he to blow into her life and tell her what was best for her? If she had been a poor country girl with the same story, he would not have thought a thing of it. Only because he thought her his equal socially did he criticize her reclusive existence. How could she explain to him that it was her very background that forced her into this life? Less-exalted families would have hidden her away until the scandal died down, then reintroduced her to society. But not her family. Oh, no. She had not behaved as a Granford ought, and that, not the particulars of her transgression, was what mattered. Her shameful actions were unbecoming a member of the family; therefore, she could no longer be treated as a member of the family.

She visualized her father standing before her that horrible day at the inn where she and her lover had been hiding. She had been such a fool, believing Harry when he persuaded her to take the eastern road to Scotland. They could be wed at Lamberton Toll as easily as in Gretna, he had said, and in the process, throw her father's trackers off their trail. She had not complained about the leisurely pace of their journey, trusting all to Harry. She was deliriously in love, and if he encouraged her to consummate the marriage that had not yet taken place, she was only too willing to agree. She spent more than one enraptured night in his arms while he awakened her to the mysteries of love.

He had gone downstairs in the morning that fateful day, to order the carriage prepared. She never saw him again, for the footsteps that echoed up the stairs and stopped outside her door belonged to her father.

When he opened the door and stood there, looking at her with a mingled look of anguish and disgust on his face, she had frozen to her chair, too stunned to speak.

"Gather your things, Elizabeth," he said. "You are leaving."

"Where is Harry?" she asked, suddenly afraid.

"You will not see him again," her father thundered.

She had never seen him so angry. Even as a child, when faced with one of her mischievous crimes, he had never looked angry, only sad or disappointed. His anger was frightening to behold.

As she entered the inn yard, Elizabeth glanced frantically about for Harry, but there was no sign of him or his carriage. What had her father done to him? Surely, once her father calmed down, once she talked to him and explained how much in love they were, he would relent and sanction their marriage. Despite her apprehensions, her mouth curved into a smile as she recalled just how delightful married life would be.

She rode the long miles south alone in the carriage, save for the company of a strange maid. Her own, she was informed, had been turned off the day Elizabeth's flight was discovered. She grieved for poor Marie, who, indeed, had helped her mistress make her secret arrangements but who did not deserve punishment for serving out of loyalty.

The coach rattled on over the long and dusty miles. Her father was ahead of her, she knew, and his refusal to travel with her sent a small stab of fear through her heart. She had expected confrontation at the inn; when it had not come, she reasoned he was waiting until they were alone in the carriage. But he had handed her inside without a word and slammed the door shut, walking away without a backward glance. At each inn, she was hastily ushered into her room and saw no one save the serving staff. When would she have the chance to talk to him about Harry?

In three days she began to recognize the road signs and knew they neared one of her father's lesser properties. Surely he did not intend to send her here? But when the carriage pulled before the door, she had no doubts.

She was greeted warmly by the staff, who had not seen the family baby since she was a girl. Her room was prepared and waiting for her. But her father never came. She was here, alone, with only the unfamiliar and uncommunicative maid.

Elizabeth finally understood her father's purposes the day the doctor arrived six weeks later. She was fully aware her courses had not arrived, but ascribed it to the strain she had been under. Certainly she was tired, but who would not be in such strange circumstances? But when the doctor had finished with his gentle but thorough examination, she no longer could ignore her deepest fear.

A plain coach arrived two days later, and she was again bundled into it without ceremony, departing for who knew where. Not until she saw the deep, forbidding moors of Bodmin did she realize where she was being sent: Cornwall, the farthest end of the island, where she would be free from prying eyes and no one would know her disgrace.

Through all those long weeks there had been no communication from her family. She wrote numerous letters to all of them—her father, brothers and sisters—begging them to write her, to tell her what they planned for her, to ask what had happened to Harry. He could be dead, for all she knew, slain in the duel the besmirchment of her honor demanded. A stab of fear raced through her. Was that why her father had not allowed them to wed once he was aware of her condition? She could not bear the thought of her handsome, laughing Harry lying cold beneath the ground. But not one word of explanation did she receive.

For seven long months she waited for word, but none was forthcoming. Until one day, while seated in the drawing room of the gloomy Cornwall house, her swollen and unfamiliar body perched uncomfortably on a chair, her father came.

"Papa," she cried in surprise and delight as he walked in. Pushing her ungainly self to her feet, her eyes bright with hope, she reached out toward him. But he stood there, arms folded, eyeing her with such a cold, glaring stare that she finally dropped her outstretched hands to her side.

"It was too much to hope, I suppose, that you would have managed to lose the brat."

"Papa?" She winced at the hardness in his eyes.

"I have made arrangements for a doctor to come near your time. You will stay here while you recover from the"—he grimaced—"birth. I have purchased you a house in a small village and you may go there as soon as you are well enough to travel."

"Is . . . is Harry . . . is he well?"

The duke gave a derisive sneer. "Your precious Harry is on an extended tour of the Continent." He raised a forestalling hand as she opened her mouth to protest. "I would not worry too much about his comfort, for his amiable wife went along to warm his bed."

Elizabeth stared in shock. "Wife?" she whispered.

"He never intended to wed you," her father said harshly. "You were only a means to some money. He had amassed a tidy sum over the years from parents eager to cover up the transgressions of their daughters. But he misjudged this time, for you can be sure I did not pay him a cent."

A cold despair swept over Elizabeth. What a fool she had been! She had given up all that was important for nothing. Harry had lied to her. He did not love her. Elizabeth instinctively placed a hand on her swollen abdomen. She had sacrificed everything for Harry; his babe filled her belly to near bursting and he would never know . . . or care. Tears sprung to her eyes.

"I want to come home, Papa."

"Harcourt is no longer your home," he responded, his voice as sharp as shards of ice. "To myself, to the rest of the family, you are dead. I no longer acknowledge you as my daughter."

"Papa, no!" She tottered toward him, grabbing his sleeve, imploring, begging with her eyes, but he refused to look at her. Instead, he shook her hand loose as if she were a pesky child.

"One does not insult the name of Granford with impunity," he announced, turning to make his exit.

Elizabeth struggled after him. "Papa, wait, please wait. Take me with you. I am so very sorry for what I did. Do not leave me here, do not.'' Her voice rose to a hysterical wail, then firm hands held her arms, preventing her from following her father down the stairs and to the door.

''Paaaapaaa,'' she cried in one long, drawn-out wail before she collapsed sobbing onto the floor.

Elizabeth looked out the window, listening to the rhythmical drip of melting snow from the eaves. She shook her head. Somers thought a total stranger could repair the breach between herself and her father. She did not want him to try, for she knew he was doomed to failure. And most of all, she did not want her father to have the opportunity of denying her again. He was proud of the family name, but she had her pride too. And she would not beg him or beseech him or enlist the help of a peer of the realm to take her back into the family again.

How lonely she had been those first two years. The death of the baby was a blow, but she admitted to her inner self that it was probably for the best. They would not have allowed her to keep him, and this way he was not doomed to a tenuous existence as an unwanted bastard. Alive, he would have been a constant reminder of his perfidious father.

Yet during those early years, as she sat at her window or in her garden, staring moodily into space, she had often thought of her son. She wondered at the type of mother she would have been, had God and her family granted her the chance. But gradually, the painful thoughts eased as she grew more caught up into the village life around her. Emily's arrival had been a blessing, for it gave her not only a companion, but an impetus to do something she had long wanted: to work with the children of the village. This plan had grown into the school they now ran together, and the light in a child's eyes when he finally looked at those letters and saw a word more than made up for all the balls and assemblies she had missed.

She had not lied to Somers. She was content with her life, at peace with her past and aware of her future. And if her contentedness was predicated on lack of change, then it would be best to get Somers and his well-meant but interfering intentions out of her life. He could rival the devil with his temptations.

7

On a day so springlike it was difficult to remember how deep the snow had recently lain, Somers took a limping tour around the yard. He could no longer offer up any more excuses to postpone his departure without them sounding patently false. It was past time for him to leave, but he had delayed, hoping one more day with Elizabeth would allow him to break through her wall of reserve, to once again see the vulnerable, hurting woman behind that barrier. She wanted, needed to be reunited with her family, yet her stubborn pride forced her to refuse his help. Well, she would find he was as stubborn as she. He had never once been denied a thing he wanted, and he would not be denied this.

The garden would be a pleasant setting in summer, he noted as he surveyed the neat flower beds, the sawdust heaped high about the roses. He could picture Elizabeth sitting under the rose arbor on a sunny summer's day, a book in her lap and a gentle breeze blowing curling wisps of hair across her face.

He shook his head wistfully. It did not help in the least that Elizabeth was a very attractive woman. But despite her age, and fall from grace, he knew she still belonged to that set of women he did not cast his experienced eye on, the set of unmarried misses. Elizabeth was as inviolate to him as any young lady dressed in white, dancing at Almack's, with a dragon of a chaperone glowering at him. No, it did not help his thinking at all to remember how lovely she had looked that night in the kitchen, her long hair gloriously unbound and falling in soft waves. Or to imagine the shapely form and creamy skin that lay beneath the bulky robe she had worn.

He stabbed his inelegant cane into the dirt. He must get control of himself before he spoke to her again. If she even half-suspected how attractive he found her, she would turn away at once. It took no imagination to know Elizabeth had little time for men.

Elizabeth and Tommy had ridden out to exercise the horses, taking Somers' pair on lead reins as well. He was waiting before the stables when the two riders returned. Leaning negligently against the open door, he approvingly noticed the drying sweat stains on his horses. They had been given a run, but their easy breathing showed they had been cooled down properly as well.

Stepping forward as Elizabeth moved to dismount, Somers caught her about the waist as she descended, and set her lightly on the ground. His hands lingered for a fraction longer than necessary.

"Was your ride enjoyable?" he asked.

"It was. And I think the horses enjoyed it as well. No one, man or beast, enjoys being penned up by this winter weather."

Somers transferred the reins to Tommy and took Elizabeth's arm in his, leading her away from the stable to walk again amid the sleeping garden.

"I have availed myself of your hospitality for far too long," he began with a self-deprecating grin. "My ankle is much improved and I think there is no reason for me to delay my journey further, so I shall be leaving in the morning."

She accepted all this with silent calm.

"What? No mild protestations? No feigned murmurs of dismay?" His voice was light, teasing. "Are you really so glad to be rid of me, then?"

She gave him a warm smile. "No, of course not, Somers. It is only that I know you are eager to be on your way. I realize how dull these last two weeks have been for you, and I—"

"Never dull," he said, taking her hand in his. "You have been a marvelous hostess. I assure you I am leaving with regret. But by now my friends have scared all the foxes permanently into their lairs, and there will not be a bird left within miles of Knowlton's if I do not go now."

He tucked her hand in the crook of his elbow and continued to lead her into the garden, away from the house.

"I would like to talk to your father, Elizabeth," he said with calm assurance. "Oftentimes it is better if an outsider is there to smooth the path. I could speak to him in your behalf, perhaps arrange a meeting—"

"No!" Elizabeth pulled her hand away while she struggled to remain calm, seeking to hide her dismay over his efforts to reopen a subject she had labeled closed. "I assure you I do not wish you to act so. I only wish to be left alone here."

"Are you afraid?" he challenged. "Afraid of what people will say about you? Of the gossip they shall whisper behind your back?" He looked down at her, his eyes intense. "I had not thought you such a fainthearted creature, Elizabeth. If you do not give a snap for society, why should you care what they say?"

"It is not that," she mumbled, refusing to meet his eyes.

"What?"

She lifted her face to him, tears brimming and threatening to spill down her cheeks. "What if he said no?" she asked in a whisper. "I could not bear his rejection a second time."

Somers caught her to him in a comforting embrace. "How could he ever reject you? He is only suffering from your malady—a surfeit of pride."

"Something that you are intimately familiar with as well," Elizabeth retorted, her brown eyes flashing in anger. "I did not ask for your help, Somers, nor do I wish it. Leave matters be. If you are so fired up to do good, there are any number of people in the parish who would welcome some assistance."

"I want to help you."

"Why?"

As he looked down into her puzzled hazel eyes, he asked himself the same question. And answered it as well. Because she was so damn lovely, he thought as he bent to capture her lips with his.

Time took a momentary pause as his lips met hers. Hers were soft, warm, inviting, and eminently kissable in that brief stoppage of time. His arms held her loosely and for an instant she leaned into him, her lips pressed against his in an answering response—before time started once again and she struggled like a trapped animal in his grasp.

"No," she wailed, freeing herself from his hold.

Immediately dropping his arms to his side, Somers stepped back a pace and looked at her in bemusement. The look of pure panic on her face held him prisoner before she broke the glance and fled across the lawn to the house.

Oh, God, he groaned to himself, what have I just done?

Somers was unsurprised when Miss Camberly announced Elizabeth would not come down for dinner that evening, pleading a raging headache. For all he knew, she did have one, but he realized the cause of it was that enchanted kiss in the garden. While he was no prince, Elizabeth had certainly looked as if she had kissed a frog.

He was glad he had already decided to leave tomorrow, so he would not have to slink off with his tail between his legs like some whipped cur. With his rash action, he had destroyed whatever fragile trust existed between him and Elizabeth, and his presence here would be only an embarrassment to them both. And he could not expect her to hide in her room for any longer than a night.

Would she come down in the morning? He doubted it. He would leave quickly, then; merely a light breakfast and he would be on his way. It was a terrible thing for Elizabeth to be uncomfortable in her own home.

Elizabeth sat in her darkened room, only the flickering light from a single candle keeping the darkness at bay. Curled up in her favorite chair, wrapped in a warm shawl, she sat and thought.

Somers had been right. She was fainthearted. She had grown accustomed to her dull but safe existence here in Chedford, where the locals accepted her as a valued part of their lives. Accepting Somers' offer of help would only open her up to new hurts. Every time she attended a social gathering, there would be the agonizing moments of introduction where she would not know if she would be accepted or cut. Eventually, of course, she would learn where she was welcome and where she was not. But it would be a painful educational process.

And then there was her father and the rest of the family. Elizabeth was uncertain whether she could endure a second repudiation at their hands. It was far better for her to remain here, cut off from her family but still relatively happy. Her days might not bring her transports of delight, but neither were they full of black despair. Here, she was safe.

Somers, she decided, was ultimately a frightening man. He was doing his utmost to turn her world upside-down again, and she did not like it one bit. He acted as if he alone knew what was best for her. A spurt of anger filled her. She was the only one qualified to make those choices. She would not be bullied into acting against her desires.

And if a small portion of her anger was directed at herself, as she remembered those brief seconds of stunned surprise when his lips had touched hers and she had not resisted, it only served to increase her relief that he would be gone on the morrow. Yes, Somers was a very dangerous man.

He entered the breakfast room warily in the morning, un-certain of the reception he would find within. But he was the first person at the table.

"Good morning, my lord. Here's your breakfast."

At least Sally was pleased to see him. Of course, his departure meant she could have her room back. That would be enough to bring a smile to anyone's face.

He ate his meal in silence—not a difficult task unless he wished to converse with the walls or the table. Miss Camberly, no doubt, had been informed of his despicable behavior and avoided him as well. Such an ignominious end to his lengthy and admittedly enjoyable sojourn.

He was pleased to discover he was wrong on one count, for no sooner had he reached that conclusion than Miss Camberly joined him at the table.

"Elizabeth is still feeling poorly," she announced as she poured herself a cup of tea. "I fear the ride yesterday was too much for her after such a long spell. But one can never tell her how to go on."

That was an understatement. "I am sorry to hear she is still unwell," Somers said. "I regret making my departure without thanking her again for her generous hospitality. You will have to extend my thanks to her. And to yourself. Why, I have packed your socks in the place of honor in my portmanteau."

Emily colored slightly. "Are you returning to London, my lord?"

"Eventually. I thought I would travel on to my original destination," he replied, reaching for another muffin. "There may still be a remnant left of the house party I was to join."

Suddenly eager to be away and in no mood to exchange further pleasantries with Miss Camberly, he rose from the table. "I need be off if I am to reach my destination today. I will assist Tommy with hitching the team, then return for my portmanteau."

Tommy was a dab hand at the duties of an hostler, and Somers knew he would not need his help hitching up the curricle, but he could not remain in the house a moment longer. It saddened him to part from Elizabeth on such a bad footing. When he returned to town he would send her an apologetic note, begging pardon for his well-meant offer to interfere in her life. Or would she rather he apologized for that kiss?

With the team hitched and ready, Somers returned to the cottage for his bag. Sally had placed it in the hall, next to his coat hanging on the hall tree. She stood to one side, shyly.

"I baked you an extra batch of muffins for you to take," she said, blushing, as she handed him a square box.

"Delightful! Just the thing I need to make my journey more pleasant." He chucked her under the chin. "If Miss Elizabeth's plans for you as a maid do not work out, write me. I shall hire you as chief muffin maker."

She giggled at his offer and fled into the kitchen.

Emily stepped out from the parlor into the hall.

"Good-bye, Miss Camberly," he said, executing a gracious bow. "Please extend my thanks to Eliza—"

"Surely, you can thank me yourself?"

Somers whirled around. He wanted to flinch at the sight of her pale, weary face, knowing he had been the cause of her distress.

"You did not think I would be so ungracious as to allow you to leave without saying my farewells?" she asked in a subdued tone.

"I am pleased to see you up," he said, extending his hand. "I am sorry you were not feeling well."

"A day of quiet will restore me to health, I am sure."

"I must thank you again for all you have done for me," he said, a hint of pleading in his eyes. He wished to repair the breach between them. "You have been most kind."

"But you have adequately repaid any kindness with your amiable company," she replied. "You were a pleasant guest, my lord."

He nodded a brief thanks. "I shall say *adieu*, ladies." He shrugged himself into his greatcoat and picked up his bag.

Elizabeth opened the door and stepped out onto the flagstone path with him.

Somers turned and looked searchingly into her face. Had she forgiven him for his impetuous kiss? She did not look angry, at least, he noted with relief.

Neither spoke for several moments as they silently regarded the other. Somers scanned her expression for some clue to her feelings, but she presented him with her usual calm, unruffled exterior. She was too damned skilled at hiding her inner emotions.

"Good-bye, Elizabeth." He finally broke the silence. "If you change your mind, if there is anything I can do . . ."

"No," she replied, offering him a faint smile. "But thank you, Somers. God speed you on your way."

Elizabeth watched as he limped slightly toward the stable and disappeared around the corner of the house. She heard the faint sounds of the carriage pulling out of the yard, and turned expectantly to face the road beyond the fence. He passed slowly, raising his whip in salute. Then he was gone.

She turned back to the house, wondering why she suddenly felt so very alone again.

It was hard to believe, Somers thought as he tooled his grays down the lane that less than two weeks ago this road was ankle-deep in snow. The mud engendered by the thaw had dried, and it looked much as it had before that fateful day when his trip to Knowlton's had been postponed.

Had he missed much? If the snow had not extended that far, the shooting might have been passable. The company would certainly have been pleasant, for Knowlton never invited any geusts who were not close friends. No purely social entertaining there. Somers gave a low sigh. He probably had missed an excellent time. But he would not have traded the last two weeks for anything. Knowlton would have to be content with the hastily scribbled note Somers sent the previous week, explaining his absence.

For he had no intention of continuing on his journey. The instant he reached the main road, Somers planned to head his team to London. There was a mystery to be unraveled here, and since Elizabeth would not give him the answers he wanted, he would have to scrape up the information on his own. He knew London was the best place to start. In fact, he knew the one person there who could probably answer most of his questions.

Lady Wentworth was not merely a society gossip, for that implied an addle-pated female with nothing more on her mind than scurrilous tales and ridiculous tittle-tattle. His mother was far more sophisticated than that. She might know nearly everything, but she never spread malicious gossip and had used her authority as an admired hostess to squelch more than one unpleasant tale that served no useful purpose. She also had a razor-sharp memory, and if anyone would recall a young girl seduced and abandoned, both by her lover and by her father, it would be Somers' mother.

He snapped the reins imperiously, urging the horses to quicken their pace. London was still a long journey away and he was eager to have his questions answered.

8

When Somers finally tooled his carriage across Grosvenor Square the following evening, the lamplighters were already busy at their task. It had been a hard two days of traveling and still he had not arrived as early as he wished. His mother was very likely out of the house, and he did not relish the task of chasing all over London in what would undoubtedly be a futile attempt to locate her. With three or four parties to choose from in an evening, she could be anywhere.

"My lord," greeted the imperious butler. His face did not reveal one hint of his surprise at seeing the master of the house reappear so unexpectedly after such a long and, according to servant gossip, strange absence. "Welcome home."

"Thank you," Somers replied, stripping off his gloves and tossing them onto the hall table. "Is my mother still in?"

"I am afraid Lady Wentworth has gone out for the evening, my lord."

Somers nodded. "Check with the kitchen and scare me up something to eat then, Halford. I shall be in the library."

The butler bowed and retreated down the long marbled entry hall. Somers strode off in the opposite direction, but before he could reach the library door, a hastening footman slipped ahead of him.

"The fire must be lit," he explained apologetically.

Somers agreed, noticing the chill in the room. It would have been uncharacteristic of his mother to have spent any time in this room during his absence. She was not the least bit bookish to begin with, and regarded this room as his private preserve, as it had been his father's before him. Somers poured himself a generous glass of brandy from the decanter on the side table, then drew his chair up in front of the newly blazing fire.

"Inform Peters I have arrived and tell him I shall want a hot bath after I eat."

The footman bowed his way out of the room.

Somers had to grin. It was quite a change from the cottage in Chedford, where he had not only lit the fires but hauled in the wood and built them. He imagined it must have been difficult for Elizabeth at first, accustomed as she no doubt was to an army of servants to be at her every beck and call. She would have had her own personal maid and probably an abigail as well, in addition to the rest of the household servants. Now she survived with only a partially trained farm girl. And he had been so affronted that first night when he had been forced to sleep on the sofa. He grimaced at the memory of his doltish reaction.

The arrival of a cold collation from the kitchen halted his musings and he dug into the food with relish. The room grew warmer as he assuaged his hunger, and when he sat back again, pleasantly full, to nurse his brandy, he felt warm and contented. It was good to be home.

The following morning was almost an unimaginable pleasure for Somers. He had his best sleep in weeks, at last snug in his own bed. There were his fresh and spotlessly clean clothes, donned with the help of his hovering valet, who kept shivering in horror as Somers regaled him with his tale of living with only two changes of clothes and no starched neckcloths. As if to show this had done nothing to damage his skills, Somers deliberately tied the proffered cravat in an impeccable mathematical before he ventured down the stairs to breakfast.

He was just slicing his ham when his mother fluttered into the room.

"Somers," she cried in delight as she ran to him and planted a motherly kiss on his brow. "Why ever did you not tell me you were arriving last night? I would not have gone out had I known."

"I was not certain when I would arrive, and did not want you to wait for me unnecessarily. But I am here at last."

"Do tell me about this adventure of yours. Your letters were so short and cryptic I almost suspected you of mischief. What is this tale of snow and a sprained ankle?''

He laughed, allowing her to take a seat and accept the cup of coffee he poured.

"There is little adventure to it, I am afraid. I was foolish enough to set out for Knowlton's with a snowstorm in the offing, and slid the curricle off the road two miles from some god-forsaken country hamlet. Fortunately, there was a cottage nearby where I could take shelter. By the time the roads were passable again, I had sprained my ankle and was confined to my chair for a week. I spent several more days hobbling about with a cane, then drove directly home as soon as the doctor allowed.''

She eyed his twinkling eyes with suspicion. "You tell a simple tale, but your face says there is more to this. Out with it.''

"Well, if you must know, I spent the last two weeks in the company of three very nice women who cosseted and coddled me until I grew fairly spoiled from the attention.''

The countess set down her cup with a start, spilling some of the liquid into the saucer. "That sounds like a bouncer to me, Somers. Now tell me, what really happened.''

He put up his hands defensively. "I swear, it is the truth. Miss Elizabeth, Miss Camberly, and their maid, Sally, were my generous hostesses.''

"Putting you in a house with three women is like putting the fox into the henhouse,'' she said dryly. "I suppose it is too much to hope that they were all elderly ladies with ear trumpets and spectacles.''

He laughed. "Sorry, Mama. It was not quite that dreadful. Sally is a delightful farm girl who is training to become a fancy lady's maid. Miss Camberly is one of those poor relations who is called in to lend countenance to a situation, except that she is a very amiable lady. I should guess she is not a few years older than I. And she knits. I have the most marvelous pair of socks as a souvenir.''

"And?''

He looked at her quizzingly.

"You said three women, Somers.''

"So I did. The mistress of the house is Miss Elizabeth, and I assure you she does not have an ear trumpet or wear spectacles. She is in her mid-twenties, I would guess, and has the most gorgeous chestnut hair that falls nearly to her waist when she lets it down at night and—"

"Somers!"

He grinned at his mother's discomfiture. "I know that only because I discovered her making cocoa in the kitchen one evening. It was a totally innocent situation." His face suddenly grew serious. "It is she I wished to talk to you about. I want to know who she is."

"You spent two weeks in her home and you do not know who she is?"

He nodded. "All I know is her first name. She would not tell me her last, for I fear there is a scandal attached to it. What I wish from you, Mama dear, is for you to use that remarkable mind of yours to recall whose daughter caused a major stir with an abortive elopement six or seven years ago. Someone high-placed in society, who subsequently disappeared from sight."

"Goodness, Somers, how can you expect me to remember back that far? Not every shocking tale reaches my ears, you know."

"I doubt that. Think upon it."

She furrowed her brow as she tried to remember every tidbit she had gleaned. "There was one girl who ran off to Gretna the year you were cavorting with that odious French dancer . . . But no, I seem to recall she did marry the fellow. And Falkingham's daughter kicked up quite a dust some years back, but I do not think she ever attempted an elopement." She stopped and increased her concentration.

"Oh, gracious, there was the Duke of Harcourt's youngest. Let me see, that must have been six, seven years—"

"What happened?" He leaned forward eagerly. Could Elizabeth be the daughter of a duke?

"She ran off with some fortune-hunter—you might recall him, he had a reputation even worse than yours with the ladies—but I seem to recall he never wed her and she returned home to her father's. He fled the country in fear of his life and he still lives abroad. The poor chit was quite ruined; I never saw her out in society again."

"Do you remember her name?" Somers asked eagerly.

She shook her head. "But I daresay there is a Peerage Index in the library. I shall have someone fetch it."

Somers leapt to his feet. "I will go."

She eyed him with apprehension. "Is it good for you to dash about like this on your weak ankle, my dear? You do not wish to reinjure it."

"My ankle is fine," he called over his shoulder as he left the room.

He quickly scanned the library shelves for the necessary volume. It was not a book he had any particular cause to use and he was unsure of its exact appearance, except that it was very thick. It took him several frustrating minutes to locate it.

Somers carried the volume back to the breakfast room, almost afraid to verify his mother's story. He opened the book, quickly searching out the Harcourt name. Finding the entry for the latest of that line, he scanned down the page until he found the children.

"Let me see. Augustinia . . . too old. Charlotte . . . she's my age, too old. Rich . . Here it is!" His voice rose with excitement. "Elizabeth Carolina, born 1790. That would make her twenty-six, and that sounds about right."

His mother was staring at him as if he had lost his wits.

Somers shut the book with a triumphant thud. "I think, dear Mama, that my hostess was Lady Elizabeth Granford."

"Harcourt's daughter?"

He nodded. "The tale you told me dovetails nicely with hers: she attempted an elopement with a notorious fortune-hunter, it was foiled, and her family has not spoken a word to her since. She says her father pays her expenses. Her house is very stylishly furnished and her clothing is all the mode, but it is quite a come-down for the daughter of a duke, I must say. She has only the one girl who helps in the house and a farm lad for the outside tasks. She runs a village school for the girls, where she teaches three days a week, and then she plays Lady Bountiful for the parish. A horridly dull existence."

"It is a sad tale, I agree."

"She deserves a life more fitting to her station." Somers announced emphatically. "Now that I know who her father is, I will speak to him."

"Do you think that wise?"

"I must do something."

Hope leapt within Lady Wentworth's breast. Could it be that

her son, who had spent all his adult life in the pursuit of heartless pleasure, had finally felt that organ touched?

"Did you discuss this with her? Does she wish you to intervene?"

He frowned. "In truth, she does not. But I do not think she is an objective judge of what is best for her."

"You seem to be taking an unusual interest in her affairs, Somers." His mother tried to keep her voice casual.

He gave her a shrewd look. "Always the optimist, aren't you? No, it is not like that, precisely. She was a very gracious hostess in a deucedly awkward situation, and I should like to do something for her in return. Although, I must admit, I would not mind seeing her again."

"She might never be totally accepted in society, even with her father's backing," his mother reminded him. "There could always be doors closed to her. You could only bring her more pain."

He considered her words. "I should not like to do that," he admitted slowly. "But I wish to help her, Mama."

"Let me think about it for a while, dear. At this point, it is all speculation. You do not know what Harcourt will say and the girl herself may oppose your actions. Let some time pass and we shall discuss this again."

He nodded his agreement. While he finished his breakfast, his mother caught him up on all the gossip he had missed, and when he went into the hall to call for his carriage, he knew all that he should.

Somers did not bring up the topic of Elizabeth with his mother for some days, but he found his thoughts were often on his enigmatic hostess. Seeing a stylish bonnet in a shop window, he imagined how it would look on her. He carefully eyed the fashionable evening gowns at the routs he attended, trying to decide exactly which ones would suit her coloring. And if he could not buy her bonnets or gowns, he could at least let his inclinations run wild at Hatchards and he purchased her numerous books. For Miss Camberly, he bought some very expensive and very fine wool, and for Sally, who had given him her bed, a totally inappropriate lacy nightrobe. He most wanted to see Elizabeth in that.

He was not surprised at his physical attraction to her, for he was invariably attracted to women in that way. Those who were available and willing, he bedded; those who were not were admired briefly and forgotten. Elizabeth fell into a special category, however, for she was certainly not available for that type of liaison, yet at the same time he found he could not easily dismiss her from his mind. That was a new experience for him.

It was her difficulties that made her impossible to forget, he reasoned, and he resolved anew to carry out his campaign to have her restored to her family and society. Once she had been reestablished, her image would not torment him so.

"I do not see why you desire me to write you a letter of introduction to Harcourt," his mother complained when he cornered her in her dressing room early one morning. "I barely know the man."

"But I do not know him at all," Somers pointed out. "He would find it odd for a total stranger to seek an interview. But if a casual acquaintance makes the request on behalf of her adored son, it would look less striking."

"Her somewhat adored son," she corrected with a fond smile. "For I cannot agree with your plan, Somers. If your Lady Elizabeth was willing to have you act as an intermediary, I would not be so hesitant. But you confess you are going against her wishes, and I find that difficult to countenance."

"There is more to it than mere reluctance to contact her father. She was also out of sorts with me at the time, and that contributed to her opposition. She might be more amenable now."

"Goodness, what did you do to the poor girl?"

He had the grace to color. "I kissed her. Very briefly," he added as his mother shook her head in dismay.

"You are incorrigible."

"You will write the duke?"

She reluctantly nodded her assent. "But do remember I warned you."

Two weeks later, Somers found himself on the road again, heading northeastward this time in the direction of the ducal estate of Harcourt. He had spent more than one day at his club, making discreet inquiries about the duke. Much he heard was interesting, but did not give him a clue whether his mission had a hope of succeeding.

The duke was in his mid-sixties and was still reckoned to be a powerful force in both society and the Lords. A staunch Tory, he was rigid in his conservative views, and was always consulted on any matter of policy. He was known to be a high stickler for proper behavior—just the type of man who would toss his daughter aside during a scandal.

Somers rehearsed in his mind again what he planned to say to the duke; he hoped to play on the man's sympathies, painting a bleak picture of Elizabeth's forlorn existence, her humble cottage, her menial labor. He was certain the duke would not like the idea of his daughter carrying wood and tending the horses, as she had done during the snow. Somers could tell of her hidden but still persistent longings for home, and the pain she still bore from her father's disavowal. Surely, the man would be moved.

Somers did not precisely gasp when his carriage started down the long, sweeping entry drive to Harcourt. He was, after all, an earl, and his estate at Kempton was a handsome property. But he was forced to admit that this was the most impressive sight he had ever seen. There were perhaps fancier houses or more attractive vistas, but he had never seen the two combined so well together. The drive, he was sure, had been designed to present the house with maximum impact. The track swept along a long, tree-lined avenue, where one could catch only tantalizing glimpses of the house and park. Then, suddenly, the trees parted and there stood the house in the perfect center of the vista. The wooded park continued off to the left, and on the right, the gently rolling lawn dipped down to the lake.

The impression of calculated design was continued in the entrance. A wide stone stairway led to the front door, which opened into a hall that was palatial in its size and decor. From the black-and-white marble floor to the domed, second-floor ceiling, all was designed to attract and impress the eye. Somers was glad when he was led from this overpowering display of wealth, taste, and power into the comparatively modest hall leading to the duke's private apartments.

Somers wondered, briefly, at the location of the picture gallery, where Elizabeth had danced in the moonlight so long ago. What must it have been like, growing up in a house such as this? He could better understand her nocturnal wanderings, for it would be a less intimidating residence when shadowed in the darkness of night. He wished he could avail himself of those comforting shadows as well. A tiny shred of doubt crept into the back of his mind. His grace would not be easily intimidated.

The servant ushered him into what was obviously the duke's private study. He was seated behind a massive desk, but rose when Somers entered. Despite the iron-gray hair and deeply lined face, the Duke of Harcourt exuded an aura of strength and power that filled the room.

"I appreciate your willingness to see me, your grace," Somers began, executing a polite bow.

"I must admit, you have piqued my curiosity. It is not every young man who uses his mother for an introduction."

"I thought you might be more willing to speak with me under the circumstances," Somers replied, gratefully sitting at the duke's invitation. He looked around the elegantly furnished room as he gathered his nerve to speak.

"I am acquainted with your mother," the duke agreed. "And I knew your father tolerably well. Pity he was taken so young."

Somers nodded his assent. "This is a magnificent house. I had heard of the splendor of Harcourt, but it truly must be seen to be believed. Did not Adam redesign most of the interior?"

The duke nodded. "My father undertook that project when I was a stripling. But, come, Lord Wentworth, you have not come here on a matter your mother described as 'delicate' to discuss my house. What is your concern?"

Somers had struggled for an appropriate opening gambit, but decided to take the direct approach.

"I should like to discuss Elizabeth with you."

"Elizabeth?"

"Your daughter."

The duke stiffened. "Her name has not been spoken in this house for seven years."

"I am aware of that fact, your grace, and that is why I a here. I wished to discuss a reconciliation between yourself and your daughter."

A shocked silence followed his words.

"I do not think you are fully aware of how she is living," Somers went on hastily. "You have provided for her financially, but even so, I can hardly think you would approve of the manner in which she lives. Her house is pleasant enough, but it is a mere cottage. There is only one serving girl and a farm lad to help. Elizabeth must handle some of the household chores herself. She lives in virtual isolation; the highlight of her week is dinner at the vicar's. And she occupies her time training farm girls to be ladies' maids."

The duke looked out the window and Somers could see he was struggling for control.

"I do not see," the duke said at last, coldly, "where this is any interest of yours."

Somers took a deep breath. "Your daughter took me in during a raging snowstorm and probably saved my life. During the course of my stay, she revealed her situation and the breach with you. Despite her protestations, I know she is not happy and I would like to see the estrangement resolved, for her sake."

"Elizabeth made her choice the day she climbed into that coach for the north. She must live with the consequences."

Somers' anger rose. "She was only eighteen! A mere child. I would say she was sadly lacking in proper chaperonage if she was able to effect such a brazen elopement. That crime cannot be laid at her feet."

A dull flush crept up the duke's cheeks.

"Are you saying I am responsible for what she did?"

"Most girls of that age are watched closely enough to prevent that kind of incident. Or did you think your great name would make her immune to the charms of a practiced schemer?"

"Elizabeth was well aware of the proper behavior for one of her name and station. She chose of her own volition to ignore those strictures. Therefore, I washed my hands of her."

The duke silently rose from his chair and walked to one of the glass-fronted bookcases that lined the walls. He returned with an enormous volume, setting it on the table before Somers. Flipping quickly through the pages, the duke did not pause until he found the section he wanted. Turning the book around, so Somers could read the entry, he spoke.

"As you can see, I have no daughter of that name. What you wish to do about her has no interest for me."

Somers looked down at the ornately bound family Bible. Scanning the list of marriages and births, he located the line where Elizabeth's name should have been. It had been neatly and methodically obliterated with black ink.

Somers raised his head, his eyes blazing in anger, to look at the duke.

"You are a hard-hearted curmudgeon," he said, carefully enunciating each word. "Elizabeth is a wonderful woman, kind and gentle. She made one mistake and you are forcing her to pay forever. She was betrayed once by the man who seduced her, but she was betrayed worse by you, her own father."

Somers trembled with rage and gave not a care to the insults he directed at the duke. He stood up, clutching the back of his chair for support.

"She still speaks fondly of her childhood. She was happy here, yet when she needed you the most, you threw her out. I told her I wished to speak to her father and she asked me not to. She feared you would reject her again. By God, she was right. You have no right to be called her father."

Somers turned and stormed from the room. Once in the hall he took deep, calming breaths as he strove to master his feelings so as not to present a suspicious appearance to the servants.

The Duke of Harcourt visibly slumped in his chair after Somers left. He stared unseeing out the window until he heard the crunch of carriage wheels on gravel, which announced the departure of his petitioner. Turning back to the desk, he sank his tear-streaked face into his hands.

9

"I do not see where you could have expected anything different, my dear." The Countess of Wentworth was never one to mince words with her son. "It seems to me that if the duke was willing of a reconciliation, he would undertake it on his own."

"It was not his refusal to reconcile that so riled me." Somers restlessly paced the room to dispel the agitation that arose within him whenever he visualized that horrible blacked-out name. "It was his manner. He was cold as ice, denying the duaghter he sired, the girl who had been his favorite for eighteen years. The man is made of stone."

His mother sighed. "Perhaps it is for the best. You yourself said Elizabeth did not wish you to speak with him and was not interested in returning to society. You can now let matters lie."

"Oh, can I?" He whirled and pierced her with an angry stare. "I may not be able to persuade her father to smooth her way back into society, but I can certainly undertake that task myself. And I expect you to help."

The countess answered him with an incredulous laugh. "I fail to see where I have a part to play in this scenario. Goodness, I had no idea you had such a fondness for interfering in other people's lives. Is this a newly developed tendency or have you felt this urge often?"

"It is an inherited trait," he said dryly, and his mother had the grace to blush.

"I want you," he continued, "to extend an invitation to Elizabeth to visit Kempton."

"I fail to see why the invitation must come from me. Why cannot you invite her?"

He gave her a look of mild reproach. "It would not do at all. I am shocked you could suggest such a thing, Mama. It is highly improper for a bachelor such as myself to invite an unmarried lady to my house. But if the invitation came from my mother . . ."

She shook her head in resignation. "I cannot know what to do with you, Somers. To badger an old woman so brutally . . ."

He laughed and bent to give her a hug. "Gammon. You are in high alt that I would even consider bringing a lady to Kempton."

"I find it difficult to believe you have never entertained a woman there."

He sobered. "I never have," he replied, then his face broke into a wide grin. "How could I, when you were always present, checking on the propriety of the situation?"

"I told you years ago I would be content to remove to the dower house."

"And I told you that you shall not go there until you are truly the dowager. Now, will you write Elizabeth and ask her to come?"

She nodded. "Against my better judgment, of course, but I shall do as you ask. When shall I plan for this visitation?"

"Soon," he said. "And . . . Well, there is another favor I should like to request."

She looked at him expectantly.

"Would you ask some of your friends—discreetly, of course—to visit when Elizabeth is there? Ones who will not raise a fuss and would treat her normally. If she sees that she can be accepted by at least some members of society, she may not be so reluctant to leave her hiding place."

"Do you think she is hiding, Somers?"

He considered. "Yes, I do. Why, she refuses to go out in society even in Chedford, where she would be accepted everywhere. I think she needs to discover that it is not so bad and she can still enjoy herself."

The countess uttered a resigned sigh. "Can I do anything else for you?"

After Somers' departure, she no longer made any attempt to

hide her pleasure. She had never known Somers to take such an interest in any gently born female. He might feel sorry for the girl at present, but she would wager a monkey there was more than just pity in his feelings for Lady Elizabeth. Hopeful that one of her fondest dreams might at last be realized, she went to her desk to pen the letter of invitation. She was deeply curious to meet the woman who had so captured Somers' interest.

"It is out of the question," Elizabeth stated flatly. "How could he ever think I would consent to such a thing?"

"The note is from the countess, not her son," Emily pointed out.

"He made her write it, I know." She turned the letter over in her fingers. The bold scrawl spelling out "Lady Elizabeth Granford" stood out as if written in red ink. "And how did he discover my name?"

"What, exactly, is your objection to the visit? It would do you good to go on a journey, my dear. It has been far too long since you have set foot out of this county."

"I have no need to go visiting. I do not want to go visiting." Elizabeth jumped up out of her chair and began to pace the floor.

"Ah, well, then, if you are firm in your decision. I had only hoped . . ."

"Hoped what?"

"I had thought to visit my brother this spring." Emily smiled apologetically. "Anne is nearing another confinement and she would like me there. If you went to Kempton, I thought I might—"

"Has Somers been working on you too?" Elizabeth sat down again. "I feel I am a victim of some gigantic conspiracy."

"What nonsense. He certainly did not arrange Anne's pregnancy."

Elizabeth laughed. "No, I agree that is out of his power." She looked pensive. "What shall I do, Emily? He thinks me a fool for living here in the country and will not accept that I am content to remain."

"Are you?"

"A fool? You know I could never go out in society."

"I think you place too much importance on nothing. Society's memory is very short, Elizabeth. Your past is beyond being even yesterday's news.'' She raised her hand to cut off Elizabeth's attempted protest. ''And even if you do not want to partake of London society, there is no reason you cannot visit within a small circle of friends. Lady Rockingham invites you to her house yearly, yet you still refuse. Do you wish to be a recluse all your life? To always know from one week to the next where you will be, the people you will see, and what you will say to them?''

Chewing on her lower lip, Elizabeth pondered her cousin's words. She had not admitted it, even to her inner self, but there was a discontent gnawing at her, a growing sense that her quiet country life was no longer all she wanted. Drat that man! He had arrived on her doorstep, a physical representation of all she had left behind, and had sown this discontent in his wake. Very well, then, if he was determined to pitchfork her into social life again, she was equally determined to show him that she did not need that life. And if she needed to prove it to herself as well, that was something she was not about to think on now.

''Pack your bags, Emily,'' Elizabeth announced brightly. ''For you are off to your brother's and I shall travel to Kempton.''

Elizabeth lay back comfortably against the thick velvet squabs. There were some compensations to being the guest of the Earl of Wentworth. It was certainly more pleasant making the journey in his lordship's personal traveling coach than in a hired conveyance. She should have guessed that Somers would travel only in the highest degree of comfort. And she was appreciative of his thoughtfulness in booking ahead her rooms at the inns where she broke her journey. Now, if he could only manage to find a carriage with wings that could travel across the county in the space of a few minutes . . .

Elizabeth recalled how she had never much cared for coach traveling. It was invariably a long and boring process, and even if the roads had improved a hundredfold from the last time she had taken an overnight journey, it was still as tedious as she remembered it. If it was not for Sally's wide-eyed excitement at every new sight, Elizabeth would have been bored to tears.

For the hundredth time she consulted the watch pinned to the bodice of her pelisse. Less than an hour now until . . .

Elizabeth shook her head as if to clear it of all thought. She was not going to think about what would happen once she reached her destination. She was not going to think about the countess and what she would think of the estranged daughter of a duke. And she most definitely was not going to think about Somerset Graham, the Earl of Wentworth. That always proved a most frustrating exercise.

Her reverie was broken by the slowing of the coach. Elizabeth looked about in surprise.

"Oh, I just know it's a highwayman, Miss Lizzie." Sally was round-eyed in terror.

"Nonsense. Highwaymen do not ply the coaching roads in broad daylight. Perhaps something is in our way." She moved to open the door, but it suddenly was opened from the outside.

"Stand and deliver."

Elizabeth's laughter drowned out Sally's shriek of terror.

"Somers," Elizabeth cried in exasperation. "You are frightening the poor girl to death."

His face broke into a broad grin. "Accept my apologies, Sally. I do not wish to disturb my favorite muffin maker." He climbed into the coach with a skillful grace and took a seat next to Elizabeth. "I thought you would feel more comfortable if I rode the last part of the way with you."

She was not as certain of that, but she appreciated the gesture. "Thank you, Somers. It has been a marvelous trip. I shall let you arrange my travels in the future if you can guarantee all the journeys will be as free of mishap."

"Easily done," he replied. "But do not talk of journeying on so soon. You have not yet even arrived."

Elizabeth smiled and almost forgave him his interfering ways. She admitted she was pleased to see him again. Those mischief-filled blue eyes were captivating.

"Coo, look, Miss Lizzie! It's a regular palace."

Elizabeth peeked out of the window to catch her first glimpse of Kempton. It was not a palace, but it was a very impressive house.

"Tudor, is it not?"

Somers nodded. "Not quite as grand as some people's homes," he said with a pointed look at Elizabeth, "but it does very well."

"I never did ask, Somers, how you learned my name."

"It was simple," he replied with a feigned nonchalance. "I merely went through the Peerage Index, looking for all daughters named Elizabeth born before 1800, and wrote them all. You were the only one to respond to my invitation, so I knew I had gotten it right."

His face was a mask of bland innocence, but Elizabeth was not fooled. She never believed his story for a moment. She had gone to great pains to keep her identity a secret from him, and he would have needed to use equal pains to discover it. Why had he gone to so much trouble?

Stepping into the entry hall at Kempton, Elizabeth was struck by its welcoming appearance. No cold marble grandeur here. The polished woodwork and thick carpeting bespoke an equal elegance, but in a friendlier manner. This was a home, not an exhibit.

As Somers escorted her up the stairs, Elizabeth finally allowed her apprehensions to run wild. How would Somers' mother treat her? Would the countess be polite, but distant? Or, worse, would she be so attentively sweet that Elizabeth would feel smothered? For the hundredth time since she made the decision to come, she wished she had not.

Somers held open the door to the drawing room and Elizabeth walked into a chamber that was decorated in a tasteful manner. But before she had time to absorb more than a fleeting impression of the room, the countess was before her, her hands outstretched in greeting.

"I am so pleased you have come, Lady Elizabeth."

Elizabeth executed a neat curtsy. "It was kind of you to invite me, Lady Wentworth."

"I hope you have a lovely visit with us." Now, please . . ." She led Elizabeth over to the sofa and motioned her to sit. "I do hope your journey went well. Somers usually does such a marvelous job of arranging things so one suffers only slight discomforts."

"It was very pleasant," Elizabeth replied. "If all journeys went so smoothly, I would not hesitate to travel often."

Somers leaned negligently against the mantel, a picture of unconcern. But his sharp eyes watched every subtle nuance of the conversation between the two ladies.

"Of course," Elizabeth continued, "there was the slight problem of the highwayman at the end . . ." She cast a teasing look at Somers.

"Somers!" The countess was torn between exasperation and amusement. "Aren't you a bit old for that sort of thing?" She turned to Elizabeth. "We spent one dreadful summer the year he was ten. He waylaid every coach on its way here. It is a miracle some overzealous coachman did not shoot him."

"Did you collect any booty?" Elizabeth asked.

"Alas, no one found a ten-year-old highwayman fearsome enough to part with their jewels. I did receive a thrashing when I heldup the Duke of Devonshire. My father was not amused."

"Somers was a dreadful rogue," his mother stated. "And, unfortunately, he still often is. Now, my dear, you must let us know what you wish to do while you are here. The neighborhood is rather quiet, as most of the neighbors are still up in London, but there are enough people about to afford us some amusements. Lady Claring stops by nearly every day, and we could get up a small card party one evening. I believe Viscount Harries has come down and—"

"Please," said Elizabeth, laying a forestalling hand on the countess's arm. "I . . . I do not know what Somers has told you, but I am not at all accustomed to going out in society. You need not plan any special entertainments for me."

The countess gave her a shrewd stare.

"I do know of your situation, Lady Elizabeth. And of course I sympathize with your reluctance to reenter society. I do not wish to force you to do anything you do not wish. I had only thought . . . Well, that perhaps a few quiet country entertainments might be acceptable."

Elizabeth looked to Somers for support, but found him staring in rapt fascination at his fingernails.

"I . . . I would be amenable to anything you care to plan, Lady Wentworth."

The countess patted Elizabeth's hand in a comforting way. "We shall take great pains to see that you enjoy your stay with us. But please, call me Catherine. We do not stand on formality here. And may I call you Elizabeth?''

She nodded.

''I, however, would prefer to be called Lord Wentworth,'' Somers interjected.

''I find it best to ignore him when he is in this mood,'' the countess said, rising from her seat. ''Now, I shall take you to your room, as I am sure you would like to change from your traveling clothes. I've arranged for a light luncheon and then Somers will take up his duties as host. I always rest in the afternoon.''

Left alone at last in her room, Elizabeth realized where Somers had acquired his tendency to bend others to his will. She doubted even he could resist his mother for long. And the worst of it was, she was so sweet and kind that one felt utterly unable to say no to her. By the time she was through, the countess could make anyone believe they actually wanted to do her bidding. Did Somers have the same power?

Elizabeth stepped toward the long windows, flanked by their curtains of rich blue brocade. Her room looked out over the back lawn and she spotted the corner of a formal garden before the grass sloped off toward the wood. Where was the lake where the youthful Somers had splashed and frolicked in the moonlight? The image of the ten-year-old highwayman flashed before her eyes.

Somers was a mass of contradictions. When he had first arrived at her doorstep, covered with snow, looking every inch the outraged aristocrat, she had labeled him a top-lofty town dandy. But as she grew to know more of him, she realized there was much more to the man behind the facade. He liked his creature comforts, but he did not complain at their lack if there was no choice. He was managing and interfering, but he had a delightful sense of humor, coaxing the usually sober Emily into uproarious laughter with his wit. And he was persuasive— Elizabeth's presence here pointed to his success in that area.

Yet she was unsure of his motivations. Despite that kiss in the garden, she did not think he was interested in her for anything beyond a mild flirtation. What man of the *ton* would be, after her unfortunate past? So, why was he taking such pains to invite her to his home and force her out into company again? Was it merely the whim of a bored, jaded aristocrat?

And, more important, why was she here? Dissatisfaction with her life in Chedford, probably. She had Somers to thank for that, for she had never been restless before. But she had enjoyed his lengthy visit, reveling in the opportunity to match wits with a man who was her equal in mind as well as in class. And, admittedly, she enjoyed the slight hints of flirtation. She had been skilled at that art, so many years ago, and it was pleasing to know she had not forgotten how to talk with an attractive man.

A sudden tremor shook her body. Elizabeth did not like the way her thoughts were drifting. She was firmly aware of her awkward position and what life held in store for her, and men were not a part of it. They were a charming sex, to be sure, but never to be trusted. She must be on her guard, for Somers had a knack of disarming all her defenses with that warm, lazy smile of his. And it grew more apparent that she needed strong defenses when Somers was near.

10

The racing horses swept across the gentle slope, matched stride for stride in a flat-out gallop. As they neared the unfenced dirt lane that neatly sliced the field in two, the black gelding shot forward at the urging of his rider, crossing the road a half-length ahead of its companion.

"I won," Elizabeth shouted gleefully over her shoulder.

Somers screwed up his face into a scowl, but he was not one whit disappointed at his loss. This new, joyful Elizabeth was a source of delight to him—whether racing him across the field, with her wind-whipped hair tumbling from beneath her hat, or teasing him over cards in the evening. The serious, reserved, and rather sad woman he had met in Chedford had become a witty, cheerful, and most entertaining guest.

Her gaiety pleased Somers. Any lingering doubts he held about the wisdom of his invitation had long vanished. The visit was doing her a world of good. Even yesterday's tea with Lady Webberly had done nothing to ruffle Elizabeth's newfound happiness. He had known she missed life in society; now she was well on her way to returning to it. She would no longer have any need to hide herself away in Chedford. He felt a sense of smug satisfaction at having shown her.

"I understand now why you have such beautiful horses at home," he said when he drew up his mount alongside hers. "You are a skillful rider."

"Thank you, my lord," she replied with a saucy grin. "Your own stable is certainly not lacking."

"One of my weaknesses," he explained. "Despite the manner

of my father's death, neither I nor my mother could bring ourselves to sell his hunters. He was a prime judge of horse-flesh, and I like to think my own choices would not have displeased him.''

"Did your mother never wish to remarry?"

Somers thought for a moment. "I am not certain. There have been one or two gentlemen I wondered about.'' He grinned. "I think she decided that supervising me was a full-time occupation.''

"No doubt," Elizabeth responded dryly. "It is terrifying to imagine what you would have been like without her steadying influence.''

"You sound just like her," he lamented. "I know I could have managed well on my own.''

Elizabeth laughed aloud. She enjoyed her teasing relationship with Somers. Matching barbs with him became her biggest pleasure of the day. As the youngest child, she had never developed a close relationship with her elder siblings. She thought this was what it would have been like had she grown up in a house with a close-knit family. Somers would have made an admirable older brother.

After the long years of exile in Chedford, it was exciting to live the life of an aristocratic lady again, even if for only a short time. Elizabeth frankly admitted she enjoyed the luxury of servants to answer her every want and need. And it was exquisitely wonderful to awake in the morning with no more pressing thought than what she would wear that day. Somers and his mother thoroughly spoiled her, and she loved every minute. It was a marvelous holiday, and for brief moments, Elizabeth wished the visit would never end. But then she would recall she was only a guest and one day would go back to her old life at the cottage with Emily.

Not that she minded that, she hastily reminded herself. No amount of coddling could make up for the satisfaction of helping a girl like Sally achieve her heart's desire, or teaching a young farm lad to read. If only . . .

"What has my mother arranged for you today?" Somers arched a teasing brow, wondering what had caused the small frown that crept across Elizabeth's face.

"I believe we are taking a drive to visit one of the neighbors for tea. And there was the mention of a small card party tonight."

"I am surprised she has not planned a full-fledged ball," he half-complained. "I am sure only the lack of participants has stilled her hand there. She is not overly fond of the country; London is her element. Anything else than a house party of ten is abhorrent to her."

"Then why is she here?"

"Because I asked her to come. I do not entertain a lady without a proper chaperone."

"Hardly necessary in my case." Despite Somers' verbal insistence on her respectability, his utterance did not make it true.

"Oh, but most necessary," he countered. "I am a proper gentleman and do not wish to sully my reputation in town. I would be sunk beyond reproach if I did not observe the proprieties."

"Are you ever serious?" Elizabeth shook her head in fond exasperation.

"Rarely." He smiled wickedly.

Somers, to Elizabeth's surprise, chose to accompany them to Lady Worthing's in the afternoon. When she saw him dressed impeccably in a snug-fitting coat of deep-blue superfine, an elaborate patterned waistcoat, and immaculate buff pantaloons, Elizabeth had difficulty remembering the shabby gentleman who had graced her parlor for so long. Yet, if it had not been for those two weeks, she would have been dreadfully uncomfortable in his presence, for there was no question he was a leader of the *ton*. And quite elegantly attractive. Had she encountered him now for the first time, he would have frightened her witless. Handsome, aristocratic men were anathema to her. But knowing the man behind the well-tailored clothes, she held no apprehension of him.

Somers leaned negligently against the mantel, his cup and saucer balanced in one hand while he watched Elizabeth chatting with his mother and Lady Worthing. She looked every inch a duke's daughter today. He had wondered, when he stayed with her in Chedford, at her stylish clothes. He now suspected it was

Elizabeth's secret extravagance, the major luxury she allowed herself in her exile.

She had exquisite taste. The high-necked blue gown she wore, with its puffed and gathered sleeves, ruffled collar, and elegant lines, was in the first stare of fashion. Whatever allowance her father grudgingly bestowed upon her, it was ample to keep Elizabeth in the latest styles. And she wore her hair differently today. It was still held back in the customary chignon, but higher on her head and looser, with curls escaping down the nape of her neck and framing her face. She could have stepped from the doors of any fashionable house in Grosvenor Square. Elizabeth had the air and grace of a grand lady in everything she did.

Somers was certain his mother had prepared Lady Worthing for Elizabeth's visit, for there were no awkward questions about her past, or references to the duke. The three ladies chattered on as if this was an everyday social event and not the first call Elizabeth had paid to a member of the *ton* in seven years.

"Somers?"

His mother's voice broke into his thoughts. He flushed, embarrassed at having been caught wool-gathering. He hoped they had not noticed how avidly he was staring at Elizabeth. Here, in the relaxed setting of a drawing room, he could not forget for a moment that she was a damnably attractive woman. And he always had an eye for attractive women.

"My apologies. I am afraid I was too absorbed with the elegant tableau of such three exquisite ladies to be paying attention. Do forgive me, Mama."

The countess made a noise sounding suspiciously like a snort. "I wished to inquire whether you would care to show Elizabeth the portrait gallery. I am afraid to bore her with the prattle of two elderly gossips."

Somers looked about him in mock surprise. "Where? Who?"

His mother shook her head, laughing. "As you can see, Amelia, he has not changed one whit over the years."

"I hope he has at least conquered that dreadful habit of pelting every four-footed creature with his peashooter. Lord, I shall never forget the time—"

"Allow me to escort you to the portrait gallery, Lady

Elizabeth.'' Somers hastily extended his arm. ''Before any more scurrilous attacks are pressed against my name.''

''Is the gallery here exceptionable?'' she asked as he guided her down the hall.

''Old Worthing had an eye for art, I will credit him with that.'' Somers led her down a narrow hallway that opened into a light, airy passage, hung ceiling to floor with paintings of every school popular in the last four hundred years. Lace-bedecked cavaliers hung cheek by jowl with ruffled Elizabethans; landscapes marched against hunting scenes.

''The collection is a bit jumbled,'' Somers acknowledged. ''But knowing of your passion for galleries, I thought you might like this one. Of course, it probably has to be seen in the moonlight to do it justice.''

She shot him a wistful smile.

Taking her hand, he placed it lightly on his arm and walked her about the large room, identifying the family portraits, embellishing their histories with stories Elizabeth was certain were total fabrications.

''How is it that you know so much of the Worthings?''

''Our families have resided side by side for generations,'' he explained. ''It is part of the inheritance, I think. One comes into the title and inherits the other family as well. It has been a long tradition that the families intermarry. This lady here''—he paused before a portrait from Queen Anne's day—''was an umpteenth great-aunt of mine, who married the earl.''

''Are there any Worthings in your future?'' she asked teasingly.

''It is my mother's greatest regret that both she and Lady Worthing were plagued with sons,'' he explained. ''Else I am certain I should have been leg-shackled years ago in order to provide them with housefuls of children to call them Grandmama.''

'''How like you to find some way to vex your mother.''

''I try.''

As the first week of Elizabeth's visit stretched into a second, she laughed at her previous apprehensions about her stay. Somers' mother was as kind as could be, and Somers himself was an attentive host. There were times Elizabeth wondered—

only for a moment—whether he was slightly more attentive than the situation warranted, but she dismissed the idea from her head. She must not refine too much on that hasty kiss in the garden at Chedford. She suspected Somers was very free with his kisses, for the man was an incorrigible flirt. Still, it was pleasant to be the recipient of any man's attention, even if he extended his interest because of her gender rather than any personal concern. Incorrigible flirts had their uses.

"You need not feel that you must entertain me every moment," Elizabeth said to Somers as the two sat in the drawing room. The afternoon sun streamed through the tall windows, the bright golden beams creating the illusion of summer outside. Somers had escorted them to the village in the morning and the countess had now retired for her afternoon rest. Elizabeth was certain he would rather be off pursuing his own interests.

"Truly, I wish to be here," he protested. "How could you even think I would care to abandon the company of such a beautiful woman?"

"Whom you have entertained faithfully for nearly two weeks. Honestly, Somers, I am capable of amusing myself for more than a minute. You are denying me the opportunity of taking advantage of your library. Be off with you."

"I assure you, I am here of my own free will, and I have no other plans for the afternoon."

"How about a hand of piquet, then? As I recall, I owe you something in the neighborhood of ten thousand pounds, and I need to recoup my losses."

"Hardly likely," he snorted derisively. Piquet was definitely not her game. "But if you wish to go further into debt, I will not argue." He found the cards and they settled at the table to play.

"You are enjoying your stay here?" he asked bluntly after she had made a thunderously foolish bet.

"Yes, I am. I am glad I came, Somers. I had truly forgotten how pleasant it is to be a guest in another's home."

"Should you like to come up to London in June?" He watched her face anxiously. "The Season will be winding down, but there will still be much to do."

"I do not think so," she replied hastily.

"Now, do not pucker up like that. Admit it, you were terrified to come to Kempton, and all has gone well. Think of what you could do in the city. There are the theaters, the Royal Academy. Why, you have not even seen the Elgin marbles. And do not tell me you would not give much to visit all the shops."

"Perhaps. But do not press me now. Let me enjoy Kempton without a thought to the future."

"An admirable plan. Considering how you now owe me another thousand pounds."

She folded her hand in feigned disgust. "You are an odious opponent, Somers. Winners should never gloat." She looked wistfully out the window. "If we bundle up well, do you think we can fool ourselves into thinking it is high summer outside? It looks so marvelously warm from here."

"And we both know it is actually biting cold. But come." He extended his hand. "We shall pretend it is August until our fingers turn blue."

The next day Elizabeth finally persuaded Somers to attend to his business while she and the countess sat and sewed. He grumbled at his dismissal, but admitted he was woefully behind on estate matters and could probably find something to do with his steward.

Elizabeth and Lady Wentworth were comparing the merits of threads from different London suppliers when a visitor was announced.

"Lady Peckingham is here, my lady. Are you receiving today?"

"Oh, dear," replied the countess. Lady Peckingham was not a particularly close friend. She was as fond of gossip as the countess, but the viscount's wife took delight in the more malicious aspects of talebearing. Lady Wentworth did not want the woman to meet Elizabeth without warning, to avoid any awkwardness. But if she turned her away, it would cause further talk, for the viscountess was certain to learn of Lady Elizabeth's presence and would be able to apply her fertile imaginaton to that situation. Admittance would be the lesser of two evils.

"Very well, then" she acknowledged reluctantly. "Send her in. And bring a tea tray."

She turned to Elizabeth. "I am not overly pleased at this

unexpected visit," Lady Wentworth explained. "For she is a gossip and scatter-wit of the worst sort, and one never knows what she will say. Yet I am afraid to turn her away, for she would twist that into who-knows-what."

"Catherine," the viscountess said as she imperiously swept into the room. Placing greeting kisses on the countess's cheeks, she settled her ample form into a softly upholstered chair and looked expectantly at Elizabeth.

"Margaret, this is Elizabeth Granford, who is visiting here at Kempton. Lady Peckingham."

Elizabeth bobbed a greeting.

"You could have bowled me over with a feather when I heard you were here at this time of the year, Catherine," the viscountess trilled in a breathy voice. "I could not believe you would leave London before the end of the Season." She cast a sly look at Elizabeth. "But I see there is more to the story. Are we to expect some felicitous news soon?"

Elizabeth colored slightly at the implication.

The countess laughed. "Believe me, I have not totally given up hope yet for Somers. But Elizabeth is a dear friend of mine. She has a quite successful school near Gloucester for the village children, and you know how I am so interested in tenant welfare."

"Indeed," said the viscountess, her disappointment in the lack of matrimonial news palpable. "Are you perhaps thinking of starting a school here?"

"It is a possibility." The countess greeted the arrival of the tea tray with relief. Eating and drinking had such a nice way of limiting conversation.

"You live near Gloucester?" Lady Peckingham asked Elizabeth with obvious curiosity.

Elizabeth nodded politely. How she wished they had not chased Somers off. He would say something utterly outrageous to draw attention away from herself.

"I was not aware of any Granford families in Gloucester. Distant cousins of Harcourt, I presume?" The viscountess wrinkled her brow as she puzzled the relationship.

"There is a slight connection," Elizabeth replied uneasily. "You live near Kempton?"

"The Peckinghams have lived in Dorset nearly as long as

the Wentworths,'' the countess interposed. ''More tea? I know Somers will be delighted to see you again, Lady Peckingham. Elizabeth, perhaps you could roust him from the estate room and ask him to join us.''

Elizabeth rose to do her bidding.

''Lady Elizabeth Granford,'' the viscountess announced in a triumphant voice. ''That's it! You're Harcourt's daughter, aren't you? I thought that name sounded familiar.'' She gave the countess a pitying look. ''Catherine, I fear you have been sadly misled.''

''Oh?''

''Surely, you would not have sponsored her in our county society if you knew the whole story. She has cozened you quite thoroughly, I am afraid.''

Elizabeth stood as if rooted to the floor, mortified at the viscountess's reaction and yet unable to flee the room. She had known that someday there would be a scene like this, known she would never be completely free from her past. These last weeks had lulled her into a false sense of security.

''I do not quite understand your meaning, Margaret,'' the countess responded icily.

''I, for one, remember the tale quite well.'' The viscountess directed a sniff of disdain toward the immobile Elizabeth. ''She is Harcourt's youngest, the one who ran off with some wretched fortune-hunter. Harcourt all but tossed her out on her ear after that.'' She turned to face Elizabeth. ''You stand there looking as if butter wouldn't melt in your mouth, young lady, but you cannot pull the wool over my eyes. At least I have a sense of who can properly be accepted into society.''

''Are you implying I do not?'' Lady Wentworth's voice was like ice.

The viscountess's eyes reflected a slight flicker of uneasiness. ''Now, Catherine, I am certain you did not deliberately set out to place your friends in an awkward situation.''

''That is quite enough, Lady Peckingham. Elizabeth is a guest in my house and I shall not hear you cast slurs upon her character. I assure you, I am well aware of who she is and I have not taken any measures to hide her identity. And it will please you to know, I am sure, that with your exception, she has been graciously received in every house we have visited.

A courtesy I do not think I shall be able to extend to you in the future.''

The viscountess stared at her aghast.

Elizabeth, suddenly finding her limbs responding to her will again, quietly left the room with as much dignity as she could muster.

The countess hastily crossed to the far wall and yanked the bell pull.

"Send Somers here immediately," she ordered the responding footman. Fixing Lady Peckingham with an disdainful stare, she added, "I believe you said you were leaving?"

Taken aback by her abrupt dismissal, the viscountess was unable to do more than utter a haughty sniff as a second footman arrived to escort her to her carriage.

Lady Wentworth sank back into her chair. Drat that woman. She would spread the tale far and wide, and all their efforts to bring Elizabeth into society gradually had gone for naught. It would have to be a frontal attack from here on out. Where was that ramshackle son of hers?

11

"Goodness, Mama, what is wrong?" Somers had entered the drawing room, expecting to find his mother and Elizabeth engaged in a peaceful coze. But Elizabeth was nowhere in sight and the agitation in his mother's face filled Somers with concern.

"I could cheerfully strangle Lady Peckingham. She recognized Elizabeth and then had the audacity to accuse her of foisting herself onto an unsuspecting world. The nerve of that woman!"

Somers' eyes turned icy blue with anger. How dare that spiteful woman hurt Elizabeth! "Damn. Elizabeth was so afraid something like that would happen, and I promised her it wouldn't. Where is she?"

The countess shook her head. "She made her escape during the debacle."

"And you did not go after her?" Somers glared at his mother.

"I was too busy giving Margaret the set-down she deserved. At least one good thing will come out of all this, for I doubt she will set foot across our doorstep again." She let out a deep sigh. "We were too complacent, my dear. This was bound to happen sooner or later. I only regret it occurred so soon."

"Or at all." He distractedly ran his hand through his hair. "Lord, this is my fault. I've got to find her."

Somers dashed from the room. He was bitterly guilty over what had happened, knowing he was fully as responsible as Lady Peckingham. He had dragged Elizabeth here, against her better judgment, offering her bland assurances that she would enjoy

herself. He had thought to smooth her reentry into society and
instead had forced her into an encounter every bit as horrible
as any she had imagined.

Quizzing every servant he encountered as to Elizabeth's
whereabouts, he finally discovered someone who had seen her
darting out the back. Looking for a sign of where she had fled
in her anguish, he crossed the terrace in long, easy strides and
loped down the stairs into the garden.

A flash of color at the far end of the rose border caught his
eye, and he quickened his pursuit. She was there, sitting on a
bench, her face flushed scarlet from her mad flight. Yet,
surprisingly, no tears fell across those reddened cheeks. He
stood and watched quietly, listening to the gradual quieting of
her tortured breathing.

"Some people," he said angrily, "are fools."

She turned and looked at him. "Yes, that is quite true. For
I am one of them."

"That is not what I meant," he protested.

"Nevertheless, it is true. I was a fool to come here, a fool
to listen to you, and a fool to believe what happened seven years
ago is no longer important to anyone but myself."

"Elizabeth, no one but a handful of spiteful gossips gives a
rap about seven years ago. Do you think you are the only
member of the *ton* who has sinned?" He laughed sardonically.
"Would Emily Cowper dare to cut you, when her children bear
a startling resemblance to a certain cabinet minister? The Prince
Regent is a bigamist, half the marchionesses are as virtuous as
whores, and England's leading poet is rumored to have fathered
a child with his sister. And you worry because your elopement
failed?"

Elizabeth did not respond, only twisted her fingers in
agitation, wanting him to go away, to leave her alone again.
She did not want his sympathy.

"Elizabeth," he said, his tone softer, inquiring. "Most people
will not care a whit about what happened seven years ago."

"It was not precisely a failed elopement, Somers," she said,
sighing. It was best to get it out, to have the whole ugly story
laid before him, so he would know how impossible it all was.
She stood up, glancing at him quickly before she turned away.
She saw the concern in his eyes, but knew it would be replaced

with shock and disgust when he heard the whole. "There was a child, later. He died at birth, poor thing. I only wish I had too."

"No," he said, stepping behind her and placing his hands on her slumped shoulders. Her pain sliced into him. He kept his voice steady, even. A baby did not change matters. It was over and done with. "You must not say that, Elizabeth. Even that does not alter things. It was all a very long time ago. And certainly no one knows that part of the tale."

She shook her head and the tears she held at bay for so long began to spill out of her eyes. "It has been a wonderful visit, Somers, and your mother has been most kind. But I think I should like to go home now."

His hold on her shoulders tightened. "I did not think you such a coward."

She wrenched free from his grasp and whirled to face him. "I am a coward, Somers. I only want to go home to Chedford, where I can live the life I please and no one cares about my past."

"Your position would not be so awkward if you were married. You would have the protection of your husband's name, his title."

She laughed harshly. "I do not wish to marry."

"Easy to say. How many offers have you rejected?"

"Several," she snapped, anger washing the tears from her eyes.

"I meant acceptable offers, Elizabeth. Country doctors and squire's sons do not count."

"Of course not," she snapped. "Even the tainted daughter of the Duke of Harcourt must look higher for a husband."

"Why do you keep insisting no one would want you? You are young, beautiful, witty. You have much more to offer than most of the Season's beauties."

"Except my virginity."

"Oh, damn your stupid virginity. It would be gone in a night anyway. Any sensible man would not care."

"Well, then, parade your troop of sensible men before me so I can make my choice." She glared at him.

"Would the idea of becoming Countess of Wentworth tempt you?" He blurted out the words.

She stared at him with stunned surprise. She scanned his face for some sign of his feelings, but his expression remained impassive, providing no clue to the sincerity of his words. He was joking, of course. "Enough of your teasing, Somers. I am not in the mood."

"I am serious. Marry me, Elizabeth."

"What possible reason could you have for wanting to marry me?"

He smiled enigmatically. "Several. I find you attractive, witty, and charming, which is more than I can say for most of the women I know. With my name, you would have *entrée* into every level of society. You need a man, Elizabeth, to look after you. And I can give you babies, to replace the one you lost."

"How dare you!" His condescending words infuriated Elizabeth. "You are doing this because you feel sorry for me. 'Poor Elizabeth, who has led such a sad life. I shall marry her and do a good deed.' I do not desire your pity."

Her vehement reaction irritated Somers. Certainly he felt compassion for her. It was an admirable sentiment. It was as good a reason as any for marriage. If his hasty offer had surprised even himself, upon reflection it did not seem a bad idea at all. It would shield Elizabeth from further hurt. Why should she take offense? He had never offered for a woman in his life, and she treated it as an insult.

"I realize an earl is a bit of a come-down for a duke's daughter, but—"

"I could care less about your title or social standing. Is this another part of the famous Wentworth hospitality? Do you offer for all your guests?"

"I have never asked a woman to marry me before."

"Could you not find one for whom you felt sorry enough? No one who was so desperately in need of your name and protection? I should feel flattered that my situation is so dire it has moved you to such lengths. But do not fear, Somers, I will not insist you follow through on your rash proposal. I have no need of your pity."

Without a backward glance she stalked across the garden toward the house.

Somers stood a long time, staring after her, long past the time she reentered the house. Every time he and Elizabeth grew closer, he managed to bungle things. First that kiss at Chedford, now this. Where were his wits? He had had no intention of asking Elizabeth to marry him when he had chased after her into the garden; he blurted out that offer with little thought as to his reasons. It had seemed the logical thing at the time. A respectable marriage would do much to stifle any lingering gossip about Elizabeth's past. And if he had not bothered to think through the ramifications of such a move, the lifelong commitment, the intimacies of marriage, and the obligations . . . Well, he was too angry and confused to give his motives much inspection now. He would be lucky if Elizabeth ever spoke to him again.

At dinner, it was apparent to the countess that something untoward had transpired between her son and Elizabeth. Elizabeth looked tired and wan, understandable after that horrible incident earlier, but the tight lines around Somers' mouth indicated he was on edge as well. Their feigned nonchalance did nothing to fool her. She was not surprised when Elizabeth excused herself shortly after dinner and retired to her room.

"Well, Somers, what have you done now?" his mother asked after she was settled in front of the drawing-room fire.

"Nothing."

"Do not try to gammon me. You and Elizabeth are wound up as tightly as clocks. You were supposed to comfort her, not to make things worse."

"I tried," he protested. "She did not want my comfort. A more ungrateful woman I have never met."

"Perhaps it was your manner that set her off. You can sometimes be a bit overbearing."

"Overbearing? I was the perfect gentleman. I offered to protect her, to take care of her, and she threw my proposal in my face."

"Just what exactly did you offer?" The countess was suspicious. "Do not tell me you tried to set her up as your mistress?"

He gave his mother a searing look. "I offered her my name."

The countess could not disguise her surprise. "And she refused?"

"Adamantly. Said it was carrying hospitality a bit too far and she didn't want my pity."

"Do you pity her, Somers?" Lady Wentworth eyed him critically. "Most men offer out of a more suitable emotion—admiration, affection, or even love."

"I don't know what I feel for her, besides anger at the moment." Somers paced frantically across the floor. "Of course I feel sorry for her; she has had a difficult time. She needs someone to take care of her, to protect her. I thought if I married her, there would be no more incidents like today. No one would dare insult my wife."

"I think you place too much importance on your position, my dear. Even your exalted name is no guarantee."

"I thought you would be on my side," he muttered peevishly.

"I might have been, if you had handled this properly. But unless you want her out of an abiding love and sense that you cannot live without her, I think she is well rid of you."

"You have been reading those dreadful romantic novels again," he said accusingly. "No one but the veriest fool marries for love."

"Yet I cannot see the point of you marrying without some feeling for the woman beyond sympathy. Elizabeth certainly deserves more. You would be chasing after your opera dancers and married ladies again in no time." The countess looked thoughtful. "No, I shall have to introduce her to someone with more sensitivity than you. I wonder who I could invite down . . ."

"I would not worry yourself too much, for she told me she wishes to leave."

"Somers, how dreadful of you to drive her away. Perhaps you should leave. I would like her to stay."

"Fine," he said, striding toward the door. "If that is what you wish, I shall go back to London." He slammed the drawing-room door behind him.

The countess made no attempt to suppress her smile. Somers may have botched things royally, but he was on the right track. To think he actually offered marriage! If only he had not insulted

Elizabeth beyond repairing . . . Matters would need a delicate touch for the next few days.

Lady Wentworth was less optimistic the next morning, for Elizabeth was adamant in her intention to leave. Despite all her pleading and cajoling, the countess was unable to change Elizabeth's mind. Even Somers' muttered remark about leaving for London did nothing to alter the situation. The countess accepted this temporary defeat with good grace and turned her attention to some effective method of punishing Somers for his idiocy.

Elizabeth stared out the carriage window. It was funny how return journeys always seemed to take less time than the outbound ones. She and Sally had fairly flown over the Cotswolds, Chedford was less than an hour away and they would be home again in the cozy little cottage.

She gave one last sigh. She had enjoyed her visit to Kempton, except for those last two days. Perhaps in the future, when tempers had settled, she could continue her friendship with the countess. As long as her odious son was away.

Elizabeth had thought Somers was truly her friend, but that insulting offer of marriage had shown her his true colors. All along he had viewed her merely as an object of pity. His charitable cause. She thought he accepted her and her past, when he only felt sorry for her. She would rather he viewed her with disgust than pity.

As the carriage covered the last quarter-mile toward her home, Elizabeth was filled with relief. This was the one place where she truly felt at peace. It was a relief to be back where she belonged.

As Somers' coach pulled up in front of the stable, Elizabeth was cheered by the sight of Tommy racing to meet them, his eyes alight at the sight of the magnificent equipage. The lad would love to be a coachman, she thought, and began weaving her plans anew.

"Miss Lizzie, Miss Lizzie! There was a man here yesterday, looking for you. I told him you was gone away, but he left a note for you. Said it was very important."

Elizabeth was puzzled and intrigued. For a moment, she thought Somers might be up to one of his tricks, but then she dismissed that thought. She had seemed thoroughly chastened when she left him, and she doubted if she would hear from him in some time, if ever. She walked eagerly toward the house. The mysterious note would answer her questions.

She spotted the envelope on the hall table, but it was the letter beside it that caused her to freeze, the scrawled frank at the corner staring out at her from the past. Dead God, she thought, after all these years . . .

Ignoring the note, she took the letter in hand, carrying it into the parlor and sitting down in her favorite chair. A sense of dread filled her. Why, suddenly, had he finally written? She stared at the letter while she held it in her hand, turning it over and over as if to absorb its contents without having to read it. Then, with a sigh, she broke the seal.

There was only one piece of paper inside. And it was not from the man whose signature had authorized its free journey across the country in a speeding mail coach. It had been written by his secretary, she saw, glancing at the closing. Taking a deep breath, she at last looked at the words.

And halted, abruptly, closing her eyes for a brief moment as the shock washed over her. Then she turned her eyes back to the paper, quickly scanning the remaining contents. With a cry of dismay, she flung the paper to the floor and ran to the hall table, fearing beyond all words to read the note that had only been delivered yesterday.

Elizabeth breathed a sigh of relief as she read the news, only two days old. There was still time; she would not be too late. She ran out the door, yelling for Tommy.

As the coach jounced and rattled over the bumpy road, Elizabeth gave a wistful thought to Somers' elegant equipage, which would have floated over the ruts with more grace. He would not have uttered a word of censure had she taken it on this trip. But she refused to take advantage of the situation and had dispatched the earl's coach back to Kempton. Luckily, Squire Reeves had loaned her his vehicle. If she had had to wait for one from the nearest posting house, her journey would have been delayed another day. And she could not afford to wait. Even now, on the last leg of her trip, she could barely contain her anxiety lest she be too late. She would have driven the coach herself if it would have sped her on her way.

Sally slept easily in the seat across, her young face untroubled by the constant traveling of the last four days. To her it was an adventure. Elizabeth smiled softly at the thought of how Sally had been so thrilled at the sight of Kempton. What would she say of their new destination?

The shadows were growing long across the road two days later when the carriage turned off the main way and through the outer gates of the estate. The couchant lions atop the gate posts stared back at her with their stone-gray, ever-open eyes. Elizabeth could not tear herself away from the coach window as she strained to catch a glimpse of the house through the trees. It all looked the same: timeless and unchanged as if she had only left the day before. The coach negotiated the final turn and Harcourt lay before her, the last rays of sun slanting across the upper windows, lighting the glass with a blinding blaze of fire.

12

Without waiting for the liveried footman to open the door, Elizabeth sprang from the coach the moment the wheels stopped. She stood unsteadily, unaccustomed to the sudden lack of motion. The footman stared at her in frank curiosity, as if wondering why this travel-weary lady acted with such urgency.

"Please see to my maid and the luggage," she said briskly, and sped up the steps in unladylike haste.

"Lady Elizabeth!" The butler's voice expressed his pleased surprise.

"Hello, Crispin." Elizabeth smiled warmly at the imperious guardian of Harcourt. He did not look one day older than she remembered.

"We have been expecting you daily," he explained as he guided her up the long marble staircase that had so intimidated Somers on his earlier visit.

"I was away from home when the letter came. He is . . . he is all right still?"

He nodded, his face grave. "The marquess wished to see you as soon as you arrived. They are all here now, with the exception of Lord Richard." Silently, he opened the door of the front drawing room.

The nerves she had fought against for two days threatened to overcome her at last. Elizabeth felt paralyzed, unable to move. She had never been close to her brother Frederick, the twelve-year gap in age too wide to overcome. He had always been stern and critical with her. She did not truly know what he thought

117

of her, whether he agreed with her father's condemnation of
her behavior. No one spoke out against the duke, not even his
heir. Yet none of her siblings had contacted her over the years,
so perhaps they had willingly acquiesced to her father's denial.

Forcing her leaden legs to move, Elizabeth stepped across
the threshold. A sea of faces turned toward her, and she felt
their sharp gazes, probing, questioning.

"How fortunate you have finally seen fit to arrive." The
harshness of her eldest brother's voice awoke her from her
trance.

"I was not at home when the letter came," she said, hating
her defensive reaction. They could not hurt her anymore, she
reminded herself. "I have been traveling for four days straight,
Frederick, from Dorset to home and from there to Harcourt.
I came as soon as I knew."

Frederick Granford, Marquess of Slate, silently set down his
cup of tea.

"When may I see him?" Elizabeth asked eagerly.

Frederick recrossed his legs and gave an elegant shrug.
"When it is convenient, I suppose. I shall tell him you have
arrived."

Something in his tone caused her to pause. "I thought he
wished to see me."

"He is very ill, Elizabeth, and is often asleep. Some days
he is willing to talk at length and on others he does not want
to see anyone. And as I am sure your presence will do little
to improve his condition, we may deem it necessary to postpone
things for a bit."

Elizabeth flushed at his insult.

"Join us for some tea," her sister Augustinia, Countess
Soames, offered tactfully.

Flashing her a grateful smile, Elizabeth sat down and accepted
the proffered cup. Feeling the curious stares of her siblings and
their attending spouses, it was all she could do not to stare back
in return. She formed her face into a polite mask and silently
sipped her tea.

They were all there—Frederick, Augustinia, and Charlotte,
all looking remarkably the same as when Elizabeth had seen
them last. She noted how Charlotte's husband, Lord Choate,
had run to fat over the years.

Suddenly Elizabeth felt the walls of the room closing in around her. She did not want to sit there a moment longer, waiting for them to begin the inevitable questions about her life. The polite smiles pasted on the faces in the room did not fool her; behind those smiles were minds filled with accusation and condemnation. There had been no contact for seven years; several hours more would not make any difference. She hastily drained her tea.

"I am very weary from my trip, Frederick. I should like to rest before dinner."

"Certainly," agreed her brother. "I shall have someone escort you to your room. Dinner is at seven."

"I was born in this house," Elizabeth informed him in icy rage. "I have not forgotten the way."

A tightness rose in her chest as Elizabeth looked around the achingly familiar confines of her old room. The curtains, the furniture, the pictures, were all as she had left them when she departed for London in that fateful spring. She was taken aback to discover the chamber had been left untouched. It would not have surprised her in the least to find her things gone. But they were still here, as if they had known she would one day return.

Elizabeth slowly walked around the room, touching every object in turn, as if fearing they would disappear like wisps of smoke before her eyes. Her dressing table, with its gleaming mirror. Her collection of tiny china figurines, all in a precise row and spotlessly dusted. She ran her fingers over the blue brocade curtains, tracing the curling curves on the ornately carved wardrobe. They were all real. She was here, at Harcourt, at last.

A soft knock at the door caught her attention. A maid entered.

"Lady Choate wishes me to assist you." The girl's tone was almost sullen.

"I have brought my own maid," Elizabeth responded firmly. "You will send her to me, please."

The maid sniffed. "Lady Choate said you need a real maid, miss. Not that country girl."

Elizabeth drew herself up and pinioned the girl with a glare worthy of a duke's daughter. "When you speak to me, you shall address me as Lady Elizabeth, or my lady. Is that clear?"

"Yes, my lady."

"Now, you are to go downstairs and find Sally and send her to me at once. And you may tell Lady Choate that I am mindful of her kindness, but I prefer to have my own maid."

Elizabeth was furious. Charlotte's condescension was the outside of enough. How dare she imply Sally was not fit to attend her mistress? Must she have to endure these petty insults for the entire length of her visit?

She wondered again why her father wanted to see her. The rest of the family were obviously not eager to have her here. Did they reflect her father's attitude as well? Was she home at last, only to endure further insult and hurt? She fervently prayed it would not be so. She was tired of running and hiding from her past. It was beyond time for her to start living for the future once again. With a wry grin, Elizabeth realized she was parroting the words she had previously condemned Somers for. Perhaps he was right, after all.

After a short nap, Elizabeth felt refreshed and ready to endure the ordeal she knew dinner would be. Sally assisted her in her toilette, and when the first dinner bell sounded, Elizabeth was ready to make her entrance into the drawing room.

She knew she had no need to apologize for her appearance. The traveling clothes she had arrived in were unexceptionable, but she knew her dinner gown was the equal of any worn by her relatives. Elizabeth gave belated thanks to her vain insistence on dressing as a woman of fashion even in an isolated corner of Gloucestershire.

Though her family had not corresponded with her all these years, Elizabeth had kept track of their activities and domestic situations. Her three sisters were already wed when Elizabeth had made her come-out, with several children among them. Elizabeth noted the announcements heralding the arrival of subsequent nieces and nephews, and had always sent gifts for the christenings, although they were never acknowledged.

Frederick had married the year before her London Season, to a woman Elizabeth had disliked even then. Sarah Armtrett had struck the then-seventeen-year-old Elizabeth as a bit of a bore, but perfectly suitable for her prosy oldest brother. They had a house full of daughters but, to Elizabeth's satisfaction, no son to inherit the title. She would much rather have her brother Richard's son become duke after Frederick was gone.

The thoughts of succession turned her mind again to the man who lay in the large bedroom above. She had rushed here in a frenzy, stopping only briefly to eat and sleep, fearing she would arrive too late. And now they forced her to sit and wait. Was that what he wished? Or were they keeping her from him out of spite?

Once again, all eyes turned her way as she entered the drawing room. Too bad she was not fond of grand entrances; this would be the ideal opportunity.

"Elizabeth, dear, tell us about your school." Augustinia turned to her husband, the Earl of Soames. "Elizabeth has established a school in her village for the foundlings or some such thing."

"It is for all the children of the parish," Elizabeth explained. "It grew out of the Sunday school. We teach the children their letters and numbers, and the girls learn sewing and cooking."

"Damn foolish idea, teaching a lot of farmers' brats how to read," grumbled Charlotte's husband, the Earl of Choate. "Gives them ideas above their station."

"It also prevents them from being cheated by their landlords or tradesmen," Elizabeth retorted. "And certainly, with such uplifting reading material as the Bible, they cannot acquire too many radical ideas."

"Is Emily Camberly still with you?" Charlotte inquired politely.

Elizabeth nodded. "Her sister-in-law was close to her confinement, so Emily joined her while I traveled to Dorset."

"Ah, yes, your visit in Dorset. I hope you had an agreeable time," Augustinia inquired.

"Yes," said Elizabeth. "Yes, I did."

"With whom did you visit?"

"The Countess of Wentworth was gracious enough to invite me to her home."

All heads nodded. The countess was well known to them.

"However did you meet her?" Augustina, Elizabeth's eldest sister, inquired. "I thought you never left your village."

"We were introduced by a mutual acquaintance."

"The countess is such a marvelous hostess," Charlotte enthused. "And I hear her house parties are always entertaining. Who else was in attendance?"

"I was the only guest." Elizabeth paused, then continued casually, "the earl was there, of course."

"Wentworth?" Charlotte sounded aghast.

Elizabeth gave her a puzzled look.

"That is a lovely dress, Elizabeth." Frederick's wife hastily changed the subject. "I did not know there were such skillful dressmakers in Gloucester."

"I have all my clothes made in London."

"You must give me the name of your dressmaker, then," Elizabeth's sister-in-law said with a polite nod. "She obviously has a great talent. Is she reasonable?"

"Horridly expensive," Elizabeth replied with a bland smile.

"Dinner is served," Crispin announced.

Elizabeth went limp with relief. At least at dinner there would be food and drink to break up the conversation. This was not going to be a comfortable stay.

When the ladies at last regained the drawing room after the meal, Elizabeth nearly laughed. Rather than continuing their interrogations, her family had virtually ignored her at the table, concentrating their talk instead on news from London and the country. Elizabeth could have entered into the conversation quite capably, for although she lived in isolation, she read most of the London papers avidly and was quite *au courant* on town gossip. But she chose not to. She much preferred to observe the interactions and undercurrents that swirled among the occupants of the room. The rest of the family might be united in their cool treatment of Elizabeth, but that was the only matter they agreed on.

"How is dear Emily?" Augustinia inquired as she settled herself into a chair and drew up her embroidery.

"She is well," Elizabeth replied. "She quite enjoys working at the school. Last year she knitted mittens for all the children; this year I believe they are getting scarves."

"I heard you had some dreadful weather there in early spring."

"Yes, we were snowbound for several days."

"How utterly frightening," Charlotte murmured. "I daresay I would not know how to get on if we were shut up for even a day. How did you ever endure such privation?"

Elizabeth smiled to herself. Charlotte, with an army of servants, would not have been inconvenienced in the least. The Countess of Choate had never hefted a log in her life, Elizabeth was certain. "Oh, we managed," she responded airily.

As conversation drifted to more domestic topics, Elizabeth turned to the marchioness.

"Tell me, Sarah, how is Papa? How long has he been ill?"

"He is not well at all, I am afraid. He took a bad turn last spring, and although he rallied over the summer, this last winter did not sit well with him."

"Did he . . . Was it his idea for me to come?"

The marchioness nodded.

"Has he said why?" Elizabeth finally voiced the question that had tormented her mind ever since she read the summons.

"I do not think even Frederick knows," Sarah replied.

"And what is it that Frederick does not know?" The marquess had caught the last words as the gentlemen rejoined the ladies.

"I am wondering why Papa asked me to come home," Elizabeth said in a high, clear voice. Several heads turned her way.

"He said nothing to me until the letter had been sent," Frederick replied slowly, managing to indicate his displeasure with his father's action. "We shall all have to wait until he feels well enough to see you."

"Does he even know I am here?"

An awkward silence settled over the room.

"I left word that he be informed." Frederick's words were abrupt.

Elizabeth was suddenly suspicious that he did not speak the truth, but what could she do to prove it? If her father was as ill as they said, barging into his room unannounced might be dangerous. And what possible reason could Frederick have for refusing her admittance to her father? She shook her head. She was merely being oversensitive. The rest of the family might be dismayed by her presence, but they would never deliberately throw obstacles in her path. The duke would brook no opposition. Her siblings would bow to whatever her father wished. She only hoped she would soon learn what that was.

13

"Why do you tiptoe around like an idiot, Crump?" Even in illness, the duke's voice was commanding.

"I had not thought you awake, your grace," his valet of many years replied.

"I am always awake," he grumbled. "Is the weather tolerable this morning?"

"The sky is clouded, but I do not think it will rain, your grace."

"English spring. Bah. Are the vultures amusing themselves still?"

Crump concurred with the duke's assessment of his offspring. "Lady Elizabeth arrived yesterday."

"What? Elizabeth here? Why was I not told?" Even illness could not hide the anger in the duke's voice.

The valet cringed. "Lord Slate felt you needed more time to rest from your last attack, your grace. He knew how difficult the interview might be for you."

The duke raised his frail frame from the pillows. "I want her here at once. At once, do you understand?"

The trembling Crump bowed his way out of the ducal chamber.

Elizabeth, exhausted from her long days of traveling, was deep in slumber when Sally came to rouse her from her bed.

"Miss Lizzie, Miss Lizzie, you must wake up. They say it is important."

Elizabeth looked about her in sleepy confusion. "What?"

"They say the duke wants to see you right away."

Elizabeth awoke instantly and scrambled out of bed. "Is he all right?"

Sally nodded. "But they say he wants you, so we must hurry." She grabbed a dress from the wardrobe while Elizabeth struggled with her nightclothes.

"I shall look a fright," Elizabeth moaned as Sally frantically did up the buttons on the dress. "Where is that hairbrush?"

While Elizabeth sought to tame her unwieldy hair, Sally strove to fasten the cuff buttons on the opposite hand.

"Miss Lizzie, you have to sit down." Sally took the brush from her mistress's hand. "I will tend to your hair and all else."

Grateful to let Sally take over, Elizabeth nearly collapsed into the chair. Her hands trembled so strongly she could barely hold the brush. Sally managed to bring a semblance of order to Elizabeth's tangled locks and produced a reasonably competent chignon.

While Sally looked to her hair, Elizabeth's mind raced ahead to the upcoming interview. What would her father say to her? Did he wish to reconcile, to apologize for the way he had treated her? Or was he merely desirous of personally telling her this would be the final break? Was he seeking only to soothe his conscience on his deathbed, thinking a last-minute apology could make up for the last seven years? Elizabeth was not certain if it could.

Slipping into her shoes and grabbing the shawl Sally held out to her, Elizabeth stepped breathlessly into the hall.

"I shall take you to your father now, Lady Elizabeth," Crump offered.

"How is he, truly, Crump?" she asked as they wound their way toward the west wing.

A sadness crept into the man's eyes. "He is not well, my lady. A lesser man would have succumbed long ago. He fights it as best he can, but I fear there is only one outcome."

"Did he really wish for me to come?" After the way the rest of her family reacted to her presence, she was no longer certain of her welcome.

"That he did, and there were those opposed to it, as you have probably guessed. But he insisted, and he is still the duke."

He stopped before the door and turned to look at his employer's daughter. "He has been sad these last years, Lady Elizabeth. But he has a fearsome pride."

As do I, she thought before she stepped into the chamber.

The tall windows were tightly girded with long, dark curtains and it took her a few moments to adjust her eyes to the dim light of the room. The large four-poster bed was placed against the far wall, and she knew the shadowed form that lay upon it was her father.

"Damme, Crump, where is that girl?"

"I am here, Papa." She slowly walked over to the bed.

"I need more light so I can see you properly," he ordered in a thin, wavery voice. "Get those curtains open. They keep it dark as a tomb in here. There will be an eternity enough of that later."

She quietly complied with his command, lifting the heavy velvet aside to allow the early-morning sunshine to stream into the room.

"That's better. Now back here next to the bed."

She stood patiently while he carefully examined her. She did the same. He looked so dreadfully old, his face gaunt and his unfashionably long hair was thin and white. His wan countenance was so different to the hearty man she had known.

"You are looking well," he announced, apparently satisfied with what he saw. "Now don't go telling me I look the same, for I don't." He paused, as if renewing his strength, and motioned for her to sit. "Why did you take so long to come?"

"I was away when the letter arrived, Papa. As soon as I reached home, I left for Harcourt. I have spent the last four days in a traveling coach."

"Where did you go?"

"I was visiting with the Countess of Wentworth in Dorset."

"Was that impudent pup of a son of there as well?"

Elizabeth was forced to smile. Her father must know Somers. "Lord Wentworth was there as well."

"He came to see me, you know. Wanted to talk about you."

Elizabeth's eyes grew wide in surprise. "No, I did not know. He never said a word of it to me." She stood up, her hands clasped in agitation. "I did not ask him to speak with you. Whatever he said, it was without my knowledge and consent."

"Sit down," the duke rasped. "He's an outspoken young man

when he is in a temper. Called me a hard-hearted curmudgeon to my face.''

Elizabeth did not know whether to laugh or cry at Somers' blunt outspokenness.

''But it needed to be said.'' He uttered a long, drawn-out sigh. ''I am a man of great pride, Elizabeth. Pride in my family, pride in my name. But there is such a thing as too much pride. It makes it difficult to admit one's errors.''

His voice dropped to a harsh whisper and Elizabeth was forced to lean closer to hear his words.

''I cannot take back these last seven years,'' he said. ''They are gone forever. But I was wrong, Elizabeth, so terribly wrong. I know you cannot forgive me for what I did, but can we start again? I want you home Elizabeth, come home to me.''

Tears streaming down her face, Elizabeth fell into her father's outstretched arms. Even weakened by illness, his clasp was firm and strong, and she once again felt whole in the encirclement of his arms.

''Oh, Papa,'' she sobbed. ''I missed you so much.''

Stroking her hair, he comforted her, talked again about the damage done to them both by his foolish pride.

''No one told me you arrived yesterday. Did you spend a comfortable night?''

She nodded. ''It was such a surprise to see my room. It was as if . . . as if I had never been gone.''

''I kept it that way. There were times when I doubted my actions. When you are my age, Elizabeth, there are those nights, when you look back on your life and know it will be sooner rather than later when you will be held accountable for what you have done. Late in the evening, I would go to your room and sit and could almost pretend you were with me still. I would be tempted to call you home. Then, in the harsh light of day, I would look at things differently again.

''Had you written and pleaded or begged, I might have relented.'' His thin lips formed a half smile. ''But you are truly my daughter, Elizabeth, and your pride never allowed you to take such a step, did it?''

''I never thought—''

He silenced her with a flutter of his hand. ''It is too late to play 'what might have been.' I have no illusions, Elizabeth. I am dying. But for the time I have left, I would like you to stay here. Can you bring yourself to stay for a while with a foolish old man?''

Determined to maintain her dignity, Elizabeth could only nod as she struggled against the tears of joy spilling from her eyes. He hugged her close. At last, her tears stopped and she lay next to him, her head on his chest, until his even breathing told her he was asleep. Quietly she slipped from the room.

Crump, sitting outside the door, looked up as she left.

''He is sleeping,'' she said softly, a smile playing on her lips.

Her head a swirl of emotions, Elizabeth had no desire for company. Returning to her room, she ordered breakfast sent up. She suspected her sisters, at least, would still be abed, but she did not wish to see Frederick either. She wanted to bask in the memories of her father's love in private, knowing her brother would not be pleased by their father's request.

Buoyed by her meal, she donned her pelisse and quickly walked down the long hall to the rear servant stairs. Following them down, she exited the house from the rear door and stepped out into the garden.

Spring's early bulbs were already turning brown now, in May, as the summer flowers prepared to begin their display. The gardens were as immaculately well-tended as ever, she noted with pleasure. Elizabeth was glad the house had not fallen apart during her father's illness, as many did. Most of the servants were as proud of Harcourt as the family, and they would never let standards slip.

She strolled along the flagstone and gravel paths for a long while, breathing in the fresh country air and the faint scent of lilac. Elizabeth was so filled with joy she could have danced across the grass. She was home again; her father wanted her to stay, and there looked to be nothing that could mar her world. She refused to contemplate how little time her father might have left.

There was so much she needed to do. She must write Emily, of course, and invite her to Harcourt as well. If she chose to come, they would have to make arrangements for the school.

Hiring another teacher would probably be necessary. Elizabeth felt a twinge of regret at leaving the children. She would have to return to Chedford, of course, to supervise the packing up of her possessions, and could say her good-byes then. And she would press her father to start a school here at Harcourt. That was a project that could occupy her time.

She suddenly remembered her father's words. Somers! There was nothing, nothing Elizabeth could do or say that would ever repay him for what he had done. His visit had been the catalyst that finally moved her father to call her home, she was certain of it, and she would be forever in his debt as a result. He and his mother had both been wondrously kind to her. In her current mood of charity with the world, she was even willing to forgive Somers for his unfortunate proposal. At least now, reconciled with her father, she would cease to be an object of Somers' pity. How would he treat her then?

Mindful at last of the time, Elizabeth reluctantly returned to the house. Her stomach reminded her it was time again to eat, and if there was not a formal luncheon set out, she would need to scare up something from the kitchen. She smiled. She could easily grow spoiled again in this house, finding herself surprisingly pleased at the idea. Luncheon would be brought to her wherever and whenever she pleased. But Elizabeth made her way to the kitchen anyway, wondering if Mrs. Pollard was still in command there.

Elizabeth would have preferred to avoid the rest of the family for the remainder of the day, but knowing the confrontation was inevitable, she determined to have it over and done. After her pleasant, gossipy lunch in the kitchen, she trudged up the stairs, preparing herself for the reaction to her news.

They were in the drawing room again, as if seeking safety in numbers. All eyes looked toward her as she entered. Elizabeth wondered how long she must endure their constant scrutiny.

"Where have you been?" Frederick asked irritably. "You come here to visit and then you disappear. What if Papa had wished to see you?"

"We already spoke this morning," Elizabeth explained, settling herself gingerly into one of the upholstered chairs.

The silence was nearly deafening.

"What, pray tell, did he say to you?"

Elizabeth took a deep breath. "He wants me to return home to Harcourt." She saw the look of stunned surprise in the eyes of her brother and sisters. No doubt this was beyond their worst imaginings. She fought back a triumphant smile.

"Do you think that wise, Elizabeth?" Augustinia asked. "After all these years . . . There would certainly be talk."

"And we can't have that, can we?" Elizabeth retorted bitterly. "Heaven forbid that the old scandal be dragged up again. What does it matter if I have been cut off from my family for the last seven years? We must preserve appearances."

"You have only yourself to blame, Elizabeth. If you had acted like a proper lady, you would be a contented matron now."

"Oh, would I?" She glared at Frederick.

Crispin slipped softly into the room. "Excuse me, my lord, ladies. He has taken a turn. The doctor has been summoned."

Frederick bolted to his feet.

The end, when it came, was peaceful. The old duke had moments of lucidity throughout the evening, and he talked to each of his children in turn. But the pauses between grew longer and longer, until he was more asleep than awake. The doctor came, and went, for he knew that the duke was well beyond his power. Crump was at his side when he breathed his last—the whispered name of his duchess—and settled back onto his pillow for the final slumber.

Elizabeth slept fitfully, bitterly upset to so quickly lose the father she had only regained that morning. Tears fell until she was too tired to produce any more. After a few hours of rest-less sleep, she awoke, to start the process anew. It was past cock's crow when she fell into an exhausted slumber.

When she had left Chedford in such haste, Elizabeth had not packed any garment of black, and her first regret when she awoke was that she would have to wear colors until the local seamstress could prepare a gown. Elizabeth was not one to feel that ignoring the outward trappings of respect somehow slighted one's grief, for she knew how deeply she mourned her father. But her lack of black would be only one more thing her sisters and brother would find fault with.

It was difficult to think of Frederick as Duke of Harcourt. He would be a good duke, she admitted reluctantly, mindful of his position and his heritage. He would never do anything to sully the family name or bring disgrace on his wife and children. He was, in fact, a marvelous prig. Elizabeth could not imagine him behaving improperly in any situation. Their father had trained him too well.

An uneasy peace settled over the residents of Harcourt following the death of the duke. Each of his children mourned him, in their own way and for different reasons, and that emotion dominated all their thoughts. There was little time to worry about one another, the future, or Elizabeth. Children were sent for, dragged away from Eton and Harrow or their schoolrooms at home, in order to pay their last respects to their grandfather. The duke's closest friends arrived as well, but for a duke of the realm, it was a small and private funeral procession that left Harcourt for the village chuch and the family mausoleum.

The death notice in the *Gazette* dismayed Somers. He knew, despite their estrangement, that Elizabeth loved her father. How his death would grieve her. He wished he could be with her, to bring her some measure of comfort in her grief. But he had lost all right to do that after his foolish behavior at Kempton. He would be the last person Elizabeth would desire comfort from. She would ascribe his actions only to pity or benevolence.

How he regretted that ill-spoken, ill-planned proposal. He feared it had cast up a permanent barrier between them. Elizabeth would never be as open, as friendly with him again. All his words, his actions, would be scrutinized for any trace of lingering sympathy. He hardly dared send her a note of condolence for fear of arousing her ire.

He stared morosely into his glass of brandy. What a way to spend the London Season, worrying about offending a stiff-necked woman who did not care a bean for anything he would say. Why was he so concerned about scratching out a few simple words of respect on the death of one of England's leading peers?

It was not as if Elizabeth's opinion of him mattered, really. She might be attractive, witty, and utterly charming when she chose, but she could be as sharp-tongued as her father when her back was up. Why should he allow her to cut up his peace like this? London in the height of the Season was full of exquisite women who were only too eager to share in some ill-behaved pleasure. He had delayed far too long in seeking one of them out.

What did it matter if none of them had such expressive brown eyes or such thick, dark lashes? Eyes were not his main concern. No, he thought dreamily, it was skin, soft, smooth creamy skin that he wanted beneath his fingers, his mouth, his body . . . He gulped down a hasty swallow of brandy, choking on its fiery heat. He was rapidly losing control of his thoughts, a situation he found disturbing. Pouring himself another glass, he returned to his chair and weighed the alternatives in his mind. Should it be the green room at Drury Lane? Or Lady Felmore's rout? Either one was bound to turn up something of interest. With a determined look, he drained his glass and strode across the room. Mounting the stair, he barked orders to ready the carriage and called for his valet. He was not going to spend his evening brooding about Elizabeth.

14

Struggling to control the panic rising inside her, Elizabeth clenched her hands until her knuckles were white, hiding them in the folds of her mourning gown. Her world, dangerously cracked by the death of her father, now crumbled into dust. She had no world, she thought dully. She had no future.

The solicitor, droning on through the long list of personal bequests, appeared to be nearing the end, for his words came faster and less distinctly. Then, setting down the sheaf of papers at last, he removed his spectacles and looked out at the impassive faces before him. Only one stood out in its individuality, pale, wan, and drawn.

Dimly sensing the gathering was breaking up, Elizabeth numbly stood, grasping the back of her chair for support. She would have to speak with Frederick, she knew, but not now, not yet. She wanted to escape the stifling air of this room, of this house. The garden. She would go to the garden. She would be alone there.

As she turned to follow the others out, her brother's voice stopped her.

"I would like you to stay for a moment, Elizabeth. Mr. Jenkins and I need to discuss some matters with you."

She nodded resignedly. She was not to be spared this new ordeal, after all. Sinking back into her chair, she focused her despairing gaze on the solicitor's spectacles, lying atop the desk.

"I received a communication from your father, Lady Elizabeth, written the day he died," he explained. "He indicated an interest in changing his will, in order to provide for you as well as the others. Since he planned to discuss it with me when I came down, he did not go into details, and I do not know exactly what he had in mind."

"I, of course, am quite willing to see that father's wishes are carried out," Frederick announced with a tinge of pomposity.

Elizabeth glanced at him sharply. "That is kind of you, Frederick. I . . . I will not require much. I know the cost of my cottage is reasonable, and as I do not go out in society, my expenses are limited. I should not be a burden to the estate."

"Father wished you to come back to Harcourt," he stated. "It is certainly my intention that you still do so."

"But I do not wish to live at Harcourt," Elizabeth said bluntly. She could have added "now" or "with you," to explain her answer, but the coolness in her brother's eyes showed he understood her unspoken words.

"We have discussed this within the family, Elizabeth, and we all feel it is the best thing for you."

"How wonderful that you have seen fit to decide my future without consulting me." She glared at him in anger. "I do not want to live here as an unwanted guest, Frederick. I have lived on my own for seven years, and I much prefer it."

"Nevertheless, for appearances' sake, you should live here." Frederick's voice was low and soothing, as if talking to a recalcitrant child. "It would indicate to the world you are accepted back into the bosom of your family. If you returned to Chedford, any story of a reconciliation would be doubted."

"And we must keep up appearances, mustn't we?" Her voice was bitter. "Not that any of you really want 'poor Elizabeth' back. Papa and I were reconciled, but I have not heard one word of apology or acceptance or even of welcome from you or anyone else. I know you all would wish me to the devil if you dared. Chedford is not the devil, but I think it is adequate for your purposes."

"I will not attempt to reason with you when you are overwrought, Elizabeth," Frederick responded, rising from his chair to bring the talk to an end. "We are all upset after hearing the will. It makes everything so final. We can discuss this another time."

She bit back an angry retort. She would never, ever, willingly live here at Harcourt with him and his starched-up wife, but Elizabeth agreed there was little point in continuing the argument now. With a graceful curtsy, she swept out of the room, her head held high.

Reaching the sanctuary of her chamber, she allowed her fury to boil over. Flinging her hairbrush against the wall, she muttered every oath and curse imaginable upon her brother's head. How dare he decide her future for her!

Pacing back and forth across her room in restless agitation, Elizabeth rapidly considered the options open to her. She had the cottage in Chedford . . . maybe. She did not know if her father had put her name on the deed. It was not part of the estate entail, but it may have descended to Frederick as personal property. If that were the case, her situation was very bleak indeed. Elizabeth could legally argue that the contents of the cottage were hers, but she knew that even if she sold every last stick of furniture, there would not be enough for her to live on for more than a very few years.

Her only hope lay in persuading Frederick that it would be the best thing for all concerned to have her maintain her own establishment. The thought of returning to Harcourt with Frederick in residence filled her with trepidation. If she did not die of boredom in this castlelike house, she and Frederick were sure to be at each other's throats. And after tasting seven years of freedom, she was in no way willing for Frederick to set himself up as her master. As long as he held the purse strings, she was answerable to him. It was an unbearable prospect.

She held no illusions about her ability to make her own way in the world. Yes, she had all the accomplishments anyone could ever wish of a governess, but that itself would be the very bar to her employment. She had no references; her only experience was in her own school, and questions were bound to be asked. Questions that would reveal her total unsuitability for the position. No one would hire a duke's daughter as a governess, even if she were penniless. And Elizabeth honestly did not know if she could give up her independence to such a degree.

Elizabeth prayed she had an ally in the new duchess. Sarah might be her secret ace. If Frederick insisted Elizabeth live with them, Sarah would be pressed into duty as her chaperone and escort. Elizabeth had no intention of living a retiring life and would be as active in the parish here as she had been in Chedford. She doubted Sarah would last long on the endless round of visits and the work involved in establishiung a much-needed school. If Elizabeth could somehow demonstrate to the duchess the magnitude of the responsibility, that lady might be less than eager to have her sister-in-law in residence. Elizabeth determined to do everything in her power to disrupt their placid existence, so they would want to be well rid of her.

The idea of subtly tormenting Frederick and Sarah brought a ghost of a smile to Elizabeth's face. Her course of action decided upon, she ceased her pacing and finally noticed the letter upon her dressing table. Sent originally to Chedford, it had been rerouted here. She opened it with trembling fingers.

My dear Lady Elizabeth,

"I am truly sorry to hear of the death of your father. I know how deeply you cared for him.

I regret that we parted on such an awkward note. Please say you will forgive me for my odious, interfering ways. My mother grew quite fond of you and she is eager to have you visit again. I will not hesitate to stay away if that is your wish.

If there are any difficulties as a result of your father's death, please write my mother or myself. Know that we will not hesitate to do all we can do assist you.

Your obedient servant,
Somers

Elizabeth thoughtfully set the letter down. In the ensuing chaos following her father's death, all thoughts of Somers had fled her mind. How like him to have gone against her wishes and spoken to the duke. And how grateful she was that he had. She must remember to thank him. Her lips curved into a faint smile. Odious and interfering he might be, but frankly, she would like to see him again. She missed those flirtatious blue eyes.

It came as a shock to find she was not completely impervious to the attentions of a handsome male. Particularly one who had

alternately bullied and patronized her. But when he was not
trying to force her to do something against her wishes, Somers
could be a pleasant companion. She looked forward to the
opportunity of extending her thanks in person. Reaching for her
pen, she sat down to compose a letter.

Dinner that evening was a subdued affair. The emotional
strain of the day had exhausted Elizabeth, and she was grateful
there was little interest in conversation at the table. She hoped
her family would be equally silent in the drawing room and she
could retreat to her bedroom early. They had all long ago
satisfied any lingering curiosity about one another, and with
the other ladies' conversations returning to home and family,
Elizabeth found herself bored more often than not.

She was certain Frederick had spoken to the new duchess
about the conversation with the solicitor, for once they moved
from the dining room, she drew Elizabeth to her side.

"My dear, Frederick says you are somewhat hesitant to
remain here at Harcourt. I must assure you that we wish you
to stay with us. Why, it is your home as much as ours. Your
papa, bless his soul, wanted you to come home."

"It is very kind of you, Sarah, but I do not wish to impose
on your household. I know how busy you shall be with all your
new duties and I do not wish you to neglect your responsibilities
in order to look after me."

"Oh, nonsense. It shall be a delight."

"And there is Emily, of course. She is so attached to our
school, I know it would be a terrible strain for her to leave
it."

"Ah, yes, the school. Well, we could always start you another
here, I suppose. I had forgotten about Emily, in truth, but that
is no matter. She will be more than welcome. In fact, perhaps
I would do well to include her in my plans. She is fond of
children, you say?"

"Oh, yes, quite," Elizabeth responded with a twinge of
apprehension. Just what were the duchess's plans?

"There will be time enough to make our decisions during
the winter. A pity your father had to die so late in May; still,

we will be in half-morning by the time the Season starts next year so that will not affect us too much.''

"The Season?''

The Duchess beamed. "It will be a wonderful exercise. I own I was a tad doubtful when Frederick first proposed the idea, but the more I thought on it, the more confident I grew. And taking Emily along may be a stroke of genius.''

"What, exactly, are you planning?'' Elizabeth grew alarmed.

"Why, to take you to London for the Season, of course. Once you are seen to be back in the arms of your family, there will be no unpleasantness over that unfortunate incident. There is your age against you, of course, but you have kept your looks quite nicely and of course, with your dowry . . .''

"My what?'' Elizabeth was confused.

"Frederick was quite insistent that we reinstate your dowry, even if your father had not the time to rearrange his affairs. I am certain it is what he would have done. I do not think we will have too much trouble firing you off. And with Emily so fond of children . . . There are always a few widowers in town looking for a second wife.''

This was beyond Elizabeth's worst imaginings. Had her brother and his wife run mad? Taking her to London for the Season? Attempting to find a husband for her?

"Yes, it will be a wonderful time. And the experience will be invaluable for me when little Jane is ready for her own come-out.''

"Did it ever occur to you and Frederick to ask me before you made your plans?'' Elizabeth asked with icy calm.

Her sister-in-law looked at her with a perplexed expression. "You do not wish to go to London?''

"I find the whole idea ludicrous.'' Elizabeth clenched her fists in an attempt to control her anger. "I have no wish to go to London to find a husband, and I doubt Emily does either. I do not want to live here at Harcourt. I wish to go back to my home in Chedford and live there in peace.''

"Oh, dear,'' said the duchess. "I had thought . . . But certainly you do not wish to bury yourself in the countryside forever?''

"I would much rather 'bury myself in the countryside' than

parade about London in a futile and unnecessary search for a husband.'' Elizabeth shook her head with angry determination. "I have no wish to marry, Sarah.''

"Nonsense. One bad experience should not sour you on all men. I am sure there will be a veritable deluge of offers.''

Elizabeth groaned inwardly. She had never heard such ridiculous twaddle. Fortunately, nothing could be done about the matter for six months. By then, she was firmly determined to be back in Chedford. Wild horses could not drag her to London.

The rest of the family left Harcourt the next day, to Elizabeth's relief. Her sisters and their husbands had never gone beyond polite conversation with her, and in truth she found their presence wearying. In such a huge house it would be easy to keep away from both Frederick and Sarah, and she could contrive to find some way out of the mess she had landed in.

The warming weather allowed Elizabeth to spend much of her time out-of-doors. She rode daily, strolled the grounds, and walked several times to the village. The enforced inactivity at Harcourt was beginning to wear on her. Accustomed to a more active life, she rapidly neared boredom.

She cast her mind wistfully to the garden at Chedford, where the early flowers would be nearing their bloom. She hoped Tommy was keeping the grounds tidy. How frustrating to be here; trying to maintain an establishment by letter was an awkward situation. Emily had offered to return to Chedford, but Elizabeth did not wish to force that lonely existence on her cousin. Her brother's house would be a much more pleasant habitat until she could straighten out her future.

Elizabeth took every opportunity to plead her case with Frederick and Sarah, telling them how bored she was and how she needed to be busy. Sewing with the duchess was nothing as it had been with Emily. The duchess's two topics of conversation were either her children or difficulties with the servants, neither of which interested Elizabeth. Sarah laughed off her complaints, saying that once they were out of deep mourning, she would be back in society again with no time to be bored.

Frederick, who daily spent hours sorting out the old duke's affairs, did not have much sympathy for someone with too much time on her hands.

It was ironic, for in many ways Elizabeth felt as she had when her father first exiled her to Cornwall. There she had no duties, no responsibilities, nothing to mark the passing of time except the growth of the life within her. At least she had the comfort of that. Here, there was nothing to give her comfort. One dull day stretched into the next.

She began to feel the tiniest bit of resentment against her father. Why had he not provided for her earlier? Goodness, if he had died before she arrived, what would Frederick have done about her then? Would he have left her in Chedford or turned her out to make her own way? Why could he not simply give her the dowry money and let her go? She did not care a whit whether society thought her reconciled with her family or not. In Chedford it would not matter in the least.

The wisdom of this thought stayed with her and she approached Frederick that evening with her idea. "I have thought of a plan that may be acceptable to us both," she said.

He looked at her indifferently. "Yes?"

"Sarah says you are prepared to restore my dowry. I should like you to make the money over to me instead."

"But how shall you ever marry without a dowry?"

"I keep telling you, I have no wish to marry. My dowry would provide me with an ample yearly income if I return to Chedford." She looked at him expectantly.

"Elizabeth, we have been over this before. We want you to remain here with us. There is no need for you to bury yourself in the country now that you are restored to your family."

"I enjoy living in Chedford," she protested. "I was busy. I had my school and my friends. And I had responsibilities. Here I have nothing. Living here with you and Sarah is the same as if you had lived here with Papa. He would have run things while you were forced to sit back and watch. You know how uncomfortable you would have found that."

"Talk with Sarah. I am sure she would be willing to share some of the household management tasks with you."

"I do not want to 'help' in your house. I want my own home!"

"Marry, then, and you shall have one."

She gave a silent groan of frustration. Why would they not listen to her? What could she say to convince them that she and they were better-off living apart? Once again she railed against the fate that had left her virtually penniless, dependent totally on the goodwill of her elder brother.

15

"There is a caller for you, my lady," Crispin announced from the door of the library.

"For me?" Elizabeth looked up from her book.

"A Lord Wentworth, my lady."

"Show him in, please." Somers! She jumped to her feet, excited, nervous, and curious all at the same time.

Elizabeth extended her hands in greeting. She thought he looked very fine, although he normally did, except for those amazing days at the cottage when he'd limped about the house in thick gray socks and an old blanket tossed about his shoulders. From the tips of his gleaming Hessians to the ends of his stylishly cut hair, he was the picture of aristocratic perfection.

"Hello, Elizabeth."

The moment his eyes alit on Elizabeth, Somers was glad he had come all this distance. The stark black gown she wore accentuated the pallor of her face; a less charitable soul might have said she looked dreadful. But to his eye, her wan appearance served only to heighten the impression of fragile beauty. Yet the woman who lay beneath that facade was stronger than anyone could guess. He had been foolish to think she would be appreciative of sympathy or compassion. She deserved his respect, not his pity. Somers took her hands in his.

"I am so pleased to see you," she said, her face breaking into a welcoming smile. "I have been so wretchedly bored."

"And I thought you would be reveling in the luxuriousness of your surroundings, with an army of servants at your beck and call, cocoa in bed every morning, and your every whim catered to.''

She laughed, that sweet trilling laugh that sent shivers up his spine.

"I found I have grown far too self-sufficient to enjoy that for long,'' she said, and drew him to the sofa. "Come, sit and chat. How is your mother?''

"She is well,'' he replied, taking his place next to her. "And she warns me I dare not show my face in London again until I wring from you a promise to return to Kempton in July.''

The cheerfulness that lit her face vanished, and Somers looked in alarm at the distracted gaze that replaced it.

"I am not exactly certain what my situation shall be in July,'' she replied, slowly, twining her fingers together nervously. "Frederick and I are still discussing matters.''

"He does not want you to remain here?'' A flash of anger spread across Somers' face.

"He does want me here. That is the problem. I do not wish to stay.''

"But I thought . . . Your letter said you and your father had reconciled.''

"Oh, I wanted so very much to stay here with Papa. But not with Frederick.'' She turned to face Somers. "We were never close: he was away to school before I was even born and we only saw each other on holidays. And the duchess . . . the duchess is a proper matron. They both mean well, I am sure, but I cannot like the thought of living here with them, any more than they really wish me to. They only want me to remain here for appearances' sake.''

"Then you will return to Chedford?''

"I do not know. Papa . . . Papa meant to change things for me. If only I had arrived sooner!''

Somers felt a twinge of guilt. If Elizabeth had not been with him at Kempton, she would have been home when the summons first arrived and could have arrived at her father's sickbed sooner.

"He made no provision for you, then?''

She shook her head. "He sent a letter to the solicitor the very day he died, but he was not specific about what he wished to do. He made Frederick promise to take care of me, but he and I are at odds as to what that entails.''

"Do you own the cottage?''

"Frederick does. But it is not part of the entail and he could sell it if he wishes.''

Somers mind worked feverishly. He was a rather wealthy man. Although he lived lavishly and spent well, he did not fling money around willy-nilly. His numerous investments and business interests continued to produce money in an embarrassing flow. If it became necessary, he could offer Elizabeth all the funds she needed to retain her independence.

Despite the headstrong days of his youth, Somers had grown cautious of late. He botched things with Elizabeth badly at Kempton, and even if he now knew that was a result of rash thinking on his part, he was in no hurry to press her again. To offer her money now would be the height of folly. He could afford to wait. Time was his ally.

"If matters grow too unpleasant, promise you will let me know,'' he urged. "At the very least, I can always offer you the chance to escape to Kempton for a time if life becomes too awkward here.''

"Thank you, Somers,'' she replied cautiously, wondering why he made the offer. Did he still see her as an object of pity? "I still have hopes of bringing Frederick around, since I know he would rather I lived elsewhere. Out of sight, out of mind. It is easier to forget one's scandalous relatives when they are not living under the same roof.''

"They still condemn you?'' He gave an irritated toss of his head. "Have they never put a foot wrong in their entire lives?''

Elizabeth offered up a ghost of a smile. "I think not. I was quite out of step with the rest of them. Perhaps from being coddled and indulged as the baby.''

Somers took her hand and brought it to his lips. "If you were indulged, Elizabeth, it was surely because you deserved it.''

She carefully withdrew her hand, disturbed by the effect the touch of his lips had on her flesh. There was enough confusion and turmoil in her life right now without Somers adding to it.

He sensed her reluctance and fractionally moved away from her.

"Should you like to remain for dinner?" Elizabeth asked.

"No," he replied. "I only stopped to see that you were well—another one of those blasted house parties calls me."

She laughed. "If you dislike them so much, why do you always attend?"

Somers gave an artful shrug. "Must keep up appearances, I suppose. I do have a reputation to maintain."

A slight shadow crossed her face. Elizabeth wished he might stay. She needed his cheering presence. She had not enjoyed herself here at Harcourt since she arrived, and as soon as Somers left, she knew the depression that dogged her these days would resettle itself around her shoulders like a dark gray mantle.

"However," he said, brightly, "if you would like, I could stop on my return. For you have not yet promised to visit Kempton and my mother will not allow me into my own house unless you do."

"I would hate to be the cause of your sleeping in the street." Elizabeth smiled. "You may assure your mother that I shall visit her when she likes."

"Good." He rose to his feet, taking her hand again and drawing her up with him. His eyes searched her face, looking for he knew not what, but seeing nothing there that displeased him either. He bent and kissed her lightly on the forehead.

"Do not trouble yourself about your brother, Elizabeth. If he remains recalcitrant, I shall arrange a nice, quiet talk."

"Like the one you had with Papa?"

"Did he tell you much of it?"

"Only that you were an impertinent pup with an audacious tongue." She looked up into his face. "I can never thank you enough for that, Somers. If you had not spoken, I doubt he would have called me home. I can never repay you for that kindness."

"I do not wish repayment, Elizabeth. I wish only for you to consider me your friend."

"Then, thank you, friend."

It took every ounce of willpower he possessed not to pull her into his arms and kiss those sweetly shaped lips. He had deluded himself into forgetting just how desirable she was. But he dare not offend her further. He must be patient. With a sigh of regret, he let go of her hand.

"Good-bye, Elizabeth. I shall be returning in about a week."

The pang of loss accompanying Somers' departure surprised Elizabeth. Amid all the wild emotions overwhelming her since her return to Harcourt, there had been little time to think of him and what had transpired at Kempton. She was woefully unsure of her feelings for him. She had not hesitated to refuse his clumsy, ill-framed offer out of concern for her own peace of mind. She did not want his pity. But, for that matter, she did not want his friendship. After seeing him today, she thought she wanted so very much more, but the idea of trusting her heart again to one of his sex was too terrifying to contemplate. Somers was a self-admitted flirt, the wrong sort of person to lose her heart to. She must be very, very careful.

It was a subdued and thoughtful Elizabeth who joined her family in the drawing room before dinner. She knew she must resolve the question of her future with Frederick before she could dare to think of anything else.

"I hear you had a caller today, Elizabeth," her brother said as he poured her a glass of wine.

"Yes, Lord Wentworth was kind enough to stop by on his way to a friend's, to express his regrets personally." Elizabeth settled herself onto the sofa, hoping dinner would be announced soon.

"I seem to recall a letter from him as well."

Frederick was certainly watching her closely. She did not answer.

"Elizabeth, I know you have been out of society for some time and are not aware of all the latest *on-dits*. But it is particularly important for a woman in your situation to be most careful about her associations."

"I do not understand your meaning, Frederick." She eyed him warily.

He sighed, setting his glass down and leaning forward in his chair. "I mean, dear sister, it is not advisable for you to be seen in the company of men such as Lord Wentworth."

"Why on earth not?"

Frederick cast an uncomfortable glance at his wife, who silently urged him to continue.

"Lord Wentworth is known to keep company with a, ah,

particular type of woman. It would cause a certain amount of speculation for any woman to be seen with him, but for you—''

''And just what type of woman does Lord Wentworth 'keep company' with?''

The duchess broke her silence. ''Wentworth, sad to say my dear, is a notorious rake. His liaisons, with both highborn and lowborn, are legion.''

''Somers?'' Elizabeth was incredulous. He was certainly a flirt, but a confirmed womanizer? That did not seem like him at all.

''Oh, dear,'' said the duchess.

Elizabeth whirled to face her. ''You said something?''

''It is only . . . I regret that you are on a first-name basis with the man, Elizabeth. It bespeaks an intimacy that could be very unfortunate.''

''I will not sit here and listen to you malign a close friend.'' She began to rise from her chair.

''Now, Elizabeth, stay and hear this through. Lord Wentworth is, uh, aware of your past, is he not?'' At her nod, Frederick continued, ''It could very well be that he has marked you out for his dubious attentions, thinking you are the sort of woman who might make herself available to him.''

''You see, Elizabeth, once there has been an unfortunate incident in a lady's past, she must always strive to be beyond reproach in the future, lest she attract the wrong sort of admiration.'' The duchess spoke as if lecturing a child. ''If others saw you with Lord Wentworth, I fear they would assume that you and he—''

''This is ridiculous,'' Elizabeth cried, jumping from her chair. ''Somers is my friend. His only intentions toward me are quite honorable, I assure you.''

She saw the dubious look in their eyes.

''He has made me an offer. A very respectable offer, mind you, the type that involves rings and clergy.''

''What?'' her brother exclaimed. ''When?''

''At Kempton, last month.''

''Why, Elizabeth, why have you not said anything to us? This is wonderful news.''

''Because I did not accept, dear brother.''

"What foolishness is this? You rejected a marriage offer from a peer like Wentworth? Are you mad, girl?"

"I thought you said he was a lecherous rake and I was to steer well away from him."

"That is of no consequence if he wishes to take you to wife," the duchess explained sourly. "You are in no position to be choosy in your situation. There are not many men who would take a foolish girl like you to wife for any reason, with an ill-gotten brat as living proof of your folly."

Her brother's sudden indrawn breath puzzled Elizabeth. She glanced at him quizzingly, and the sudden paling of his face surprised her. What had the duchess said? A brat as living proof?

"What proof?" she demanded, swinging suddenly on the duchess. "What proof is there of the brief existence of my son? He died, before he even lived. Dumped unceremoniously in an ummarked grave, no doubt. Was he even baptized?"

The duchess's lips trembled.

"Sarah?" She turned frantically to her brother. "Frederick? What does she mean? Tell me!"

"Your child did not die, Elizabeth," he said, almost in a whisper. "It was thought best by all that you should be told that story."

There was a loud ringing in her ears, as if she had been struck a sharp blow to the head. She must have misheard him; her mind was playing tricks on her. She dimly sensed her brother pushing her gently into a chair, pressing a tumbler into her hand, and ordering her to drink. The fiery liquid burned her mouth and throat, and brought tears to her eyes, but in so doing it cleared her head.

"My son is alive?" she asked in a stunned murmur.

Frederick nodded.

"Where is he?" She looked up in rising agitation. "What have they done with him?"

"I know very little," Frederick explained, and for the first time in her life Elizabeth thought she saw a vestige of sympathy in his eyes. "Father told me once, many years ago, what had been done, but it was all arranged by others. I do not know if he even knew himself where the boy was sent."

Elizabeth took another long gulp of brandy. Her son was alive!

It was almost impossible to believe; she had thought him dead for so long. Where was he? Was he safe, unharmed?

"Frederick, I must know what happened to him. To think where he might be, what misery he could be suffering right now. I cannot bear it."

"I do not see how we can find out, Elizabeth," he said. "These things are meant to be hidden. Without the physical evidence of a child, the depth of your indiscretion would always be in doubt. It is far, far better that the child cannot be traced."

"Someone had to make the arrangements," Elizabeth said, ignoring her brother's pronouncement. Her brain whirled in an effort to sort out all her conflicting thoughts and emotions. "Who would Papa have called upon? Someone in the house would have taken care of him after the birth. There would have been a wet-nurse or a doctor or—"

"Elizabeth, it was a long time ago. Aunt Sybilla is dead and her servants dispersed. If any of them knew what exactly went on that night—and I doubt if they did—it would be deucedly difficult to find them again."

"Can we look through Papa's papers?" She knew it was grasping at straws, but she had to do anything, something, to discover what had happened to her child. It made her blood run cold to think of the horrible places her son could be in, deep in the coal mines or the stinking sewer of London's rookeries. "Perhaps there is some record, a payment for support, a letter . . ."

Frederick looked pleadingly to his wife for assistance.

"Elizabeth, at the time everyone felt it was for the best, and it still is." The duchess offered a comforting smile. "I am certain your father made suitable arrangements for the boy. It would only create awkwardness now—"

"Awkwardness? For whom? You? What about me?" Her voice was taut with anger. "He is my son. I carried him in my body for nine agonizing months. Do I not have a right to him? I am his mother. You have children. You should understand."

At last the strain of the news became too much and she slipped into choked sobs. She felt Frederick slip his arm around her in a vain effort to offer comfort, but it was an ineffectual gesture.

"I promise, Elizabeth, I shall look through Father's papers tomorrow. But I do not think we will find anything."

She nodded and turned her tear-streaked face toward him. "I should like to go to my room now," she gasped between sobs. "Call me in the morning and I shall help you." Without further speech she fled the room.

The Ninth Duke of Harcourt gave his wife a long, cold look. "Thank you, my dear, for your timely revelation."

16

Somewhere, Elizabeth knew she would find the information she sought. Despite the fruitless hours of searching through the old duke's personal papers, her determination had not dimmed.

"It is only logical that Papa would have relied on Jenkins to handle the matter, Frederick." Without giving him a chance to respond, Elizabeth hurried on, "And since you must agree the matter is too delicate to be left to the mails, my only option is to travel to London and see him."

"I cannot like the idea of you going to London alone," he replied slowly. "I am far too busy settling matters here to accompany you. Perhaps later in the summer, when I am less busy—"

"I am not some brainless child," she said, her voice tinged with exasperation. "I am perfectly capable of traveling to London without your escort. Sally will be ample company."

"You cannot go traipsing off to London with only your maid." There was marked disapproval in Frederick's voice.

"Why on earth not? Does Sarah take an army with her when she travels without you?"

"Sarah is a married lady."

"Frederick, I think it is rather late to be worrying about my reputation." Elizabeth gave a sharp shake of her head. "Even so, there is nothing amiss with a young woman traveling with her maid. I wish to go to London now." Elizabeth gave him a challenging stare. "Do I go in your carriage or shall I take the mail coach?"

"Take the carriage," he conceded weakly. "I shall send Parsons along to see to opening the house."

"Oh, there is no need for that," she protested. "I will only be in town a short time, I am sure. I can easily stay at Grillon's or the Pulteney."

"And cause untold gossip because you are not staying at Harcourt House?"

Elizabeth should have appreciated her brother's desire to put on an outward show of support for her in front of society, but the hypocrisy of his sudden turnabout left a bad taste in her mouth. He did not truly forgiven her, as Papa had, but concerned himself only with the opinion of others. As long as Frederick thought society would think ill of him for treating her harshly, she had a place in the family. She doubted he would continue his support if she found her son, for Elizabeth had already determined to keep the boy with her. That would be too much for Frederick to tolerate.

Realistically, her chances of finding the boy were slim. But as long as she maintained a slender thread of hope, Elizabeth would not give way to the despair that threatened to overcome her. She, perhaps because of her own fall from grace, was well aware of the fate of most aristocratic bastards. The luckiest ones were accepted into a parent's household and passed off as legitimate offspring, much as Lady Melbourne and Lady Oxford had done. Others, like the old Duke of Devonshire or his son-in-law, Viscount Granville, gave their children different surnames but raised them in their homes. But the unlucky ones, the majority, were cast off like last year's outmoded clothing, sent to women who specialized in tending noble by-blows, or given to farmers, who were always eager for more able-bodied workers. Elizabeth dared not even think of what worse fate might have befallen her child.

Despite the cruelty of the man she had thought to love, despite her father's rejection and her aunt's sniffing disapproval, Elizabeth had never resented the life that grew inside her all those years ago. It was the only comfort she had during her long months of exile in Cornwall. Perhaps it came of being the youngest, for children had always fascinated her. With no younger siblings of her own, the lure of babies had never paled.

Even though she grew to hate the man who fathered her child, and mourned her rejection by the babe's grandfather, Elizabeth had been eager to see the life she would bring into the world. The child's death had been a severe blow, coming as it did on top of her family's rejection. After losing all else, she thought at least she would have the solace of her child. The knowledge that strangers had been watching over her son all these years was unbearable. She prayed with every hosanna she knew that he was safe, and healthy, and that she would find him again.

Lumbering down the gravel drive, the elegant traveling coach of the Duke of Harcourt began its two-day journey to London. Elizabeth watched the great house grow smaller and smaller until it disappeared behind the trees. How different a journey she embarked upon now from the one that had brought her here. She could only hope there would be a reconciliation at the end of this trip as well.

When the carriage finally reached the outskirts of the city, Elizabeth laughed at how seasoned a traveler she had become. In less than two months she had made four coach journeys of several days each, after six years of never venturing farther than a few hours from Chedford. And if her mission here were successful, she would undoubtedly have more journeying ahead of her.

Elizabeth stared out the window of the coach at the passing street scene with as much goggle-eyed enthusiasm as Sally. It was almost seven years to the day since Elizabeth had last seen the city, and she was curious to see all that was new. For London had changed greatly from the city she had known in 1809. There were new theaters at both Covent Garden and Drury Lane. Another bridge would soon span the Thames, and the construction of Nash's new street was altering the entire focus of the city.

"I've never seen the like, Miss Lizzie," Sally said in awestruck tones. "There's more people here than you could count in a month of Sundays. And so many streets! How can you ever find your way back after you've walked away from your house?"

Elizabeth laughed. "London is very large. But do not worry, for we shall not be here long enough for you to get lost."

"Look at the swells." Sally pressed her face to the window as she watched the people on Piccadilly. "Are they goin' to a party?"

"They dress that way all the time," Elizabeth explained. "Remember how fine Lord Wentworth looked when he first arrived at the cottage? That was merely for driving across the country in a carriage. Perhaps there will be a party on the square while we are here and you can see people dressed for evening. Now that is something to see."

Harcourt House was an unimposing town residence on the west side of Grosvenor Square. A messenger from the new duke had long ago arrived, so all was in readiness for Elizabeth when she stepped into the entry hall.

The London house was much more her brother's residence, for the old duke had preferred the peace and serenity of the countryside to the bustle of town. Elizabeth wrinkled her nose in distaste at some of the redecorating initiated by her sister-in-law. The dining room, which Elizabeth remembered as having pale-cream walls, was now done up in a shocking shade of red. She was glad she would not be here long.

Entering the library, she dashed off a quick note to the family solicitor, requesting an appointment for the next day. Then she retreated to the room prepared for her, and took a much-needed nap.

Elizabeth was not unaware of the stares cast her way as the ducal coach traversed the busy streets. She wished Frederick had sent her off in one of his unmarked carriages; the coat of arms emblazoned on the coach doors drew attention like a magnet. She could just as easily have asked for a meeting at Harcourt House, but she was not embarrassed to admit she wanted to see more of the city.

From the moment she alit from the carriage, the staff at Mr. Jenkins' law offices treated Elizabeth like royalty. They immediately ushered her into the office, offered her the most comfortable chair, and presented her with a cup of tea before she could even blink. And it was only short moments before the solicitor stepped in to greet her.

"Lady Elizabeth, this is a surprise. What can I do for you?"

"I want you to know, first, that I am here with the full

knowledge and approval of my brother, the duke." Elizabeth's calm voice belied her nervous anticipation. "So you need not feel you will be violating any sort of confidence if you speak to me plainly."

"You have me intrigued," he said. "Are you concerned about the lack of provision for you in your father's will? The young duke assured me that he would deal with you as your father intended."

"That is not why I have come," she replied evenly. "You are aware, I am sure, of the difficult circumstances I was in seven years ago." At his nod, she continued, "It has suddenly been revealed to me that certain matters were kept from my knowledge at the time. In short, Mr. Jenkins, I have come to ask if you know anything concerning the whereabouts of my son?"

"Your son?" he questioned, after a momentary pause.

"My son. His grace revealed to me this week that, contrary to my belief, the boy I birthed did not die. I know my father made arrangements for him to be fostered. Since you handled all the other matters regarding my situation, I thought it only logical that he consulted you when those provisions were made as well."

Mr. Jenkins sat back in his chair, his hands clasped over his waistcoat.

"I am sorry, Lady Elizabeth, but I know nothing of the matter."

There was something in his manner, his too-eager denial, that made Elizabeth suspicious. She eyed him sharply.

"Are you quite certain, Mr. Jenkins? I assure you, there is no need to maintain secrecy any longer, since it appears I was the only one unaware of the matter. Frederick is not overjoyed at my discovery, but he agrees that I be allowed to search for my son."

"I am sorry I cannot help you."

"Is there someone else who may have handled affairs for my father? Did he ever use other agents or lawyers that you are aware?"

He shook his head. "I handled all your father's business from the moment he became the duke." He leaned forward across the desk. "It is not unusual, in a matter of such, ah, delicacy, that he would have used another. But let me suggest, my lady, you do not concern yourself with this any longer. There is no need for you to seek out the child. He is only a reminder of unhappier times. Now that you are back with your family, you will have other matters to concern you.''

"I want my son," she exclaimed, rising from her chair. "And I shall find him if I have to search every corner of this island.''

He bowed his head. "I cannot truly wish you success in this, Lady Elizabeth, for I think it is a mistake. Go home to Harcourt.''

She was trembling now with repressed anger. "Thank you for your time, Mr. Jenkins. I will see myself out.''

Elizabeth collapsed against the soft velvet cushions of the coach. There had been something too facile in Jenkins' disposition. She could not imagine a man of law lying outright to her, but he perhaps had not revealed as much as he knew about the situation. What power did she have to wring the truth from him?

After placing such hopes on this meeting, Elizabeth did not know what step to take next. Somewhere, someone had handled the matter for her father. How would she ever discover who?

Crossing Berkeley Square, Elizabeth recalled that Lady Wentworth lived nearby. Tomorrow, when the disappointment of the failed mission to the solicitor's office had faded, Elizabeth would pay her a call. During the two weeks spent at Kempton, Elizabeth had developed a great fondness for Somers' mother, and it would be a pleasure to see her again. If only Elizabeth were more certain of what she felt for Lady Wentworth's son! But that was too complex a matter to puzzle out now.

Knowing she would be in blacks for a year, Elizabeth spent the afternoon at the dressmaker's. The simple and unmodish garments the village seamstress had hastily prepared at Harcourt offended her vanity. It was, she readily admitted, her major weakness. But since her wardrobe in Chedford was as fine and up to the mark as any in London, her mourning clothes would not differ. Later, after eating a simple meal in her room, she retired early.

Looking about her in frank curiosity, Elizabeth entered Somers' town house the next morning with an air of anticipation.

Would the house reflect his personality? Kempton had been a model of grace and elegance, but she knew that was his mother's doing. Here, at the town house where he spent more of his time, would he have left his imprint? She almost felt underhanded in coming here, wondering if he would mind her visiting when he was not in residence. Then she shrugged off such a foolish thought. There was nothing amiss in paying a call to Lady Wentworth. Had he not told her his mother wanted to see her again?

The countess stood as Elizabeth entered the morning room, holding out her hands in welcome.

"This is such a pleasant surprise, my dear," she greeted, kissing Elizabeth on the cheek before ushering her to a chair. "What brings you to London?"

"I had some business matters to take care of."

"I was very sorry to hear of your father's death, Elizabeth. Somers told me you reconciled before the end. I am glad."

"I have your son to thank for that. His talk greatly influenced Papa." Elizabeth paused and looked briefly at her hands before she looked up again and met the countess's scrutinizing look. "Somers stopped at Harcourt last week, you know."

"He said he might," the countess replied casually. "So, how long are you to be in town? Goodness, it has been an age since you were here last, hasn't it? How do you find the changes?"

"Amazing. I drove past the construction along Piccadilly yesterday, nearly hanging out the window like Sally to get a better look. It is already impressive. I cannot wait to see it when Nash has finished."

"The construction has been most inconvenient, I assure you, and they say it will only get worse as the street grows north." The countess gave a slight shudder. "Do you have plans while you are here? Would you care to dine with me tomorrow?"

"Thank you, but I do not think I shall be here more than another day."

"Oh, Elizabeth, you must stay longer now that you are here," the countess coaxed. "I know you are in mourning and do not care to go out in society, but surely a quiet evening here would not be amiss."

"I cannot," Elizabeth said in a trembling voice. "There is something I must do."

"Elizabeth, my dear, what is wrong?" Lady Wentworth laid

a comforting hand on her arm. "Is it something I can assist you with?"

Elizabeth shook her head, struggling in vain to hold back the tears that trickled from her eyes.

"Enough of this nonsense. If you are so upset it moves you to tears, something is terribly wrong. Please tell me, Elizabeth."

The countess, thinking surely the girl's distress was related to her unpredictable son, was not prepared for her revelation.

"When I eloped," she began haltingly, "my father caught up with us, you know, but it was too late for . . . for me. When he discovered I was with child, he sent me away to my aunt's. I never saw the baby. They all told me he died, but now Frederick said he did not."

The countess listened to this confession with an impassive face, but her mind reeled at the revelation. Did Somers know of this? Whatever would he think?

"I have a son," Elizabeth whispered in a voice so low she could barely be heard. "I thought he was dead, but he is not and I have to find him."

Extending her handkerchief to the weeping girl, Lady Wentworth absorbed Elizabeth's words. It was not surprising news, really, for the duke's treatment had seemed unusually harsh for a mere aborted elopement. A pregnancy was different. That was a transgression that could not be neatly explained away.

"Do you have any idea where the boy is?"

Elizabeth shook her head. "I . . . I came to London to ask my father's solicitor if he knew anything, but he said no. I do not believe him," she said fiercely. "My father would have arranged everything down to the last detail, and someone had to assist him."

Lady Wentworth made comforting noises. "My dear, I can understand your concern, but if you have no clues at all, how can you ever hope to find the child? I know it is distressing, but would it not be better to rely on your father's judgment and assume the boy has a proper home?"

"He is mine," Elizabeth cried. "They took him from me and I want him back."

"Have you given any thought as to how you would raise him? I do not mean to sound callous, but if you think your reentry into society is difficult now, it would be impossible if you kept the child," the countess cautioned. "No one tolerates an unmarried mother." Even Somers would balk at that.

Elizabeth raised her head, a look of fierce determination in her eyes. "I do not care one whit about society and what it says of me. How would you have felt if they had taken Somers away from you at birth, and you only discovered years later he was alive? Would you not have moved heaven and earth to find him?"

Lady Wentworth sighed. As a mother who loved her son dearly, she empathized with Elizabeth's feelings. But she also liked Elizabeth very much and still cherished hopes of a match between her and Somers. A child could be a virtually insurmountable stumbling block to that event.

"I think you should take some time, Elizabeth, and think this matter out further. Have you given any thought to what you shall do next?"

"I planned to go to Cornwall, to my aunt's house, where he was born. She is dead now, but her servants might have stayed on. Or there may be someone in the town—the midwife or the doctor—who remembers." She twisted the handkerchief in her hands. "It is all so hazy I cannot recall exactly who was there that night, but there must be someone I can find."

"And how do you plan to undertake this search? You cannot hop into your brother's coach and speed to Cornwall on your own." The countess hoped she could temper Elizabeth's impulsiveness. "You will need someone to go with you. And what of your brother? Will he even allow it?"

"Frederick has nothing to say about the matter. If he does not wish me to take his coach—as he nearly did for this trip—I shall take the stage. I am determined to find my son, Catherine."

The countess desperately wished her son were home. He might be able to talk some sense into Elizabeth. But Somers was not due back for several days, and by then Elizabeth would have hared off on this wild chase of hers. Lady Wentworth needed some plan to keep Elizabeth in town.

"If you are truly determined on this course, allow me to help you," she offered.

"I do not mean to sound ungracious, Catherine, but how can you help?"

"There are people I know . . . people who are adept at asking the right sort of questions. Allow me to send someone to Cornwall. They can discover, at the very least, if any of your aunt's retainers are still in the area. Then, if there is someone worth talking to, you can undertake the journey. It is a long way to travel on only a mere chance."

Elizabeth smiled sadly. "It is kind of you to offer, but I think I shall do better on my own. The people in Cornwall do not take kindly to strangers."

"Then, for heaven's sake, wait until Somers returns," the countess burst out, then looked chagrined at her unladylike display of emotion.

Elizabeth rose from her chair. "Somers has helped me quite enough." Giving the countess a quizzing look, she added, "You do know he asked me to marry him when I was at Kempton?"

Lady Wentworth nodded with a wry smile. "And made quite the botch of it, from what I hear."

"No, he was most gracious. I know he was being kind, by extending his assistance, but I simply could not wed a man who offered out of some charitable notion. And having refused him, it would not be fair of me to continue involving him in my troubles."

At last, thought the countess with a weary shake of her head, Somers has met a woman who is as blind as he. The situation would be laughable if it did not so directly affect the people she cared for.

"At least give me your direction," the countess said. "And write me when you arrive at your destination, so I will not worry. You may find you require assistance, after all."

"She lived at Drumhead, near Penzance."

"Be careful, my dear." The countess rose and gave Elizabeth a hug. "I pray for your success."

Fearful she would give way to tears again, Elizabeth hastily took leave of the countess. Catherine was such a dear. Elizabeth almost wished she had availed herself of the offer of help, but she was determined not to grow beholden to Somers—or his mother. They had done so much for her already. This was something she must do on her own.

On the slim chance Somers planned to delay his return to town, Lady Wentworth dashed off a hasty letter, urging him to fly to the city with utmost speed. She seriously doubted if anyone could change Elizabeth's determination on this matter, but she was well-acquainted with her son's powers of persuasion. If anyone could sway Elizabeth's resolve, it would be Somers.

17

Somers glanced approvingly at the bulging portmanteau standing by the door. Elizabeth had often been on his mind during his country stay, and he was eager to see her again. Harcourt was only a day and a half's journey away.

He was discovering that the other women of his acquaintance no longer held his interest. How had he never noticed that irritating laugh of Lady Caldwell's? And Lady Petridge threw herself at him in a most ridiculous manner. Didn't she have any sense of proper behavior? He missed Elizabeth and her witty conversation, her knowledge of literature and politics, and her delicious delight in the absurd. These featherbrained women disgusted him.

And even more surprising, he realized he had no desire to bed them. There had been enough hints dropped to let him know he would be a welcome nocturnal visitor in more than one bedchamber. Yet the thought filled him with distaste. If he could not abide these ladies during the day, how could he frolic with them at night? It was this that worried him the most of all, for he had never been one to concern himself with a lady's behavior outside of bed.

He shocked himself when he half-hoped the new duke still treated Elizabeth as high-handedly as ever. Somers did not wish Elizabeth any more pain, but if her situation at home grew intolerable, she might look with interest on his planned offer of financial independence. He was not averse to a bit of bullying, if necessary. After all, it was in her best interest. And once he rescued Elizabeth from her brother, Somers would be free to

163

visit her as much as he liked. He looked back with longing on those peaceful weeks spent at her cottage. Only one of those days was infinitely superior to months of house parties such as this one.

He firmly tried to push to the back of his mind the images of Elizabeth that threatened to disturb his equilibrium: her pale and drawn face in the drawing room at Harcourt, her teasing smile when she had ridden about Kempton, and her glorious hair swirling around her shoulders that night in the kitchen. Somers was helpless to keep his thoughts from straying to her, and he had no idea what to do about it.

Elizabeth was unlike any of the women he had known. His successes with them had been in the matters of the flesh and not the mind. But it was not Elizabeth's body he wanted. He laughed to himself at that. Well, it was not only her body he wanted. Most of all he wanted her respect, something he had never asked of a woman before. Unsure and uncertain how to gain that accolade from her, he knew he must make the attempt.

With a sense of determination, he made his thanks to his host and set his carriage toward Harcourt. This time, he would remain longer and do all he could to further his friendship with Elizabeth.

"How could you have allowed her to leave?" Somers' irate voice carried into the hall. "You must be as mad as she."

Lady Wentworth crossed the room and gently shut the door. "Short of holding her prisoner in the house, there was little I could do." She fully appreciated Somers' anger. "I encouraged her to wait for your return, but she did not want 'to burden you with her troubles.' "

"Idiot," he muttered. When he learned at Harcourt of Elizabeth's trip to the city, he had raced his horses to town, only, to his frustration, to find her gone again. "Why, of all places, did she choose to drag herself off to Cornwall?

"I think Elizabeth had best explain that." The countess was not at all sure how Somers would react to the news. The existence of a child would not disgust him, and he would fully share her anger at how shabbily Elizabeth had been tricked. But what would he say to her fervent determination to find and raise the boy? It was one thing to shelter your own bastards, but quite another to take in your wife's.

The countess wondered, idly, if Somers had gotten children on any of his numerous ladies. Sighing, she gave an imperceptible shake of her head at her son's penchant for frolic all these years. His obvious interest in Elizabeth had gladdened her heart, and now she feared it would all come to naught over a scrap of a child.

Somers eyed his mother shrewdly. She was not telling all she knew, but he could not force the story from her.

"I am tired," he complained. "I do not want to travel the width of the country chasing after some harebrained female."

But you will, his mother smiled to herself. "Then you can escort me to the theater tonight. Lady Watkins is having a small supper after the play and—"

"I am sorry to disappoint you, but I could not possibly accompany you." He moved toward the door, resolving to at least change his clothing before he left. "I have to chase off to Cornwall after some damned impetuous female."

By the third day of her journey, Elizabeth was thoroughly sick of coaches, posting inns, strange beds, and dust. Even Sally, who had gazed out the window in wide-eyed wonder for the first two days, lost interest in the ever-changing country outside. The two women sat in fatigued silence, the rough roads too rutted for reading and all conversational topics long exhausted.

Was this truly a fool's errand? After her failure in London, Elizabeth was desperate for any clue to her son's location. Somewhere, somehow she would find a person who knew what had transpired on that fateful night. She kept reassuring herself that her father, no matter how angered, would have placed the boy in a decent home. But that had been six years ago, and much might have changed. The mere thought of her son being mistreated, starving . . . Elizabeth took several deep breaths to push down her nervous apprehension. He is all right, she told herself, willing her brain to heed the message.

With Elizabeth a full two days ahead of him, Somers knew he had to fly over the roads to catch her before she reached

Penzance. Traveling in the curricle was faster than the coach, so with any luck at all he should be able to make up the time. She would be taking the main post-house roads, so there was little danger in losing her trail.

And indeed, her path was laughably easy to follow. Ducal carriages did not often pass this way and the coat of arms emblazoned on the coach's side attracted more than cursory attention. Every hostler on the road remembered the vehicle.

He caught up to her on the first posting stop outside Devonport. Somers, who had been rising at first light each day and driving until he could barely see the road, was exhausted and angry. What had driven her to undertake such a foolish scheme?

He spotted the carriage the instant he drove into the yard of the White Hare. Leaping down from the seat, he tossed the reins to his groom and stalked off toward the inn, eager to do violence to the woman he chased.

"Where is the lady who just arrived?" he demanded roughly of the innkeeper.

"Lady?" the rotund man replied with an innocent expression.

"The one who came in the carriage of the Duke of Harcourt," Somers explained through clenched teeth. "The one I have been chasing across England for the last four days."

"Be you the lady's husband? Or her brother?"

"What does that matter?" Somers exploded. "Where is she?"

"How do I know you do not wish to do her harm?" the inn-keeper asked suspiciously.

Struggling with his rising anger, Somers strove to remain calm. "Will you tell me where she is or do I have to look into every room of this inn until I find her?"

The landlord took the threat seriously and, with a look of great reluctance on his face, led Somers to the parlor where Elizabeth took refreshment.

Startled, Elizabeth stood up when the door to the dining parlor flew open, crashing against the wall with a resounding thud.

"Downstairs, Sally," Somers ordered, jerking his head toward the open door as he strode into the room. As Sally scurried from the chamber, he slammed the door shut behind her.

"What is going on?" Elizabeth asked. "What are you doing here?"

"I might ask you the same question," Somers roared, crossing the length of the room to her. "What do you think you are doing, jauntering across the width of England with no one but your maid in attendance? Are you mad? What can your brother be thinking of, to permit you to do such a thing?"

"It is pleasant to see you again too, Somers." Elizabeth's tone was cool.

"Damn it, Elizabeth, I want some answers. I have been chasing after you for four days now. When my mother told me what you had done, I was frantic with worry. It is the height of folly to undertake such a journey on your own."

"I am sorry, Somers, but it is something I have to do. I thought, perhaps, that your mother understood my reasons, but it is plain you do not. I shall not be dissuaded from my task."

"What is your task?" He raked his hand through his hair in frustration. "That is what I have been trying to find out. It must be damned important for you to ignore my mother's pleading to stay in London. What is so all-fired urgent that you have to race across the country as if the devil were at your legs?"

"She did not tell you?" Elizabeth's eyes opened wide in surprise.

"No, she did not," he said in clipped tones.

Elizabeth turned away. She meant what she had said to the countess. She did not want Somers' aid; she did not want any more of his pity. And she was not at all certain she wanted him to know this, her final secret.

"Elizabeth?" He laid a hand gently on her shoulder. "I do not know what is wrong, but I wish to help. Please tell me."

She shook her head. "You will not understand," she said softly.

He forced her to turn and face him. "I am your friend, remember? And friends are there to help when there is trouble."

Elizabeth lifted her head and looked into his soothing blue eyes, full of concern and puzzlement. It reminded her of that night in her kitchen, when she first told him her story. Would he be as understanding now? She took a deep breath to steady herself.

"My son . . ." she began, then her voice faltered and she looked down again, unable to meet his eyes. "He did not die that night, Somers. They all lied to me. He is alive, and I wish to find him."

Somers absorbed this revelation with a stunned silence. He had not judged her when she told him of her seduction and abandonment. When he learned of the resultant pregnancy, it did not lessen his opinion of her. It had all been long ago, far in the past, and easily forgotten, by him at least. But a living child . . .

"Somers?" The apprehension in her voice was palpable.

Racking his brain for something, anything to say while he absorbed the full significance of the news, Somers mumbled, "Are you certain?"

"Frederick himself admitted the truth," she replied. Somers' obvious reluctance to speak sent a cold chill through her heart.

"Is the boy in Penzance? Is that why you are going there?" Somers leaned against the mantel, his boot braced on the fender. It was a pose of studied casualness, but he was anything but calm inside.

She shook her head. "He was born at my aunt's house, in Drumhead. My father sent me there so no one would know of my disgrace."

"Will your aunt know where the child is?"

"She is dead. But I hoped one or two of the servants might still be at the house, or in town. Or perhaps the doctor was there . . ."

"You are racing all the way across England because someone might remember something about the birth of a child six years ago? A birth that was such a disgrace to your family they sent you to the most remote corner of the island? And you expect a servant to answer all your questions?" He shook his head in amazement. "I have thought you many things, Elizabeth, but stupid was not one of them."

"What am I supposed to do?" she cried in anguish. "Forget I ever had a child? I spent seven years of hell, cut off from my family and friends, because of that boy. He is mine and I want him."

"Have you given any thought as to how you would provide for a child?" Focusing briefly at the ill-painted seascape hanging on the far wall, Somers struggled mightily to rein in his irritation at her folly. "I can hardly picture your brother welcoming him into the schoolroom at Harcourt."

"I shall manage," she said stiffly.

"How? With what? You do not have a penny to your name, Elizabeth." Her naïveté infuriated him. "If the duke tosses you out, where will you go? You have no funds to put food in your mouths, let alone a roof over your heads."

"I have friends in Chedford. They will not allow us to starve."

"Oh, certainly," Somers retorted, his voice dripping with sarcasm. "There is always the attentive Doctor Moore, isn't there? I am certain he would leap at the chance to have you—even with a bastard in tow."

He regretted the words the instant he uttered them, even before he saw the stricken look on her face.

Elizabeth recoiled as if Somers had struck her. Then a surge of anger filled her. She had trusted Somers, relied on him and his advice. How dare he turn on her like this! "Damn you, Somers! You have no right to tell me what I can or cannot do."

"Somebody needs to give you guidance. You are doing such a poor job of it yourself."

"I did not ask for your help. Now or in the past. Yet you insist on forcing your wishes upon me, determined that I shall do what you think is best." She glared at him in furious anger. "You have no business sticking your arrogant, aristocratic nose into my affairs. This is my life and I shall live it as I please."

Somers bit back an angry retort. Nothing would be served by upsetting her further. She was so damn infuriating when she got her back up like this. Elizabeth would cut off her nose to spite her face, just to show him he could not tell her what to do. He struggled to find the words to cool her wrath.

"Elizabeth, I only want to keep you from any more hurt. Do you realize what it will mean if you take the child to live with you? There would be no way anyone could forget or ignore your past. Society would cast you out firmly and permanently." His voice softened. "Your family is willing to maintain the appearance of acceptance. My mother and her friends receive you. Do you wish to throw that all away for a child you have never seen?"

Her shoulders slumping, Elizabeth turned away. She should not be so disappointed, really. Why should Somers react any differently than her family? Yet she had thought, perhaps, that he might somehow understand her deep longing, her deep need for the son who had been taken from her. Thought that he would look beyond the rigid conventions of society and understand how much this meant to her.

"I knew you would not understand," she said sadly. "I appreciate your concern, Somers. Now, would you please go? I would like to have a bite to eat before I resume my journey."

Exhaling deeply, Somers watched her, standing so quietly, undaunted by his angry words. He took a step toward her, then hesitated. Elizabeth was a grown woman, free to make her own choices, ill-advised as they were. If she wanted society to cast her out forever, it was her decision to make. But, then, how could she ever become his countess?

The thought stunned him. What was he thinking? Yet in his next breath he knew, beyond all doubt, that it was what he wanted, what he needed. He had fallen in love with the impetuous fool.

There was no guarantee she would find the boy. Elizabeth herself admitted this trip to Penzance was clutching at straws. She was impassioned now with the idea, after so recently learning of his existence. But if the search only turned up dead ends, she might lose her enthusiasm. Somers' presence would be a constant reminder of his disapproval, and she might begin to think twice about her decision. If she never found the child, her ability to rejoin society would remain unchanged. And there would be no bar to taking her to wife.

He did not relish the idea of her traveling alone, with only the very young and very green Sally as a companion. Elizabeth, for all her years, had only been out in the wide world for a short time. She had exchanged the protection of her family for the safely bucolic setting of Chedford. She was in no position to anticipate the difficulties she might encounter, traveling alone. She needed his help.

"I think," he said at last, eyeing the rigid back she still presented to him, "that you will need some assistance on this quest."

As she turned to him, hope dawning on her face, he added

warningly, "I do not mean that you have my approval for this, for I think it is the height of folly, Elizabeth. Yet I do not wish you to travel alone. I will accompany you to Cornwall."

Inexplicably, Elizabeth laughed.

"What is so amusing about my offer of assistance?" he demanded, offended by her response.

"Oh, Somers, you are obviously overset by my plan or you would have thought ahead. Cannot you see how dreadfully improper it would be for a single male like yourself to accompany us? My reputation would be in tatters if we were ever recognized."

Somers reddened. After their easy friendship at Chedford and Kempton, he had in truth forgotten to think of Elizabeth as a proper unmarried lady who required a chaperone in all her dealings with him. A broad grin split his face.

"Your pardon, my lady. It is rather foolish of me to natter on about society's strictures and then propose such a scandalous alternative. So tell me, how are we to resolve this thorny problem? I will not let you travel alone, yet I cannot properly accompany you as a male friend."

"I will be fine on my own," she reassured him. "Besides Sally, there is the coachman and the groom. I am well-protected."

"Are they trustworthy souls?"

"I assume so. They worked for my father."

"I think with a bit of subterfuge we can pull this off." His eyes glinted with amusement. "I have always wanted a sister."

"We do not look alike at all," Elizabeth protested. "Any innkeeper will see that for the bouncer it is." She flashed him a wicked grin. "I think you had better pose as my groom."

"Hardly likely," he asserted. "I have no intentions of sleeping in the stable. No, dear lady, you are about to be blessed with another brother."

"And what, pray tell, is his name?" Elizabeth thought the plan ridiculous, but doubted Somers could be swayed.

"I am Mr. Graham and you shall be Miss Graham. We are visiting our aunt—our father's sister—who is failing in her old age." Somers thought for a moment. "And while we are at it, I think we should exchange your carriage for one of the post chaises."

"Why? That is a very comfortable carriage. You certainly must have noticed how bad the roads are."

"And I have also noted how everyone who has seen your carriage pass vividly recalls the elaborate coat of arms upon the door. I have no intention of impersonating a duke."

"I don't see why not. You are certainly overbearing enough for one."

"Perhaps Prinny will reward me with the title someday. For services rendered in the assistance of harebrained females who attempt to travel the country alone."

Elizabeth held out her hand and smiled warmly. "I am glad you are coming with me, Somers."

18

The sun shone brightly on the cobbled streets of Penzance as the post chaise carrying Somers and Elizabeth rattled through the town. Elizabeth hoped it was a good omen. For how could one be discouraged on such a beautiful day? She would find the information she sought at her aunt's old home.

Stepping from the carriage in front of the house, Elizabeth breathed deeply of the salt-tanged air. It was a smell she would always associate with this place, a scent she had breathed daily for the ten months she spent in her aunt's keeping. Every time Elizabeth smelled the sea she was reminded of those long days of waiting, dreaming, anticipating, of hopes that had been so dashed the night her son was born. But now these same feelings rose up within her again, with the promise of fruition this time. Here, at the house where she once thought her son had died, she hoped to discover where he lived.

Elizabeth was escorted into the familiar front drawing room by an efficient butler, who unfortunately had come to the house with the new owners. The furnishings had all been changed, she noted with mild disgust, examining the modern-patterned wall paper and new furniture. They seemed out of place in this old house.

Lady Dorcas was a middle-aged woman, tall and stout, with a gown that, like her furniture, seemed too new for its setting. Elizabeth instantly guessed her mission was doomed. This was not the type of lady who kept old family retainers.

"I am Lady Elizabeth Granford," Elizabeth explained as they exchanged greetings. "This was my aunt's home, before she died. I was visiting nearby and wondered if any of my aunt's servants were still in residence. I spent some length of time here, and many of them became dear friends. Is Mrs. Freshett still the housekeeper?''

Lady Dorcas shook her head. ''All the old staff was gone when we took possession of the house,'' she explained. ''There was only a local couple acting as caretaker when we arrived. The place was a mess then, I can tell you. Ancient, rotting furniture and mildewed hangings.'' She shook her head in remembered disgust. ''Fortunately, the refurbishing is nearly complete.''

''I noticed the changes in this room. You must have been very busy.''

Lady Dorcas nodded. ''It was a dreadful task, I tell you. But you are not here to listen to my decorating problems. I believe one or two of the older servants may still live in the village, but where I cannot say. The vicar might know.''

''Vicar Spalding?''

''Vicar Smythe-Robbins.''

''Goodness, one would not think there would be so many changes in such a short time,'' Elizabeth said, her voice heavy with disappointment. A stab of dismay raced through her. Had her father been responsible for this, too? Had he deliberately sent away anyone who might have knowledge of what had transpired in 1810? She prayed his anger had not driven him to such lengths, or her search was mere futility.

''Cornwall is changing,'' Lady Dorcas said with a sigh. ''So many of the old families gone . . . and the young people all want to go up to the city now. It would not surprise me to see the whole place deserted in another twenty years.''

''That would be a pity,'' said Elizabeth. ''It's so beautiful here. I very much enjoyed my visits.''

''If you're going to be in the area long, I could have the vicar make some inquiries for you,'' Lady Dorcas offered.

Elizabeth rose to her feet. ''That is very kind of you, but it will not be necessary. My brother and I start our homeward journey today. I will drop at the vicar's as we go past.''

Elizabeth fought the urge to run for the safety of the carriage as soon as she reached the front door. But she held on to her dignity, walking with steady grace to the waiting coach.

* * *

Somers had remained in the coach to avoid any awkward explanations and unnecessary lies. Now they had finally arrived at their destination, he was filled with a nervous apprehension. What would Elizabeth discover here in this far corner of England? Was it possible she could get information about her son after all these years? He was torn between his selfish wish that she be thwarted in her search, and a deeper desire to have Elizabeth find the answer she sought. He wanted to see her happy. To his knowledge, he had never fathered a child—he was always careful in that regard—yet he thought even if he had, the fatherly ties would never be as strong as those of a mother. Would he race across the breadth of England to chase down any lead, no matter how small, to locate his child? What was it about the bond between a mother and child that demanded such a search? He wondered if even Elizabeth could fully explain her deep need to find her son.

He looked up with a mixture of apprehension and anticipation when he head the carriage door open. But Elizabeth did not greet him with a smile.

"They are all gone," she announced dully to Somers as she entered the carriage.

"No idea of where they went?"

"I spoke with Lady Dorcas. She suggested I talk with the vicar, but he is not the same man who was here." Elizabeth clenched her hands together. "Oh, Somers, I am so fearful that Papa had a hand in this. What if he has sent everyone away?"

"That seems overmuch, even for a duke," he said skeptically. "Was there no one in the town with whom you were acquainted?"

Elizabeth shook her head. "I saw no one outside the household the entire time I was here. Except Papa visited once."

Somers could imagine how traumatic a visit that had been. A man who could cross out his daughter's name from the family Bible would not have brought words of comfort.

"Would you like to stop at the vicar's? And you mentioned the doctor?"

"I will try anything," Elizabeth replied, but she already sensed that she would learn nothing.

The vicar was unable to help, for both her aunt's housekeeper and butler had left the area before he acquired the living. His lack of knowledge only fueled Elizabeth's suspicions about her father.

"Are you certain you still wish to try the doctor?" Somers saw how exhausted Elizabeth was; the weariness in those dark eyes reflected her lengthy travels and the strain of the search. If he could save her one more disappointment . . .

"If I did not stop, I would always wonder," she replied, giving him an apologetic glance. "The vicar gave me directions. It is not far; we could walk if you like. I am sure you are tired of being cooped up in the carriage all day."

"That is a certainty," Somers muttered. But it had been his choice. Their masquerade had worked well so far; he did not want to press their luck. Lady Dorcas and the vicar would have requested an introduction, and he did not want to lie more than necessary. Cornish villagers, on the other hand, posed no danger.

The afternoon sun was bright, with only the slight hint of a breeze as they ambled through the village. A few wary Cornishmen glanced their way in curiosity, but as strangers, Elizabeth and Somers were ignored.

"It is odd," Elizabeth commented, "after living so close for nearly a year, how I never saw the village. Even after . . . when I could have safely appeared in public, Aunt never allowed me to venture farther than the garden."

"I can't say that you missed much," Somers replied, surveying the tiny hamlet with a dismissive air. Elizabeth's precious Chedford was more picturesque than this by a long sight.

After visiting with the doctor and his wife, Somers was less ready to disparage Elizabeth's suspicions about her father. It seemed a trifle too neat to find every person who had ever had contact with her aunt's household gone. And if the duke had gone to such lengths to cover his daughter's transgression, and the child's existence, there was no hope for Elizabeth's mission.

Elizabeth forced herself to join Somers in the parlor of the Lighthouse Inn for dinner. She had little appetite and the food tasted like sawdust to her, but she preferred his company to the solitude of her room. Yet, once she was seated across from him, she found she could do naught else than avoid his solicitous eyes and push the food about on her plate.

Somers watched her with concern, but said little. There was not much he could say, at any rate. The trail was cold. No one in Cornwall had any answers for her. She was going to have to face the dismal reality that her son was lost to her—probably forever. He was truly at a loss at how to reach her, what to say that would not offend. Ever since that disastrous proposal and her condemnation of his misguided desire to help, he was wary of expressing too much sympathy. He did not want to be accused of mere pity again.

Her depression was infectious. Somers downed his fourth—or was it his fifth?—glass of claret. Normally, he was a temperate drinker, but tonight he enjoyed the dulling of his senses. The wine helped distance him from her pain.

"I am not very good company tonight," Elizabeth acknowledged, pushing her barely touched plate away at last.

"I am easy to please," Somers said with a wine-mellowed grin. "As long as you do not threaten me with daggers, I can accept nearly any behavior, from cheerfully outgoing to sullen and morose."

"Do you ever refrain from teasing?" There was an edge to her voice.

"Rarely." His eyes were bright with laughter, but then he sobered. "I have found there is very little in life to take seriously," he explained. "Laughter is as good a way as any to go on."

"You are spoiled," she retorted, semiserious.

"I know it," he said. "But so is most of the *beau monde*. Why should I be any different?"

"Most of them are silly and empty-headed because they cannot aspire to anything else," Elizabeth said. "But you are not a stupid man, Somers. Do you not think you are wasting yourself? Have you ever entertained any grand dreams?"

He shrugged. "Like every boy, I think I cherished dreams of becoming a dashing hussar or a valiant naval captain. But sixteen-year-old earls are not permitted to ship out for the Peninsula when their nearest heir is only a distant cousin."

"Yet even at home there is much you could have done." Elizabeth's tone was accusatory.

"No one in their right mind would aspire to the halls of Parliament," Somers said, a trifle bitterly. "Gouty old men holding forth on outmoded ideas, tramping down opposition whenever it arises. I could talk until I was blue in the face in the Lords and never accomplish a thing."

"Did you ever try?"

"Once or twice," he said, then smiled ruefully. "It cured me thoroughly, I assure you. I found I much preferred the less-hallowed halls of Brooks's or Watiers."

"There is Kempton to see to—"

"Kempton does not need me. Perhaps it is my fault," he mused as he poured himself another glass of the ruby-red claret. "My father hired the best estate manager, and when the man was ready to step down, he had trained his son so well, he was the logical replacement. I am superfluous at Kempton. I could not run the estate half as well."

"And what have you done for your tenants?"

"They do well." Somers grew indignant. What right did she have to sit there, implying he was subject to the sloth and indolence that pervaded their class, when she knew nothing about the things he had done? She had not been there during the bad harvests, when the rents were waived, or sat through the late-night sessions with Coke, listening to him discourse on every imaginable agricultural improvement. She automatically assumed he was like so many others, putting selfish pleasure ahead of obligation.

Somers' anger rose. He did not need to justify himself to her. She was so full of righteous indignation, this daughter of a duke. Had she not incurred her father's wrath all those years ago, she would be living the very life she sought to scorn.

"Perhaps I shall start a school like yours for the children. Would that atone for a life spent in the frivolous pursuit of pleasure?"

Elizabeth flushed at the sarcasm in his voice. "Think what you might have done if you had not wasted so much of your life."

"Who gave you the power to judge and condemn me? Can you honestly say your life has been more profitably spent? If you want to talk about wasted lives, I think you should start with your own."

"I had no choice," she protested with an imperious toss of her head.

"Cut line, Elizabeth. You did what you damn well pleased. It suited you to hide away in Chedford, cloaking yourself in your mantle of martyrdom."

"How dare you say such a thing!" Elizabeth's hazel eyes darkened in anger. "I have innumerable good works to my credit."

Somers uttered a harsh laugh. "Good works? Merely excuses to justify your selfish existence. You did exactly what you wanted to, Elizabeth. Don't try to pretty it up. You had your London fashions, your high-stepping horses and fancy furniture. You did not give up anything. You've frittered away the last six years of your life as surely as I have. But at least I do not claim otherwise."

"What would you have had me do, then?" she asked bitterly.

"Lived your life," he retorted. "You are not the first daughter to have been cast out by an angry father. There were friends who would have stood by you. And had you approached your father after his anger cooled, I have no doubt he would have taken you back years ago."

"You sound so very sure of yourself, Somers. It is easy for you to say such things. You were not there when he told me he never wanted to see me again."

"The words of a hurt and stubborn man," he countered. "He would have come 'round. But it suited your purposes to ignore that, didn't it? I think you are not happy unless you are suffering, Elizabeth. This determination to find your son is just another means of prolonging your purgatory, one more excuse to avoid life. You resent everyone who is not suffering along with you, and I refuse to let you drag me down into the gloom."

Somers grabbed for the decanter of wine, slamming it down against the wooden table after refilling his glass. He was shocked at his anger, shocked at the harsh words he had uttered. Unaccustomed to the wild emotions Elizabeth provoked in him, he had a strong urge to grab hold of her and shake her until she acknowledged her mistakes. He did not want a woman who was afraid to face life.

"And you are not happy unless you are interfering in the lives of all those around you." Her angry eyes flashed. "You have set yourself up as Somers the all-powerful, who, in his infinite wisdom, knows what is best for everyone. Woe be to those who do not dance to your tune; you will badger them mercilessly until they give in out of desperation.''

"Do I badger you?"

"Yes!"

They glared at each other across the rough-hewn table.

Somers struggled to regain his composure. The whole argument was ludicrous. They were squabbling like small children, their anger inspired more by tension and disappointment than any conviction of wrongdoing. He sought to defuse the situation.

"If I promise not to badger you anymore tonight, will you smile for me?"

Elizabeth threw up her hands in disgust. "That is exactly what I meant earlier. You are joking one moment and serious the next, and I am never certain which Somers is the real one."

"Neither," he retorted enigmatically.

An uneasy silence fell between them. Somers stared morosely at the flickering flames reflected in his glass. This was Elizabeth's fault; her gloom pervaded the room. He shook his head as if to shake off his discomfort.

"I think," he said slowly, with great effort, "that we are both tired. Perhaps in the morning we can have a more rational conversation."

She nodded but did not speak. Somers reached over and placed his hand atop hers, wrapping her fingers in his.

Elizabeth looked down at their hands, light against the dark tabletop. How warm and comforting his fingers felt, twined with hers. How easy it would be to succumb to his interfering ways. For a brief moment she wondered what it would be like to love such a man. One who accepted her for what she was, who knew of her past and did not care.

Was he right? Had she actually enjoyed her life as an outcast and done all she could to prolong it? At the time, she thought she was doing an admirable job of coming to terms with her new situation. Should she have fought against it instead? Refused to accept her father's words as final? He had finally accepted her back. Could she have achieved that goal sooner? A wave of dismay washed over her. Instead of one day with her father she could have had four or five years with him. My God, had she really been so stupid?

But he was wrong about one thing: she wanted her son more than anything on earth. Not because society would condemn her for raising a bastard, but because he was her own flesh and blood. She no longer viewed her brothers and sisters as family. That small boy was all she had left. She needed him.

Somers remained still, watching her. She sat there quietly, looking so sad and vulnerable after he had blasted her so thoroughly. He could not take back his angry words, nor did he wish to. They needed to be said. But now he wanted to soothe her hurts, smooth out the small line of wrinkles that furrowed her brow. Even more, he longed to see her in her deshabille again, wanted to bury his hands in that long, thick chestnut hair. To press her soft body against his . . .

"Somers?"

He started as if awakening from a trance. Lord, he was halfway to being foxed. Not at all good *ton*.

"Trying to decide which of your eyes is browner," he explained, flashing her his slow, seductive smile.

Elizabeth shook her head. "You are impossible," she said, with a twinge of regret for him once again ruining the mood with his teasing.

Somers made a great show of yawning and stretching. "There is a three-days journey ahead of before we reach London."

Elizabeth quickly rose. "You are right. Good night, Somers." She moved toward the door.

Somers leapt instantly to his feet and placed himself between Elizabeth and the door. "At least allow me to see you to your room," he offered. "Young ladies should not be walking about unescorted in inns, no matter how pleasant they seem."

She nodded her thanks, although she secretly wondered how good a protector Somers would be right now. Earlier, he had sounded more like he wanted to strangle her.

They said nothing on the short walk to her room. Somers paused outside while Elizabeth knocked for Sally, who opened the door.

"Good night, Somers," Elizabeth said, turning to bid him farewell.

He took up her hand, so small and delicate in his. He raised it to his lips for a salute. "Good night, Elizabeth."

Somers tossed restlessly in his non-too-comfortable bed. Lord, he had drunk too much tonight. For unless he was sadly mistaken, landlocked inns were not supposed to roll about like a wave-tossed boat. But he did not think he could have borne Elizabeth's moodiness sober. It was too painful to watch her hurt without being able to ease her pain—particularly when she persisted in wallowing in it.

She had lashed out at him in anger tonight. At least he had provoked some emotional reaction from her, although he did not think contempt was the sentiment he wanted to be viewed with. There was a modicum of truth to her words. Somers acknowledged he had spent his life in a headlong pursuit of pleasure. But why not? He harmed no one; it was his life, his money that he frittered away. If he had neglected his estates, gambled away a fortune, or mistreated his mother, Elizabeth would have a right to criticize. He punched his pillow in irritation. But he had done well by all those who depended on him, and what he did with himself was his own business.

Which, of course, was exactly what he had criticized Elizabeth for. But he had justification for his views. He was open and honest about his life; she was not. She termed his efforts to point that out "interference." He gave a derisive snort. Well, he was going to continue to "interfere" with her life until she admitted that hiding in Chedford was no longer an attractive proposition. And when she did, he would be waiting with another offer.

19

Somers sat back against the carriage squabs, admiring Elizabeth's profile as she stared out the window. She had wrapped herself in this cloak of silence ever since they left Penzance, three days previously. The lack of news there about her son had hurt her badly; their argument at the inn had left them treading on eggshells for the last two days. He desperately wanted to bring a smile to her face. But what could he say that would sound sincere when she knew he had opposed the search for her son from the start? He could not retract his angry words, for he had meant every one of them. She had wasted the last seven years of her life and it was time she put the past firmly behind her and turned her mind to her future. Now that Sally rode with his groom in the curricle, Somers could talk candidly with Elizabeth.

"Elizabeth?" he asked gently and she turned to face him. "What do you propose to say to your brother when you return to Harcourt? Has he given you any indication he might change his mind about setting you up at Chedford?"

She shook her head. "The last time we discussed the subject, we ended up arguing about something else, then Sarah blurted out the news of my son and I have thought of nothing else since." She uttered a deep sigh. "I suppose now I must."

"What were you arguing about?"

She flashed him a dimpled smile. "You."

"Me?" Somers raised his brows.

"Frederick thought a lady with a 'past' should not be seen in your company."

"And why not?" Somers was not sure if he was amused or annoyed at her brother's pronouncement.

"Because you are an 'unscrupulous rake' and our association would give people the wrong impression." She tilted her head to one side and eyed him speculatively. "Are you?"

Somers was beginning to think seriously about a future for himself and Elizabeth, and he knew he would have to be brutally honest and risk her disgust. He could not lie to her, as so many others had.

"Unscrupulous, no," he replied slowly. "But a rake? There are some who would call me that."

"Why?" The label did not seem to fit Somers. He did not remind her at all of Harry or the other men about whom there had been whispered stories.

"Some men spend their energies in Parliament, or on their estates. I, as you made so abundantly clear the other night, have other interests. I prefer to devote my attention to women. Or, rather, women like me, and I am too polite to say no to a lady. I am available, and if the lady is married, I have the reputation for being discreet. And if there is a shortage of discontented wives, there are always several lovely ladies dancing in the opera."

Despite his teasing tone, Elizabeth knew he spoke the truth about himself. She did not understand why his confession disconcerted her so. What did it matter to her if he had dallied with hundreds of women?

Somers' interest in her problems puzzled her. Why would a rake, with or without scruples, interest himself in a penniless lady who had no desire to sport in his bed? Unless he, of course, felt sorry for her and thought of her only as his charitable cause. As Somers so obviously did.

Even that day in Chedford, when he had kissed her, Elizabeth had never felt threatened in his presence. He had flirted with her, to be sure, but it was a flirtation of the harmless sort. Despite his fumbled offer of marriage, she had no idea what he thought of her as a woman. And she realized she wished to know.

"Do you have a mistress in keeping at the present?" She kept her voice light.

"Weren't you ever taught not to discuss such things?" he questioned in mock horror.

"Never," Elizabeth replied, pleased at his discomfiture. "You are not answering my question, Somers."

"No, I do not presently have a mistress."

"London must be full of unhappily married ladies this Season."

Somers opened his mouth to reply, then shut it firmly.

"I, for one, think the stories are decidedly exaggerated," Elizabeth pronounced. "Or else I am severely disappointed. Here I have been traveling for days now with the premier rake of the realm, and he never once made an improper advance toward me. How lowering!"

The sudden anger in his face surprised her.

"You are not the kind of woman meant for dalliance, Elizabeth," he said sternly. "You are meant to be a wife, and that puts you into an entirely different category. I told you once before, I do not trifle with unmarried ladies."

Turning away, Elizabeth gazed blindly out the window again. She had only meant to tease him, and his reaction startled her. She liked Somers; she valued him as a friend, but it grated on her soul that he viewed her with only pity or benevolence. Did he not find her the tiniest bit attractive?

With a sudden pang, Somers realized the lie in his words. He wanted her. Badly. This unmarried duke's daughter lit a white-hot fire inside him that threatened to spill out with every mile the carriage traveled.

He shook himself. Surely six days' close proximity to any attractive woman would have this effect on him. Ever since his forced sojourn in Chedford he had only halfheartedly pursued his normal pleasures in London. It was that lack that affected him now, he decided. Had he cut a wider swath through the nobility and the demimonde this spring, he would not be feeling these pent-up longings. Elizabeth must be treated with respect, not viewed with lust. One did not treat the woman one wanted for a wife like a doxy.

Elizabeth shifted her position and the movement brought a gentle waft of her lavender scent to his nose. Maybe just one kiss, he told himself. One to erase the memory of her terror-stricken face that day in Chedford. He did not think she would cringe from him now.

"Elizabeth," he breathed softly, edging closer to her.

The odd tone in his voice caused her to turn; the unfamiliar look in those brilliant blue eyes made her draw in a sharp breath. It was not until he reached out to stroke her cheek with his thumb and then lowered his hand to her neck to draw her toward him that she realized what he intended to do.

The touch of his lips was hesitant at first and she did not flinch, as she had before. She knew him now, trusted him. And truly, she was curious how a man who was reported to be a hardened rake would kiss.

Soft, he thought, at that first initial contact. He lifted his head and looked into her light-brown eyes, round and wide with curiosity. Then he lowered his mouth to hers again and, as he felt her relax, he was lost. Slipping his arm about her waist, he drew her closer while his other hand held her head to his. Gently, persuasively, he moved his lips against hers, touching, teasing, tantalizing, always in motion. Her lips parted beneath his and with a muted groan he slipped his tongue into her mouth.

Elizabeth's skin burned at his touch, matching the boiling liquid that flowed through her veins. She unconsciously reached up to clasp his shoulder, pulling Somers closer as she drew him inside her mouth as well. The gentle explorations of his tongue sent stabbings of flame through her body and she tentatively reached out to touch her own tongue to his.

Like a jolt of electricity, Elizabeth's hesitant response fanned Somers' desire. His fingers artfully stroked the side of her neck, drifting ever downward across her collarbone, until his hand rested on the high swell of her breast. While their tongues lazily intertwined, he cupped her breast in his hand, softly, gently caressing it through the fabric of her gown.

The light touch of his hand on her breast brought the first trace of panic to Elizabeth's mind. She should not be doing this, should not be enjoying it so. But, oh, how wonderful it felt. His thumb and forefinger massaged her nipple, teasing it into aching hardness, and she uttered a soft moan at the sheer pleasure of the sensation.

The sharp jolt as the carriage hit a deep rut catapulted them back into the world. Breathing in ragged gasps, Somers tore his lips and hands from her and held her tight against his chest.

"Oh, Elizabeth," he whispered in her hair, feeling the rapid thudding of her heart that matched his own.

Elizabeth did not pull away, content to remain within his grasp as she reined in her body and emotions. Her response to his advances stunned her. Friend or no, she was suddenly beginning to realize just how damnably attractive Somers was as a man. And the passions that had led her down her path of folly so long ago could be fanned into existence again.

"You sounded so unconvinced of my reputation," he said at last, gently stroking her hair while she leaned against his chest. "Did I adequately convince you of my rakish nature?"

Suddenly shy, Elizabeth was glad her flaming cheeks were still hidden against his coat. "Yes," she whispered, a wistful smile tugging at her lips.

Despite Elizabeth's attempts at lighthearted banter for the rest of the journey, that passionate embrace in the carriage subtly altered her relationship with Somers. There was a slight strain, a hesitancy in their dealings that had not been there before. Yet there was also a heightened awareness of him, an imperceptible physical bond that now linked them together.

What would have happened in the coach if that rut had not jolted them back to their senses? Somers had laughed off his actions as a demonstration of his prowess with women. Had that been all he intended? Her own response had startled her, but through it all she had been well aware of whose kisses and touches she was returning with such wild abandon. It frightened Elizabeth to think she was developing more than feelings of friendship for him. She knew how that path led only to disaster.

But she was too torn with despair over the loss of her son and worry about her future to afford much thought to herself and Somers. In far too short a time she would be back at Harcourt for another endless round of arguing with her brother and his wife. Then she would have ample time to think about Somers.

Elizabeth did not want to return to Harcourt, but she needed to deal with her brother. She had to find a way to convince Frederick to allow her to return to Chedford.

The frustration at having so little control over her destiny grated on her. She had railed against her fate more than once during these last years, but it was only now that she realized just how in control of her life she had been. Somers was right; she had chosen the way she would live in Chedford. It was her choice not to go out in society, when she could have; her choice to spend her time with the school, when she could have ridden about the countryside. She had been free to choose her own friends. All the bills had been paid without question.

Life with Frederick would be unbearable. With total control over her, he had the power to forbid her to even see Somers. And with a pang, she realized just how painful that situation would be. She had grown to trust and admire Somers, and even if he had an irksome habit of meddling in her life, she appreciated his concern. He was her friend, and that was something she sorely needed right now. And if a small voice reminded her how deliciously wonderful it had felt with his hands and lips on her body, she chose to ignore it.

Somers felt a nagging guilt at his pleasure in the failure of her quest. He was being utterly selfish, he knew. But where it came to Elizabeth, he wanted to be selfish. Anything that could disturb her happiness displeased him, and he was arrogant enough to think he knew best in the matter of her child. She wanted the boy now, but over time, he was certain she would realize the folly of that view.

And then, what? There was still the troublesome problem of her brother. Somers had been successful in his appeal to the old duke, but the new one might not be as amenable to persuasion. Particularly if he thought the persuader an "unscrupulous rake." In fact, it would look damned suspicious for Somers to beg for Elizabeth's right to establish her own home. He could almost hear the veiled accusations now. But what else could he do? He had no intention of pressing his suit now. Elizabeth would once again accuse him of pity and sympathy. One passionate embrace in a carriage would not erase that concern. No, she would take careful handling. He blasted himself again for his stupid proposal at Kempton. He knew it would take a great deal of work to convince Elizabeth of his sincerity the next time he spoke.

And he was now very certain he wanted to speak. Elizabeth

aroused in him all the emotions and feelings no other woman had. Somers was fiercely protective of her, wanting to shelter her from all hurt and pain. He found he liked—actually liked— the thought of seeing Elizabeth across the breakfast table each morning. He could see himself looking forward to sharing a glass of wine before dinner while they talked about their day. He wanted to escort her to exclusive routs, and to the theater, showing off her elegant beauty to all the *ton*. And most of all he looked forward to the glorious nights together in bed.

He expelled his breath slowly. He must not refine too long on that aspect, or he would be driven mad. Better to think of how he should proceed with the slow process of winning her trust. He could not endure failure this time.

The exhausted condition of the two travelers when they reached London appalled Lady Wentworth.

"Elizabeth, this time I will not take no for an answer." She firmly drew the younger woman into the drawing room. "You will stay here with me until you are fully rested. Why, the duchess would be horrified if I sent you back to Harcourt in this condition."

Elizabeth was too tired to argue and gratefully took to her bed only moments after dinner.

"Well?" the countess arched an eyebrow at her son, who was swirling the wine in his glass in a most annoying manner.

"She learned nothing in Cornwall," he replied. "I think that will close the matter, for I do not think she has any place else to look." He studied his mother intently. "You know why she went there. What do you think of her plan?"

Lady Wentworth remained silent for several moments. "There are two sides to everything," she finally said. "As a friend, I think her idea was folly, and I told her so. But as a mother . . . I cannot argue with her desire to be reunited with her son."

"It would destroy her in society."

"We both know Elizabeth is content to live without society. To give it up would not be a sacrifice to her."

Somers stood and crossed the room, his impatient movements betraying his agitation. "Even if it causes pain to others?"

She eyed him shrewdly. "Elizabeth must do what she thinks

is right for herself. She is under no obligation to think about the needs of another.''

He gave a self-conscious laugh.

"But surely, the whole question is moot at this point. She has no other place to look. She will be returning to Harcourt with no harm done.''

The countess noted her son's deliberate casualness with a hopeful gleam in her eye.

20

Despite her original intentions, Elizabeth could not face the thought of returning immediately to Harcourt. She gratefully accepted the countess's offer to remain in London "for just a few days." Elizabeth needed the time to think and prepare for the upcoming confrontation with her brother. She was under no illusions that he would permit her to remove from Harcourt without a fight.

Elizabeth stared out of the tall morning-room windows, oblivious to the bright July morning outside. Somers' presence in the house provided a distraction in the extreme. Elizabeth could not erase from her mind the memory of that burning kiss in the carriage, or her own response to it. Her feelings then had been almost frightening. Yet Somers thought she was a fool and a coward. Not very loverlike sentiments. But at least more acceptable than pity.

As if sensing her confusion, Somers had kept away from her for the most part, allowing Elizabeth to sit quietly in the drawing room, reading, or walking in the small garden behind the house. Most of the *ton* had already left the city, fleeing from the dirt and grime to the more agreeable climes on their country estates. Lady Wentworth received an occasional caller, and Somers came and went as he pleased, but for Elizabeth it was a peaceful respite from the chaos of the last month.

Elizabeth was startled from her musings when Somers bounded into the morning room, an eager grin on his face.

"We are going driving today," he announced, taking the open book from Elizabeth's hands.

"We are?"

"You will turn into a hermit if you do not ever leave this house." He gave her a comforting smile. "The park will be nearly deserted at this time of day. You need not worry about encountering any acquaintances."

"I am not worried about being seen," she interjected hastily as she rose to her feet. "It is only that I was enjoying the solitude."

"Five minutes," he said, looking pointedly at the mantel clock.

Elizabeth scurried from the room.

"This was a marvelous idea, Somers." Elizabeth turned her bonneted head to flash him a radiant smile. "Thank you."

"My pleasure." He smiled back. There was still much that lay unsaid between them, but at least the awkwardness was gone from their conversation. In time . . .

Elizabeth surveyed the park with greedy delight. They had the tree-lined pathways nearly to themselves. Even the small children and nursemaids who usually dominated the park at this hour of the day were conspicuously absent, having departed to the country with the rest of aristocratic London. She could almost close her eyes and remember that heady spring in 1809, when a daily drive in the park with a handsome gentleman had been an accepted part of the routine.

"Wentworth! I thought that was you. What are you still doing in town?"

Somers peered curiously at the approaching rider, a wide grin creasing his face in recognition. Lord, he had not seen Barnet in years. Rumor held him to be tactfully residing on the Continent, to the despair of his creditors. Other rumors, more scurrilous, had spoken of a misalliance that barred most of London's doors to Barnet. Yet he appeared as immaculately dressed as always. On closer inspection, however, Somers could not help but notice the subtle signs of dissipation in his old acquaintance's face.

"Barnet!' Still riding the same bone-crunching—"

Elizabeth's audible gasp startled Somers. Turning toward her, he was appalled by her ashen face. She looked as if she would swoon—and Elizabeth was not the swooning type.

"Elizabeth?" He lay a protective hand on her arm.

"One could only expect that it would be a lady that kept you in town," Barnet joked as he reined in his horse. "Am I to be granted an introduction to this fair charmer?"

Somers eyed Elizabeth with concern, ignoring Barnet. She was staring straight ahead, looking as if she was carved of stone. "Are you feeling all right?"

She turned slightly, and one glimpse of the stricken anguish on her face told him all was not well. He turned to make his apologies to Barnet, who was staring at Elizabeth with a puzzled expression on his face.

Instantly, everything fell into place for Somers. Elizabeth's blanched countenance, Barnet's curious look and old reputation. Without a word, Somers flicked the reins with a flourish and drove past the startled Barnet.

"It was Barnet, wasn't it?" he asked wearily, slowing the carriage at last.

He saw Elizabeth's brief nod from the corner of his eye.

Somers uttered a mirthless laugh. "Trust me to take you to the park and encounter the one person you never wanted to see again. I am sorry, Elizabeth." He shifted uncomfortably in his seat, finding her quietness unnerving.

Elizabeth exhaled slowly. "You cannot be blamed for the encounter, Somers," she said in a voice taut with strain. "There was always the chance that I would encounter him at some time."

The pain in her voice sent a wrenching ache through Somers. Elizabeth had been so low after failing to learn of her son; now, she was brought face-to-face with the man who had caused her all that agony. Somers could cheerfully tear Barnet apart with his bare hands for what he had done to Elizabeth. He had lied to her, seduced her, gotten her with child . . .

And there was nothing, nothing Somers could do to ease her pain except say that he was sorry. Sorry that their ill-timed drive in the park had brought the past back to her in living detail. She had held up so well through everything: the death of her father, the knowledge of and loss of her son. At what point would she break?

"Somers?"

He started and looked guiltily at Elizabeth.

"We are at the end of the park," she pointed out with a wan smile.

He looked around in surprise. "So we are," he said slowly. He halted the team. "I fear my mind was occupied devising creative methods for torturing Barnet."

Elizabeth smiled. "Is not the cut direct from a man of your stature punishment enough?"

God, she was so strong. He was so filled with despair and regret that he could barely function, and she was already joking about that earth-shattering encounter. Despite her light words, he knew how shaken she was.

His eyes must have reflected his surprise, for she placed her gloved hand over his.

"Somers," Elizabeth said gently, "I must own it was a shock seeing Har—him again. But I have had seven years to come to terms with what happened. It simply does not matter anymore."

Despite her light words, he did not believe her. It more than mattered to him. But perhaps it was best if Elizabeth did not know exactly how much right now. There was time and enough for that later.

"You greatly relieve me, my lady," he said with forced casualness, turning the team toward the park exit. "I was dreadfully afraid you might call him out and I would be forced to loan you my prized pistols. I hate for anyone to touch my pistols."

Elizabeth's lighthearted laugh softened his gloom. But he could not forget that Barnet had a very large debt to pay. Somers' only concern was the price to be extracted—and how best to do it. He had never been a vengeful man, but he discovered a wicked pleasure in planning Barnet's ruin. The man must pay—as Elizabeth had paid for the last seven years. And only Barnet's total disgrace would provide adequate recompense. The moment Somers returned to the house, he would set the wheels in motion.

Not until she reached the sanctuary of her room did the heart-stopping numbness that had surrounded Elizabeth since the encounter in the park wear off. For a moment, when she first recognized Harry, she actually thought she would faint for the first time in her life. Shock was too mild a word to describe her reaction. But then soothing oblivion had descended and she had been barely aware of the return journey home.

Harry. Her feelings for him had undergone so many changes during the past seven years. Pain had dominated at first, followed by a white-hot anger at how skillfully he had duped her. She had spent months rehearsing just what she would say to him if their paths ever crossed again. Yet, when at last they had, she sat tongue-tied with shock. Elizabeth realized with a start that even had she been able to find her tongue, there was really nothing she wanted to say to him anymore.

With the wisdom of years, Elizabeth wondered how she could ever have been so young and foolish to be taken in by a rogue like Harry. She had been warned about him, told to steer clear of his type. Ruefully, she admitted that was probably his principal attraction for her: pure rebellion against the strictures placed upon her by her family and society. Everyone had said no and Elizabeth willfully ignored them.

Elizabeth had not precisely lied to Somers. She had come to terms with Harry and what he had done to her. But she was more disturbed by the meeting than she had let on, and it had nothing to do with seeing Harry again. It was Somers' reaction to Harry that concerned her. It was one thing for Somers to lightly dismiss some nameless seducer, long in the past. But to know exactly to whom she had yielded brought her downfall into the immediate present again. Particularly when he was acquainted with the man.

Despite all Somers' protestations of disinterest in her tarnished status, it had to be a concern for him. Men were brought up believing in the same rigid code of behavior for women as any young girl was. They might take advantage of the male prerogative to toss up the skirts of any willing female who came their way, but when it came to the matter of choosing a wife, they were as demanding as the strictest dowager. It was that knowledge that convinced Elizabeth marriage would never be in her future.

She shoved her musings aside. Her concerns were absurd. Somers had no intention of making her his wife. He was kindness itself in his dealings with her, but his actions were motivated out of concern and friendship, not a lover's desire.

Friendship could stand the strain of her scandalous past and the reappearance of her seducer. She reminded herself firmly that friendship was all she wanted from Somers.

Somers retreated to his study, his mind still reeling from that encounter in the park. It was Barnet who had ruined Elizabeth's life, estranging her from her family and forcing her into a life of seclusion. It was a disgrace that the man still walked the streets.

Somers ached to call him out. He was stunned to discover how pleasurable the idea of putting a ball through Barnet sounded to him. But that avenue of revenge was not open to Somers. That action should have been undertaken by a member of Elizabeth's family. Their dereliction of duty rubbed like a raw wound on his sensibilities. It was only another example of how they had all failed Elizabeth so miserably when she needed them the most. By God, he would not fail her now. He would make Barnet pay.

Somers took a long sip of his brandy, wishing it were so easy to dispatch the other thoughts spinning through his brain. Elizabeth's original confession of her fall from grace had not shocked him. He was not hypocritical enough to castigate her for a pleasure he had never denied himself. But Somers had never stopped to think exactly what that fall had entailed. Now, with Barnet's face fresh in his mind, Somers could achingly visualize what had transpired. The thought of that louse making love to Elizabeth, touching her, caressing her . . . The intensity of the emotions coursing through him caught Somers off-guard. He should have been the one who led Elizabeth down that path of discovery, showing her the joy and pleasure of physical love.

That initially teasing kiss in the carriage had shaken him more than he was willing to admit. To his pleased surprise, Elizabeth hid a passionate nature behind her tranquil exterior. He realized how badly he wanted her, how badly he wanted to make her his, to imprint his name and face and body upon hers so that it would be indelibly burned upon her brain forever. Yet between them always would be Barnet, another memory for Elizabeth that Somers would always wonder about.

He did not even want to think about Elizabeth's true reaction to seeing Barnet today. She had laughed the encounter off, but he knew how shaken she had been. Barnet had used her horribly and made a shambles of her life. But she was bound to remember what she had once felt for him, if only for a moment.

It was not fair. Somers had never held any intention of falling in love with Elizabeth. But now that he had, it seemed there was always one more thing coming between them to prevent their perfect happiness. First it had been the boy, now Barnet. Two people to whom she would be unalterably tied for the remainder of her life. Her lover and her son. How could he ever hope to supplant them in her life? Somers had no illusions that Elizabeth viewed him with the same intensity that had led her to run off with a man against the wishes of her family. And he desperately wished she did.

He shook his head to clear it of his disturbing thoughts, taking a long, deliberate swallow from his glass. He could do nothing about what had passed between Barnet and Elizabeth in the past. But he could deal with Barnet in the present. He laughed mirthlessly at his previous longing for a duel. Death would be too good for Barnet. His fate called for something infinitely more painful and slow, something that would dog him for the rest of his life. It would be a small price to pay for what he had done to Elizabeth.

Somers moved to his desk and uncapped the inkwell. Scratching a few hasty lines on a sheet of paper, he sealed the missive and rang for a footman. The sooner he started Barnet down the road to his destruction, the better.

Should he tell Elizabeth of his plans? He hastily dismissed that notion. She need not know. It would only cause her to dwell further on the matter, while Somers wanted it out of her mind as soon as possible. He did not openly admit that he feared she might not want any harm to come to Barnet.

Two days later, Somers treated himself to a small smile of satisfaction as he surveyed the papers spread out before him. It had been a long, expensive Season for Barnet and he was badly dipped. The tailors and hatters, bootmakers and tradesmen were only too glad to have the Earl of Wentworth buy up Barnet's notes. It had taken a bit more trouble to ferret out the gambling chits as well, but Somers thought he now owned the majority of them. It was time to plot his next move.

Financial ruin was not a thing to laugh at. Much better men than Barnet had been forced from England's shores for fewer debts. The problem for Somers was how to impel Barnet's forced departure in such a manner as to make it widely known and highly permanent—with no hint of the old scandal involving Elizabeth. Which meant that Somers' role in all of this had to remain hidden. No one but Barnet should know that what was to befall him was retribution for Elizabeth.

It was unfortunate that the Season had ended, as there would be fewer ears to hear of Barnet's departure. But Somers had dropped enough hints among those he had been able to find to ensure that word made the rounds of the great houses over the summer. In fact, this would even keep the news alive longer than if it had taken place during the height of the Season, when other and perhaps even juicer tales would vie for attention. The only thing left to do was to call in the bailiffs and offer Barnet the opportunity to chose between exile and the Fleet. Somers had no doubt as to the man's answer.

By the following day, Elizabeth could not deny that the encounter with Harry in the park had strained her relationship with Somers. How could it not have? Worse, it was not even something she could discuss with him. They had been open with each other about so many other topics, but on this subject he was strangely silent. It could only be interpreted as a sign of his distress, the knowledge that he could no longer ignore the truth of her past. As much as she disliked the idea, it was time for her to return to Harcourt. She could not bear to watch Somers' attitude toward her change. She resolved to tell him of her plans to depart.

"Your mother said I might find you here," she said hesitantly, stepping over the threshold of the study.

Somers rose from his chair, greeting her with a warm smile. "So you have. And what is your boon, Lady Elizabeth?"

"I . . ." She dropped her eyes before his cool blue eyes. "I believe it is time that I return to Harcourt. Frederick will think I plan to stay away forever."

"Why don't you?"

"You know that is not possible, Somers. I have abused your hospitality long enough."

"It is an abuse I do not mind," he said quickly, his mind racing at how to persuade her to stay, if only for a short while longer. There were still so many things they needed to say.

Elizabeth fumbled nervously with the paperweight on his desk. "It is past time for me to deal with Frederick. Now that I know I will not . . . will not find my son, I at least know what I will ask of my brother. It is time I settle my future."

"What do you plan for your future?" he asked lightly, although his heart was pounding. Did she still long for Barnet? If only she would give him a clue as to how she felt.

"I wish to be allowed to return to Chedford." She turned and walked to the window. "It is not the expense he objects to, but what people will say if I do not live at Harcourt. I do not understand how he can be so hypocritical, when it is plain as a pikestaff that he does not really want me there."

"Perhaps he feels it will ease your return into society if you appear to be on good terms with your family. One should not turn up one's nose at a duke, you know. They are possessed of enormous consequence."

She smiled. "And how depressing for you to know you are only an earl! You would have made a devastating duke, Somers, dampening the pretensions of the rest of us mere mortals."

He did not smile, although he appreciated her teasing. He had to know what she felt for her former lover. "Is it because of Barnet that you wish to leave?"

She looked at him with surprise in her hazel eyes. "No," she replied firmly. "I own that seeing him was a great shock, but once I had time to think on it, I realized that it really mattered very little."

"Oh," he replied, the doubt in his voice obvious.

Elizabeth took a deep breath. "Does it matter to you?"

"Yes," he said evenly. "It does."

Her shoulders slumped; all her false bravado withered at his words. But even if Somers could not easily dismiss her youthful folly, she wanted him to know that she had.

She averted her head slightly, so she would not have to look in his eyes. "It was surprising," she said at last. "To find out how indifferent I was. I would have thought there would be at least anger. But there was not even that anymore."

"Yet you gave up everything for him once."

She shook her head in amazement. "I find it difficult to even identify with the stupid child I once was. I am quite certain it was someone else, not me." She glanced at him from the corners of her eyes, startled at the bemused expression upon his face.

"His wife is dead, you know."

"The poor soul," she said softly.

Somers was uncertain whether she referred to Barnet or the dead woman.

"Do you know what was my foremost thought upon seeing Harry?" Elizabeth faced Somers. "I thought how terribly old he looked."

Somers heart leapt at her words. If she spoke the truth—and there was no reason to doubt her—then he had no cause to fear Barnet. He would not be an invisible barrier between Elizabeth and himself. There was no reason for his insane jealousy.

He laughed aloud in relief. "He is nearly my own age," Somers protested.

"Perhaps you have lived a less-taxing life." She flashed him an impish smile. "Or, like French brandy, you improve with age."

"I have been so worried about your state of mind these last days, thinking you were either pining for Barnet or plotting his death." His eyes widened with amusement. "You never cease to surprise me, Elizabeth."

"Nor do you. How could you even think I felt anything beyond anger at that man?"

He offered her a deliberately casual smile. "They always say that a woman never forgets her first lover."

"Only if the succeeding one is less memorable."

Somers remembered those breathless kisses in the coach and vowed to obliterate all memories of another from her head. He took a step toward her, halting and turning in dismay as his mother entered the room.

"Did you forget, Elizabeth dear, that we were going to call on Lady Marchmount today?"

Elizabeth's hand flew to her mouth at the remembered plan. "I shall be ready in a moment," she said, hastening from the room.

The countess settled herself comfortably on the sofa. "I have been thinking," she said pointedly to Somers.

He turned, still irritated at her interruption. "What?"

"Elizabeth's child. It would have been unlike Harcourt to have done the thing in a havey-cavey manner. He would have had the whole business arranged with utmost precision."

"She said his solicitor denied all knowledge."

Lady Wentworth looked pointedly at her son.

"You think he lied to her?"

She gave an enigmatic shrug. "Solicitors are slippery creatures at times." She looked up at the opening door and rose to her feet. "Ah, Elizabeth, how speedy you are. Have a delightful afternoon, my boy."

Somers could only stare after his mother, the seed she had planted in his mind growing with every moment.

21

After his mother and Elizabeth departed, Somers sat in the drawing room for a long time, watching the dust motes dancing in the sunlight. Was there still the chance Elizabeth could find her son? Would a man of law lie to her out of a conviction of rightness? Somers ruefully judged that very likely. For had he not made the same judgment of Elizabeth's quest? That it was a mistake and she would best let matters rest? That he, in his unmitigated arrogance, knew what was best for her?

The thought filled him with shame. He could not make Elizabeth's decisions for her. The woman he loved, the proud, independent and even stubborn lady she was, demanded his respect. And he did not respect her if he allowed himself to interfere in her life. She must be free to make her own choices. And if she chose to reunite herself with her son, it was not for him to say it was wrong. He had to do everything in his power to facilitate her search. He owed her that much.

Grimacing, he rose and walked to the desk. In London, everything was for sale, be it merchandise or information. Prying confidential papers out of a solicitor's office was not quite as easy as buying a horse, but anything could be had for a price. Hastily, he composed another note to the man who had assisted him in ferreting out Barnet's difficulties. Somers only hoped Elizabeth would appreciate his efforts. For if he was successful, it might ruin all his plans.

Nursing his brandy in the near dark of the study, Somers stared at the paper he held in his hand. When he had engaged

Rogers two days ago to make one final inquiry into the whereabouts of Elizabeth's son, Somers had not expected—or wanted—results. Yet, here he sat, with a name and a village on a piece of paper, and he did not know what to do.

He loved Elizabeth. He knew that with a ringing finality now. There was no other woman on earth for him. In her, there was a passionate nature to match his own, for he did not delude himself, that was an important requirement for him. When he wanted to cosset and coddle her, she rebuffed his attempts, insisting in her pride and independence that he meet her as an equal and not a dominating protector. It was this strength he loved so well, the one thing he had never found in another woman or even thought to seek for.

It had been stupid of him to offer her his name that once, for all the wrong reasons. It would make it even harder to convince her of his regard, for he was certain she still held a lingering suspicion of his motives. He laughed. Perhaps it would be better if he sought liberties with her body, for he suspected she would look more tolerantly on lust than on sympathy.

But the boy . . . It was an ironic situation. If the child were his own bastard, society would say nothing about his inclusion in their household. Yet, as her child, he would serve as a reminder to everyone of the events of his conception. Somers was under no illusions the lad's parentage would remain a secret. One could not marry a woman of Elizabeth's lineage without attracting attention, and to set up marriage with a six-year-old child would dredge up all the old gossip. Particularly with Barnet back in town. And worse, Elizabeth's insistence on keeping the child would shock and disgust most society leaders. Bastards were to be discarded and forgotten. Married women were allowed their affairs, and their bastards. But unmarried women were not. Even the noted scandals of the past—from Lady Holland and the Duchess of Devonshire to the Marchioness of Anglesey—had all been married women when they bore their lover's offspring.

Elizabeth would never be accepted in society. Even the name and title of Wentworth would be no guard against that. And he was not quite certain he could resign himself to the strange life they would be forced to lead. In the country, in his house, Elizabeth would reign supreme. But in public, she would be invisible. If they went to the theater, there would be no one else in their box. He could not hold her in his arms and waltz across the floor at fetes and assemblies, for she would not be invited. He was uncertain if even his mother would be so willing to flout convention and acknowledge Elizabeth as a guest.

Yet the fool wanted her son. Somers held the key to his happiness—and hers—in his hand, and he knew what he should do. What he ought to do. And what honor demanded he do.

With a regretful sigh over all that might have been, he slipped the piece of paper into the top drawer of his desk, carefully locking it away. The rest of the house was asleep. There was time and enough for this tomorrow.

Somers paced back and forth across the breakfast room, his feet beating an agitated rhythm. He wanted to catch Elizabeth before his mother came down.

"There you are," he exclaimed as she entered the chamber. "I thought you were going to sleep the morning away."

"This from the man who once told me I had the waking habits of a farmer?"

He smiled, but it was a hollow sensation. "I need to talk to you for a moment. In the library, where we can be private."

She sensed the seriousness of his tone and followed him with some apprehension into the room he called his own. Taking the chair he indicated, Elizabeth watched impatiently as he unlocked his desk and drew out a piece of paper. He looked over her with such an expression of anguish that she grew alarmed.

"Somers, what is it?"

"When you returned to London, I hired a man to make some inquiries about your son. You were right, Elizabeth. Your father's solicitor lied to you. He made the arrangements with the family and set up an annuity to pay for the boy's keep." Solemnly, he handed her the paper. "That is the name of the family who is taking care of your son, and their direction."

Elizabeth reached for the paper as if afraid the touch of it would burn her fingers. Carefully, cautiously, she ran her fingers over the scrawled letters, as if absorbing their information into her body. Lunny. Steep. Hants. Then she burst into tears.

Sommer knelt before her in an instant, pulling her into the

comforting circle of his arms as he had done that night in Chedford.

"Easy, easy," he whispered, fumbling for his handkerchief.

"Oh, Somers, how can I ever thank you for this?" she cried between sobs, her face lit with an incongruous smile as the tears fell down her cheeks.

And he knew he had done the right thing, even if it meant the end of all his hopes. For it was what she wanted.

Elizabeth, if she had been given her way, would have jumped into the carriage without even packing her bag, so eager was she to depart. But the Wentworths' wisdom prevailed, and it was early afternoon before she and Somers drove off toward the south. Even with such a late start, there would only be a short stretch to travel on the morrow. The countess volunteered to accompany them, to lend countenance to the situation, but Elizabeth demurred. Once she was reunited with her son, she knew she would have no reputation to maintain.

They said little on the journey. Somers did not wish to dampen her joy with his words of warning; Elizabeth was fully aware of Somers' disapproval of her plan. When they talked, it was of light and trivial matters.

Nearing Steep the next morning, Somers thought it wise to discern Elizabeth's thoughts—and make one last attempt to dissuade her from this course.

"Have you thought out all you plan to say?" he asked.

She shook her head. "So much depends on the family. I do not know what they were told when they took him, whether they expected him to be there forever or knew someone would come eventually."

"They may not want to give him up, you know," he said gently.

"But they must! I am his mother."

"Was the birth ever documented? Do you have any proof?"

"Somers!"

"I am trying to play devil's advocate. If they are a good family, they have raised him as their own, and it will be like losing a son to them. A son they have known for all of his six years."

"I know you think I am foolish to persist in this," Elizabeth retorted, her eyes flashing, "but if you are going to try to talk me out of it again, you may save your breath. I am determined to raise my son."

Somers thought it wise to hold his tongue for the short distance left to Steep.

The carriage stopped before the small inn serving the town, and Somers alit easily from the coach. "I shall inquire inside of the Lunnys' direction," he explained to Elizabeth.

The innkeeper looked up with joy at the sight of this potential client. "Good day, your lordship," he greeted, knowing quality when he saw it. "What is your pleasure?"

"Is there a family named Lunny living in the parish?"

"Lunny? Can't say that there is. Friends of yours?"

"A distant connection of my, uh, half-sister's. Have you lived in the area long? They were here six, seven years ago I think."

"Lunny, Lunny," the innkeeper puzzled. Then light dawned in his eyes. "Of course! You mean Reverend Lunny. Stands to reason, if he's a connection of the quality. You can see the church spire from the street; vicarage's right alongside."

"Thank you, thank you," Somers hastened, thrilled and dismayed by the news at the same time. The boy was likely in good hands, he realized as he crossed the lane to the carriage, but there may be more of a problem in taking him away than Elizabeth thought.

Passing directions to the coachman, Somers hopped into the carriage.

"He's with the vicar," he explained. "Just at the other end of town."

Elizabeth twisted her fingers into knots on the short journey. Now that she was here, was really here, and would see her son in only a matter of minutes, she was scared and elated and frightened and overjoyed.

"Do you wish me to come with you?" Somers asked when the vehicle stopped.

Elizabeth nodded, not daring to speak. Somers helped her from the coach and they walked down the flower-bordered path to the front of the house. She allowed him to rap upon the door.

"Yes?" inquired the middle-aged woman who opened it.

"I would like to see Reverend Lunny, if I may," Elizabeth gasped out.

"Margaret, who is it?" a pleasantly modulated female voice called.

"Visitors for the reverend, ma'am."

A small, delicate-boned woman with silvery-blond hair stepped into the hall.

"Do come in," she said. "I am Mrs. Lunny. My husband is busy with the boys and their lessons at the moment, but they will break in fifteen minutes. Would you care to wait in the parlor and have some tea?"

Elizabeth felt the comforting warmth of Somers' hand on her back, pushing her into the darkened hall.

"Mrs. Lunny," she began. "I am . . . I am Lady Elizabeth Granford. And I think you have my son."

Mrs. Lunny looked at her in silent surprise for a moment, then spoke. "I think this justifies an early end to lessons. I shall fetch my husband."

The housekeeper ushered them into the parlor. Elizabeth sat gingerly on the edge of a chair while Somers stood a little to one side.

"He must be here," she breathed. "She recognized my name."

"I think any woman arriving on her doorstep and asking for her son would be accorded the same degree of interest," he replied. Elizabeth's deathly pale face frightened him. Let it go well, he prayed.

In scant moments, Reverend Lunny and his wife entered the room. He was a tall man, plainly dressed, with spectacles slipping off his nose, and a shock of startling red hair. The housekeeper arrived with the tea and everyone waited patiently until she filled the cups and retreated before speaking.

"Now," said the reverend after taking a sip of the reviving brew. "What makes you think your son is here?"

Elizabeth looked to Somers, finding strength in his presence. "Six years ago I bore a child out of wedlock and was told he died at birth. Two weeks ago I discovered that he is alive." She took in a deep, calming breath. "My father's solicitor made the arrangements to have the boy sent to a family named Lunny in Steep. Is he here?"

"When was the child born?"

"The fifteenth of February, 1810. I was in Cornwall for the

birth, so it must have taken a few days before he arrived here."

"William," Mrs. Lunny whispered.

Somers, from his vantage point, saw her face, and it was a sight he never wished to behold again. If Elizabeth's pale countenance had dismayed him earlier, the sick look on Mrs. Lunny's face was devastating. How could Elizabeth put them through this?

"You say your father's lawyer made the arrangements," Reverend Lunny said. "What was that man's name?"

"Jenkins," Elizabeth replied.

The red-haired man issued a deep sigh. "I believe, then, that the boy we named William is your son, Lady Elizabeth."

A small cry of joy escaped her lips. "May I see him?" she asked eagerly.

"What, exactly, do you propose to say to him?" The vicar's concern was etched on his face. "He is aware he is adopted, of course, but he does not know the true story of his parentage. I do not think it is necessary to confuse him with your true relationship for only a short visit."

"This is not a short visit. I am here to reclaim my son, Reverend Lunny," Elizabeth said with emphasis. "I am his mother and he belongs to me. He was taken from me through lies and deceit and I want him back."

"I see." The vicar removed his spectacles and leaned forward over the desk. "Don't you think the sudden addition of a child into your family will cause comment? Not to mention the disruption to your household. Do you have other children, my lady?"

"I am not married," Elizabeth replied.

"You wish to raise him by yourself?" The man was incredulous. He looked to Somers. "I had thought you her husband."

'If I were, we would not be here," he replied dryly. "Do not think that I support her in this, for I do not. But I do not like her traveling about the country alone, either."

"May I see William now?"

"Elizabeth," said Somers, "there is no rush. You know he is well-cared-for. Nothing will be served by shocking the boy with the news immediately. We can rest at the inn and return at another time. I am sure everyone would appreciate some time to organize their thoughts.''

"No." Elizabeth set her mouth in a stubborn line.

"Your wife mentioned there were boys?" Somers tried another tack. "Might perhaps the whole brood join us for tea? Elizabeth could then observe her son without drawing undue attention to the situation."

"An admirable compromise," Reverend Lunny agreed. "We have five children here—all adopted and all with stories like William's. My wife and I were unable to have any of our own, and I knew too well the fate awaiting many of these cast-off mites."

"They are lucky children to have been taken into such an accepting home," Somers replied, looking at Elizabeth for her response.

She nodded her agreement. The Lunnys did seem like nice people and they had raised her son for six years. She owed them so much, for keeping the boy safe. After waiting six years, she could afford to wait a little longer.

All five children, three boys and two girls, were ushered into the library.

It took all Elizabeth's strength not to leap from her seat and fling her arms around William. She would have marked him instantly, even without his like-colored hair. She saw so much of herself reflected in his face, and a trace of his father as well. He looked so grown-up.

Her son. For six years she had thought him dead and now he sat before her, nervous in strange company, eyeing the cakes on the tea tray with the avaricious greed of a small boy. All the things she had planned to say, the imaginary conversations she had rehearsed over and over in her mind, vanished like wisps of fog on an early summer's morn. She could only stare with greedy eyes at the child she had never thought to see.

Somers had no difficulty picking out William. The resemblance between him and Elizabeth was marked. They had the same hazel eyes and rich, thick hair. Only the mouth differed—a lasting sign of his father. Somers was unable to look at Elizabeth as the children entered the room. For a moment earlier he had feared she would truly make an unpleasant scene, but she had reined in her emotions and was acting more like the duke's daughter she was.

If he had known before what he knew now about the Lunnys, he would never have told Elizabeth their name. The child was obviously loved and welcomed in this most unusual family, and it would be the height of cruelty to tear him away from his home. But he had selfishly wanted to please Elizabeth and had pitched them both into a situation in which no one could win.

All depended on Elizabeth. Somers hoped she was experiencing the same doubts and dismay as he. He hoped Reverend Lunny's surprise at her plan to raise the child by herself reminded her how difficult a task that would be.

Elizabeth was grateful for Somers' presence of mind, for he kept up a lively conversation while she sat tongue-tied and silent. She had eyes and thoughts only for William. But gradually, Somers' voice intruded on her thoughts and she began to listen to the conversation. It seemed to center on fishing.

"I like diggin' for worms," William piped up in his squeaky voice.

"That was always my favorite part, too," Somers said. He leaned closer in a conspiratorial whisper and asked, "I don't suppose you have ever stuck any in your sister's bed?"

The light in the boy's eyes showed he thought that a capital idea.

"I never had a sister," Somers confided. "So I never had a place to put any worms."

"You can borrow Cassie if you want," the boy offered hopefully, looking at his older sister with disdain.

"William," said the eldest boy, George, attempting to disassociate himself from the younger. "That is not a nice thing to say in front of company."

"Or indeed, at all," added the reverend.

William scowled and remained silent.

Elizabeth racked her brains for some conversational topic. Here she was with her son at last and she could not even utter the most innocuous remark. "What did you learn in your lessons today?"

"Homer," George replied with enough distaste to indicate it was probably in the original Greek.

"Ah, Homer," said Somers with a mischievous glint in his

eye. "Always one of my great favorites. Lots of battles and fighting and lovely ladies."

"I want to be a sailor like Odysseus," William announce. "When I get big enough, I am going to run off and join the navy."

"Do you think it altogether wise to run off?" Elizabeth asked, torn between amusement and chagrin. "Your family might worry."

"Oh, I would write Mama every day," he said with pride. "And I would say my prayers every night for Papa."

"I am not sure that would make amends for running off," said the vicar with a hint of a smile. "Perhaps you should wait until you are old enough to go properly."

"Have you ever been a sailor?" William asked Somers hopefully.

Somers shook his head. "No, I am sorry to say I was not, William. I fear my mama would not allow me to run away to sea when I was young, and by the time I was old enough I did not want to go to sea anymore."

"I shan't change my mind," William said, a stubborn set to his mouth.

Somers recalled the same expression on Elizabeth's face.

All too soon, to Elizabeth's mind, the children were dismissed. Somers stood.

"We have imposed on your hospitality long enough for one day," he said smoothly, tugging Elizabeth from her chair. "We are grateful you allowed us to see the boy."

"What . . . what do you plan to do?" Mrs. Lunny asked hesitantly.

"I am not certain," Elizabeth answered honestly. "May we call again tomorrow? I should like to consider the matter carefully."

The reverend nodded.

Somers lingered at the door while Mrs. Lunny escorted Elizabeth to the gate.

"Will you fight her for custody if she wishes to take the boy?" he asked the vicar bluntly.

The man shook his head. "I think a battle would be worse on the boy than any change."

Somers nodded. He gave the reverend his hand. "I cannot

order her decision. But she is well aware of my opposition, and
perhaps that will weigh some.''

"We shall pray that God will guide her decision,'' Reverend
Lunny said.

Somers nodded in agreement. He did not count himself a
religious man, but he doubted even the Lunnys' prayers would
be more fervent.

Elizabeth said nothing during the brief drive to the inn. Somers
bespoke them rooms and a private parlor before he escorted
her from the coach.

"Would you like to rest?''

She shook her head. "It is such a lovely day. Let us take a
walk.''

He took her arm and they strolled down the short center of
the village. Soon the neat buildings gave way to cottages and
then fields, and still they walked on in silence. Somers was
determined to keep his thoughts to himself, difficult as it was.
This was Elizabeth's decision, he reminded himself. She must
make it on her own.

Elizabeth walked as if in a daze. She was aware of Somers
at her side, the feel of his arm clasped within hers. Yet her mind
was back at the vicarage, with her son and his family.

His family. For that is what they were. Mother and father,
brothers and sisters. All of the world her William had ever
known was back at that small house. Dared she remove him
from it? Would he truly be better-off with her than with the
woman he had called Mama all these years? There would be
no brothers and sisters at her house, she realized with a pang,
knowing how she had always bemoaned the lack of close siblings
in her own life. Could she consign William to such a solitary
existence? True, there would be neighbor children to play with,
but it was not quite the same.

She stopped, suddenly, and turned to face her escort. "What
am I to do, Somers?''

The anguish in her face pained him. He wished he could solve
her dilemma, ease her mind. But as desperately as he wanted
to help her, he knew it was not his task.

"I cannot tell you that, Elizabeth. You must decide on your
own.''

"I cannot! It all sounded so simple back at Harcourt and in London. Now I see that it is not simple at all. He is part of a family here. Would it be right for me to take him away?"

No, he shouted silently. And not just for the prudent reason of preserving her reputation. But for the simple reason it would be best for the boy.

"You do not need to reach a decision immediately," he said gently. "Think the night on it. You must be very certain in what you decide."

She nodded at the wisdom of his words and allowed him to turn their steps back toward Steep.

And if she makes the wrong decision, he thought as he walked beside her, there was still one more card he could play. Elizabeth had not resolved her situation with Frederick. If he forbade her the house in Chedford and ordered her to Harcourt, she would be unable to keep William with her. Somers had no doubts of Frederick forbidding that. Somers himself intended to provide Elizabeth with an independence of her own, if Frederick insisted on confining her to his house. But if it meant she would be able to take the child with her . . . Somers would have to think long and hard about that. He prayed Elizabeth would come to the right decision.

22

Elizabeth lay fully clothed upon the bed, her room lit only by the moon. It was odd how the smallest incidents in one's life could have such a dramatic impact. In the Cotswolds, in March, there had been a late snow. It all devolved from that. Somers had arrived on her doorstep and everything that followed had led up to this moment in a small inn in Hampshire, where the future of several people rested in her hands. She had the power to determine the course of all their lives.

William. The very name sent a stab of pain through her heart. Her father's name. The name she had picked out for her son. Had the Lunnys been told that, or was the naming only a coincidence?

Elizabeth knew what she should do. What everyone, from Somers and his mother to Frederick and the Lunnys, wanted her to do. Let him go. Tuck away the image of a smiling, tousled-haired young boy into the corner of her heart and leave him there. But why? Why had his existence been revealed to her if she was meant to give him up? She had endured enough pain already in this lifetime. Why must she endure more? Wasn't she entitled to some happiness too?

Yet her happiness could be bought only with the pain of others. She had not missed Mrs. Lunny's stricken expression when she realized the purpose of Elizabeth's visit. She had raised William as her own, lavished a mother's attention on him, never imagining his real mother would one day want him.

But she had other children. William was all that Elizabeth had. Blood of her blood. Flesh of her flesh. Were not those ties stronger than any other? Did she not have a right to William, after carrying him in her body for nine months, enduring the pain and suffering necessary to bring him into the world? Her claim was the strongest.

She and Wiliam could make a happy life together in the cottage at Chedford. The six years of separation would be erased. There were children aplenty in the village for playmates, and classes with the vicar. In Emily he would find a doting aunt.

The more she struggled to justify her desire, the more she strove to paint a rosy picture of their life together, the more Elizabeth knew she fought a losing battle with reality. She had nothing to offer William, except her heart. She did not have a home to call her own, or a penny to her name. Frederick would never allow her to bring William to Harcourt. What if Frederick refused to allow her to return to Chedford? Where could they go? There was no jobs waiting for a genteel woman with a young son.

The foolish, simpleminded dreams she had built about her future life with William faded away under the cool moonlight. She knew she could not tear him away from the Lunnys. If he were younger, if they were an unpleasant couple, she would not hesitate. But they were caring, compassionate parents who loved him as if he were their own. She could not give him half of what he had here. She had no money to provide his support, no brothers and sisters for him to play with, and no father for him to look up to.

In that moment of decision she felt a peaceful relief. Deep in her soul she knew it must be this way, and if it was the most painful decision in her life, she could console herself with the wisdom of it in the long years to come. There would be moments of regret, but there would be no agonizing days of remorse either. It was, in those oh-so-simple words that gave no hint of the agony involved, "the best thing to do."

Her decision would please Somers, she knew. And although his opinion had not influenced her choice, she was glad to think he would admire her action. For it was suddenly very important for her to have his admiration.

She loved him. It had taken her this long to realize it, but now that she acknowledged the fact, it seemed the most obvious thing in the world. Her feelings for him had been such a jumbled

mixture of gratitude, exasperation, and delight that she had not
been able to sort them out properly. Ironically, seeing Harry
again had jolted her into recognizing just how much she did
care for Somers. Why else would she have worried so about
what he thought of her? Somers had stood by her side throughout, despite his opposition to her search, and it was perhaps
that loyalty that appealed to her the most. He had never judged
her for past actions, but had treated her as a lady from the first
moment they met.

In fact, she thought, he treated her far too much like a lady.
After that passionate embrace in the coach, he had indicated
no further interest in her that way. She was afraid he still viewed
her as an object of pity and sympathy. And that was the last
thing she wanted from him now. She needed him, his strength,
his wisdom, his understanding. What other man would have
stood at her side through this whole terrible ordeal?

Yet here she was, posing again as his sister. Was that how
he viewed her? She was partly to blame, for she had relied
heavily on him these last weeks, turning to him for help as if
he were a brother. Or her husband, a small voice reminded her.

But a husband would not be sleeping across the hall, she
reminded that small voice. And all her pent-up longings for love,
companionship, intimacy, and friendship burst forth as if a dam
had broken. She wanted marriage, she wanted a husband and
a family and all the joys and sorrows those things brought with
them. She had been living a lie in Chedford all these years and
only now finally admitted the truth to herself.

And the bitter irony was she had fallen in love with a man
who treated her like a fragile piece of china, who had offered
his assistance in her times of need. And she realized with a pang
that she no longer had any need. William would remain in Steep,
she would return to Harcourt, and Somers would be gone from
her life, satisfied he had neatly taken care of matters. He would
go back to his opera dancers and bored wives without a backward thought.

Other women might have flung themselves at his head, or
flirted and simpered until he took the hint. But Elizabeth's pride
forbade such blatant actions. She could point out that his
unchaperoned company as they crisscrossed England these last
weeks obligated him to marry her. If word ever reached the

ton that they had spent a night at an inn together . . . But what would be the point of a marriage of obligation? It would be infinitely worse than no marriage at all.

Perhaps, in time, she would find another man. One who was less managing, less sure of the rightness of his ideas. One who was not such a wicked flirt. One who found the idea of liaisons with married women abhorrent. One whom she did not love quite so much.

"You had a restless night." Somers offered Elizabeth a sympathetic smile as he joined her in the private parlor for breakfast.

"Do I look so dreadful?"

"I have seen worse," he responded cheerfully. "But I think if you keep your face heavily veiled, no one will think aught is amiss."

She offered a woebegone smile, knowing he tried to cheer her with his teasing. "I should like to return to the vicarage this morning," she began. "I have decided to . . . to leave William with the Lunnys. It is the best thing for him."

Somers winced at the pain in her voice. Despite his conviction that it was the right action, he felt a pain nearly as sharp as he knew hers must be. He wanted to gather her into his arms, to take away some of her pain, to offer her comfort and solace. Reaching across the table, he cupped her hand in his. "I appreciate what a difficult decision that was for you, Elizabeth. I wish I could ease the hurt for you."

"You have done so much already. I need to tell the Lunnys of my decision, and I should like to see him one more time."

"Do you want me to go with you?"

Elizabeth shook her head. "I had best go on my own. Would you have the carriage ready, though, so we can leave immediately? I do not think I could remain another minute in this town afterward."

"I will meet you outside the vicarage, then. In about an hour?"

She nodded her assent and rose from the table, her breakfast untouched. Pausing at the door, she turned and looked back at Somers. He sat immobile in his chair, watching her intently. As their gazes met, he gave her a brief nod of salute.

She had done it. He had known Elizabeth to be a woman of deep, inner strength. How could she have endured so much without breaking? Yet she had faced each crisis in her life with a resiliency that astounded him. He did not know how she did it.

He experienced a strange mixture of sadness and elation. He ached with empathy for her pain at leaving her son, but her decision filled him with joy as well. It would make it all much simpler when the time came to court her properly. He wanted to dash after her, to declare his love and beg her to become his wife. But it was the worst possible moment for him to demonstrate anything but friendly sympathy. If he asked for her hand now, she would only ascribe to him all the motives she had charged him with that first time at Kempton. The next time he proposed, he wanted to make certain she clearly understood his reasons.

Somers quickly alit when the coach pulled in front of the vicarage. Mrs. Lunny had apparently been watching for his arrival, for she was out the door in an instant.

"I shall tell her you are here, my lord."

He shook his head. "Let her come in her own time. She will know how long she needs to stay."

"We are ever so grateful for her decision, my lord. Like all the others, we think of William as our own and—"

"Tell her, not me," he said abruptly.

She nodded, as if taken aback at his brusqueness. Curtsying, she returned to the house.

Somers leaned against the coach, booted feet crossed, arms folded across his chest. Outwardly, he portrayed a picture of calm, but inside, his mind was in turmoil. Now that Elizabeth had made her decision, he was consumed by guilt. Had his opposition influenced Elizabeth? Had it all become too much: Frederick's insistence she live at Harcourt, his own disapproval of her search, her uncertainty about her future?

He was not sure he could live with himself if she had not made this decision willingly. He should have made his plans for her more clear, earlier. Told her he was willing to give her the money to return to Chedford if Frederick would not. Told her that . . . that he loved her, even if she was so harebrained as to want to flaunt her illegitimate son before the world.

Somers kicked at a rock in the road, raising a slight puff of dust where his boot met the dirt. Once he had been so certain of his views, confident he knew what was best for her, and himself. Now he did not know. If Elizabeth had bowed before his disapproval, how could she ever look favorably upon him? He would always be a reminder of what she had given up, and why.

Should he never have tried that last time to find the boy? But would a future always filled with doubt and worry have been a better fate for Elizabeth? She could at least grasp some happiness in the knowledge that her son was well-cared-for and loved.

There was little point in worrying over what had already transpired now. It was the future that concerned him. A future he wanted to share with Elizabeth at his side. And he was dreadfully unsure whether she felt the same.

The soft murmur of voices broke into his thoughts. Looking up, he saw Elizabeth at the door, making her good-byes to the Lunnys.

He would never cease to admire her for what she had done. He could only guess at how wrenching a decision it had been for her. And his conviction that it was the right one did not make him any less sympathetic. Elizabeth seemed to have an unfathomable well of strength inside her that allowed her to endure what would have crushed lesser women. How he longed to shelter her from any more grief and pain.

As she reached the end of the flagstoned path, he offered her his hand and helped her up the steps into the carriage. He bowed a farewell to the Lunnys and climbed in beside her. The coachman snapped the reins and the carriage slowly lumbered down the road.

"They promised to write, occasionally," Elizabeth said after they had traveled for long minutes in silence. "To let me know how he is and what he is doing."

"That is kind of them." He paused, wondering if a clean break would be best.

"I shall feel better knowing, I think. Else I would worry,"

"There is still much you can do for him, you know, even from afar."

She looked at him with a quizzical expression.

"I doubt the Lunnys could afford Eton or university. You could easily provide him that, and an *entrée* into whatever career he chooses."

"How?" she asked bitterly. "I have no money to call my own."

"I would not be surprised if your brother agreed to such a thing. And if he did not, I would not be averse—"

"I shall speak to Frederick when I return," she said, ignoring Somers' offer. She did not want more charity from him.

They lapsed into silence again, which was not broken until they stopped for the midday meal.

Elizabeth had paid little attention to her surroundings ever since they left Steep, so it was with surprise that she noted they entered the outskirts of Portsmouth.

"Where are we going?" She turned to Somers, puzzled.

"I thought that no matter the outcome of your journey to Steep, you would not wish to return to London, or Harcourt, immediately. I am taking you to Kempton."

Odious, interfering man, she thought fondly. How like him to do this without asking. And how wonderful of him to know she needed this time to come to terms with all that had happened.

"My mother should be arriving about the same time as ourselves," he continued. "So you need not worry about the impropriety of staying alone at the house with me."

Elizabeth laughed. "The matter concerns me greatly, I assure you. Particularly since we have at least one more night to spend together at an inn. Your misguided sense of propriety never ceases to amaze me."

To his chagrin, Somers discovered his mother had not preceded them to Kempton, and as the afternoon shadows grew longer, it became doubtful she would arrive that day.

"Since my mother has obviously been delayed, I shall need to make some arrangements," Somers announced to Elizabeth. "I thought Lady Worthing might be willing to stay with us this night, as I am certain Mama will be here on the morrow."

"Do not be absurd, Somers. It is not necessary. I assure you I am much too exhausted for any form of impropriety. In fact, if you do not mind, I would rather dine on a tray in my room so I can retire early.''

He opened his mouth to rebut her argument, then closed it again. Frankly, he was too tired to rush over to Lady Worthing's this night. If Mama did not arrive tomorrow, he would do something about the lack of proper chaperonage. Tonight he agreed with Elizabeth: he had no energy to even contemplate behaving badly. Maybe tomorrow . . . With a mischievous smile, he nodded his acceptance of Elizabeth's wishes.

He managed to persuade Elizabeth to join him for dinner, which they ate in the cozy comfort of the small drawing room. A warming fire took the chill out of the cool summer night.

Somers motioned for Elizabeth to join him on the sofa while the dinner trays were cleared. Pouring himself a glass of wine, he relaxed against the cushions, one booted foot across his knee. How he would like to have many more nights like this. With just himself and Elizabeth, alone, chatting after dinner, sharing their experiences of the day.

He noted that Elizabeth, whose conversation had been less than animated at dinner, remained quiet and pensive. Somers studied her carefully, unsure how troubled she was. Since her brief remarks when they left Steep, she had said nothing about her decision to leave William with the Lunnys. Somers desperately wanted to offer her solace, yet was unsure exactly how to approach her without making a mess of things.

Elizabeth shifted slightly and turned to face him. "I am rather tired," she began apologetically.

"I know." He reached out and took her hand, rubbing his thumb across her knuckles as he spoke. "I . . . I admire what you did yesterday. I know it cannot have been easy."

She let out a long breath and looked toward the fire. Somers could see her lower lip trembling.

"Elizabeth?" He held out his arms and she came into them, burying her face against his chest.

I will not cry, she told herself, taking long deep breaths in an effort to maintain the rigid control she had envinced throughout the last two days. She felt Somers' arms tighten around her and she derived strength from his nearness.

"My brave, brave Elizabeth," he whispered soothingly. He

began stroking her back in broad, lazy circles, feeling the tension gradually draining from her.

Elizabeth lifted her head and met Somers' unwavering blue gaze. She wanted to pour out her feelings, her longings, her desires, but shrank from exposing herself to any more emotional upset. She felt limp and exhausted, and Somers' presence was nearly as disturbing as William's absence.

"Better?" he asked.

Elizabeth nodded. She could not resist a final gesture, a final thanks for all he had done, now, before the deep bond she had felt with him throughout their wild journeys was severed at their return to normality. She reached up and lightly touched her fingers to his cheek. "Thank you, Somers."

He cupped his hand over hers and carried it carefully to his mouth, gently drawing her fingers to his lips. His eyes locked with hers and he imagined he received her silent acquiescence. Bending his head, he covered her mouth with his, pressing light, teasing kisses on her lips.

Elizabeth responded eagerly, knowing she should not, but dashing caution to the winds. She wanted his kisses, the light play of his hands on her back. Placing her own hand behind his neck, she pulled him closer, showing him her want.

Somers had never struggled so mightily for control. The woman he wanted, the woman he loved, was in his arms, her lips locked against his, her mouth and tongue warm and accepting, and her fingers doing devastating things to the back of his neck. He was excruciatingly aware this was Elizabeth he held, her warm, soft body pressed against him.

The heady, sweet taste of wine on Somers' lips intoxicated Elizabeth as if she had partaken as well. This was madness, insanity, but for one last time she wanted to hold him, to feel herself crushed against him. Just for a moment she wanted to pretend that all was beginning, not ending, that Somers, her rock and her strength, would always be there with his support. Oh, how she needed him!

It would be so easy, thought Somers, to ask her now. To end the burning agony. But it was too soon. He must know, with utter conviction, that she freely chose him. That marriage was not merely an escape from her brother. He needed the total certainly that she wanted him for the same reasons he wanted her. As she responded to his touch, he kept reminding himself of this, promising after only one more kiss he would release her. Just one more kiss . . .

With a groan of dismay, Somers finally tore his lips away. Breathing heavily, he strove to lighten the moment while he regained control over his raging desires.

"I fear I had more energy left than I thought," he teased, running his fingers lighty up and down her back. "I should have sent for Lady Worthing, after all. If Sally sleeps outside your door, shall you feel safe enough tonight?"

"I always feel safe with you, Somers."

He kissed her softly on the tip of her nose. "I promise I will be a perfect gentleman until my mama arrives."

Elizabeth hid her sense of disappointment. She had thought, that . . . that perhaps he felt more for her than pity—or lust. After such a spirited demonstration of his prowess at love-making, she had hoped for something more than an apology.

"In that case, as a perfect gentleman, you will allow me to retire to my chamber. Else I fear I will fall asleep in your drawing room."

Somers rose from the sofa, drawing Elizabeth to her feet. "I shall escort you to your room, my lady."

Elizabeth almost feared to go down to breakfast, knowing that her emotions lay far too close to the surface. She could not face Somers and keep her feelings hidden for long. She no longer had the strength. Lady Wentworth's early arrival was most welcome. In the presence of another, Elizabeth was able to joke and tease—in a subdued manner—and she hoped that her slight hesitations would be credited to her decision to leave William.

Lady Wentworth was sympathetic and supportive on that matter, and her presence filled Elizabeth with gratitude. There were too many unresolved issues between her and Somers to make him an effective source of consolation. In fact, his presence only increased her agitation, and she did what she could to stay away from him during the day.

Somers retreated to the library after the ladies had retired for the evening. Pouring himself another brandy, he settled himself into the worn leather chair at his desk and applied his thoughts to Elizabeth.

He still possessed no inkling of what she felt for him, beyond gratitude and exasperation at times. That passionate lovemaking in the drawing room last night . . . She had been tired and vulnerable. If he could be certain of her affection, he would not hesitate to ask her to marry him tomorrow. But in the back of his mind was a niggling suspicion that she was no more than fond of him. And foundness was not the emotion he wanted from the woman he wished to make his wife.

The sensible thing would be to allow her to return to Harcourt, and when she began to return to society after her six months of deep mourning, to gradually increase his attentions. But with a sudden pang he thought of all the other men who would be vying for her attentions as well. Impudent puppies, most of them, but there were still a few bachelors in the country who could offer her as much as he—or more. Why, among men of his own rank alone there was Knowlton or Penhurst. Not that he thought either man was interested in riveting himself for life, but neither had Somers been before he met Elizabeth.

No, he did not wish to wait until Christmas to declare himself. He had never been in the habit of waiting for anything he wanted, and he was not going to start now.

Mentally he listed all the advantages he could offer Elizabeth. Companionship, sexual intimacy, and if they were lucky, children. A restored position in society. An escape from her brother. But as he made his list, his frown increased.

In the end, it all came back to the present Duke of Harcourt. He wanted Elizabeth to remain at the family home; she wanted her independence. Did she want it so badly she would do anything to escape Harcourt? Even marry where there was not love?

The thought pained Somers. He had known from an early age that women were mainly interested in him for his position and wealth. And that had been fine at the time; he had sought no emotional attachments with any of them. But now he wanted to know, with utter certainty, that Elizabeth came to him out of want and desire and love, and not desperation. And there was only one thing he could do to ensure his piece of mind.

Elizabeth was surprised to find Lady Wentworth alone at the breakfast table the next morning.

"Goodness, you are up early today. Did Somers ask you to chaperon our morning meals too?"

"No, the London papers have been delivered and I am sadly behind in my reading." Lady Wentworth gestured at the pile beside her. "I fear I simply cannot abide the isolation of the country without them. Although," she added with a sigh as she flipped through the pages, "there is so little of interest in the summer."

Elizabeth knew she meant there was little gossip, with the town emptied of the aristocracy. The *on-dits* of the summer would travel more slowly, spread by letter rather than word of mouth or the daily papers.

Reaching for the *Chronicle*, Elizabeth decided to follow the countess's example. Ignoring the advertisements, Elizabeth scanned the news, passing quickly over the pages until she, too, reached the gossip. There was little in the reports of the comings and goings to interest her, until her eyes were caught by a short paragraph. "After returning only a short time ago from an extended residence on the continent, the restless Mr. B*rn*t is off again, this time to North America. Perhaps he will find adventure—or an heiress to repair his sadly tattered pockets. The bailiffs were disappointed at the departure of their quarry."

Elizabeth sat back in her chair. Could they mean Harry? A smile stole over her face at the thought. She had wished him to Jericho from the moment she had seen him in the park. North America was not Jericho, but it would do as well.

"An amusing item?" Lady Wentworth asked.

Elizabeth nodded briefly but did not explain. "Has Somers made any plans for us today?"

The countess looked at her uncertainly. "Did he not talk to you?"

"About what?"

The countess frowned. "He has been called away on a business matter. However, he assured me he will be back within a sennight."

"Oh." Elizabeth felt sadly deflated to learn he was gone—and without even telling her. Then she bravely shrugged. She knew this would happen eventually. It had been ever so kind of him to bring her here; she should not expect more. In a short while she would be back at Harcourt, without Somers. She would have to grow accustomed to his absence.

Yet she had not wanted it all to end so suddenly. She had hoped, while they were forced into close contact here at Kempton, that she might gain an inkling of his feelings for her. She needed to know if it was still only sympathy that guided his actions. She ached to know if those embraces in the drawing room had only been the act of a confirmed rake and not something more. But with Somers gone, she had no way to find out.

23

As Somers' absence stretched from one day into the next, Elizabeth's discouragement grew. As much as she had intellectually accepted Somer's eventual departure from her life, the reality of it was something different. She felt as if a part of her was missing, a teasing, joking part that made her feel alive and vibrant. With growing sadness, she realized how much she needed him. They had shared an experience that few people ever would, but it was not until he was gone that she discovered just how close they had become.

She was grateful for the countess's tactfulness. Ascribing Elizabeth's moodiness to the relinquishment of William, the woman did not probe. She talked when Elizabeth felt like chatting, sat silent when that was most helpful, and knew when to absent herself when Elizabeth needed solitude. In short, she was a godsend, and had it been only William who tore at Elizabeth's heart, it would have been enough. But she knew that she wanted, needed Somers, and knowing she would lose him as well made the pain nearly unbearable.

As each passing day unfolded, Elizabeth spent more and more time out-of-doors, riding across the estate with a groom in attendance or walking in the gardens on her own. But even that innocent occupation filled her with pain, for she could not look at the roses without thinking of that encounter with Somers and his clumsy proposal. She had been quite correct to refuse him. But, oh, how she wished he had asked for the right reasons so she could have said yes.

Lady Wentworth kept her own counsel, but she watched Elizabeth carefully, worried the girl would sink too deeply into despair. She had weathered all else in her life, but she seemed to be particularly overset now. Why had that detestable Somers chosen this time to run off? The countess swore she would forgive him half his sins if he returned soon.

Elizabeth was carefully snipping flowers to carry into the drawing room when a shadow fell across the rose bush. She turned and nearly dropped the clippers and the basket.

"Hello, Elizabeth." Somers reached out and took the basket from her hand. "Mama has put you to work, I see. You need to be more forceful with her, you know. Tell her you are not a servant to be ordered about."

Elizabeth did not exactly stare at him openmouthed, but she was quite unable to speak. He looked so wonderfully handsome as he stood there looking at her, an amused half-smile on his face. She knew she appeared a fool, but she was at a loss for words.

"Other people would, of course, say things like 'Hello, Somers' or 'Glad to see you, Somers.' That is what I like so much about you, Elizabeth. You never do the predictable."

"I was surprised to see you," she stated baldly, finding her tongue at last. "Did your business go well?"

"It depends," he replied. "It is not quite finished. I have hopes for a successful conclusion, but some additional negotiations are in order."

"Oh." He would be gone again, then.

Transferring the clippers from her hand to the basket, he offered her his arm and escorted her slowly back to the house. Depositing the flowers on the table inside the door, Somers led Elizabeth toward the library.

"I have some matters I need to discuss with you," he explained after he shut the door behind them, "and I think it is best done in here." Motioning for her to sit, he leaned against the desk, waiting for her to get settled.

Elizabeth looked at him with curious expectancy. He seemed nervous and on edge, a Somers she had never seen before. Were his business problems serious?

Turning quickly, Somers drew a sheaf of papers off his desk and handed them to Elizabeth.

"I know I ran off abruptly, but I did not wish to tell you where I was going until I knew if my mission would be successful. I have been at Harcourt," he explained with a hint of hesitation. "Your brother is a most amiable host."

"What! Whatever were you doing there?"

"Look at the papers."

She bent her head and thumbed through the pile on her lap. All dull legal documents, she noted, quickly scanning one and then the others. But the words written on them were not dull at all. In one stroke he had once again done so much for her and dashed all her hopes as well.

She finally raised her eyes to his. "You did this for me?" She could not keep a trace of disappointment from her voice.

"I could not bear the thought of you returning to unhappiness at Harcourt. This way"—he gestured at the papers—"you are free to do as you wish."

She looked again at the words before her eyes. The title to the cottage at Chedford. Her dowry money, invested in the percents and annuities, providing her a tidy annual income. All that she had wanted after her father's death. Once again, Somers had used his wicked powers of persuasion to give her what he thought she wanted. But this time, he was wrong. Yet how could she tell him?

"You are not pleased?"

"I am overwhelmed. What strange power do you have over the Harcourt men that you can talk them 'round to anything?"

"The famous Wentworth charm," he teased. "Seriously, I think even the duke was beginning to see the foolishness of forcing you to remain against your will. I fear he does not have the stomach for battle."

Elizabeth looked down again at the pile of papers in her lap. It was almost unnerving, to think she was free at last of her family.

"Your brother asked—I think he explains it in the letter—that you return to Harcourt first. I think there are some signatures and such to be taken care of. And he and the duchess both want to see you."

"Did you tell them about William?"

He nodded. "I mentioned schooling to him and he was amenable to sending him. The boy shall be able to take up any career he wishes—even the navy."

Elizabeth stood up quickly and walked to the windows, carefully keeping her back to Somers. He had been so wonderful, so generous with his time and help, neatly arranging a comfortable future for her. But this gentle dismissal hurt as deeply as if he had abruptly asked her to be gone.

"Elizabeth?" He could barely raise his voice above a whisper. He thought she would have been wild with elation at this turn. Yet she acted if he had dealt her a blow. Was she angered at his interference? Surely, with the rseults he had achieved, she would not belabor the point.

When she did not respond, he stepped closer, until he caught a tantalizing hint of her lavender fragrance. He had planned to wait until she was settled back at her cottage, with her independence restored, but impatience seized him. *She has a choice now. Take the chance.*

"There is one other matter," he began hesitantly. *The most important moment of his life; he must not bungle it again.*

"Yes?" She still stood with her back turned.

"It would involve your leaving Harcourt and Chedford. But I thought that perhaps you would not find Kempton too terrible a place to live."

Elizabeth froze at his words, afraid to even breathe. Was he . . . ?

"I wanted you to have a choice." He was nearly babbling now, but he had to get it all out. The words turmbled out in a rush. "I did not want you to think that it must be either me or Frederick. But knowing you can return to Chedford if you wish, that you will have an adequate income to live on, might you consider . . . would you ever . . ."

She had turned suddenly and was looking at him with such a curious look on her face that he could not think for a moment.

"I love you," he said, with a most frustrated, unloverlike expression on his face. "I want you to be my wife. I may not have truly felt that the last time I asked, but I mean it with all my heart now. Please, Elizabeth, say that you will." He took another step toward her, reaching out his hand.

The pleading tone in his voice wrenched Elizabeth's heart. Reaching out her own hand, she took his. "I had hoped you would ask me again," she said, smiling through the tears that misted in her eyes.

"You did?" The joy in his voice was unmistakable. "You will?"

She nodded and felt herself crushed against his chest in a bruising embrace that nearly forced the air from her lungs.

"Oh, Elizabeth, I was so worried you would say no. I thought you would accuse me of offering out of sympathy or politeness again."

"You are never polite," she mumbled against his waistcoat.

He tossed back his head and laughed. "You have spent far too much time in the company of my mother, I see. How shall I ever keep you apart after we wed? You two will conspire against me constantly."

"What would life be without a little danger?" She pulled away enough to lift her head and look into his eyes. She had seen so many emotions there—sympathy, exasperation, admiration, and frustration—that changed them from glacial blue to azure and back again. Now, filled as they were with love, she thought them the most glorious color of all.

He tilted her chin up, and his eyes lingered a moment on her deliciously shaped mouth before his lips descended on hers. A flooding warmth filled his body as he pulled her closer still.

"You do not know what a strain it was," he told her, later, when they cuddled cozily on the sofa, "keeping you at arm's length all those days we were together."

"I thought you did not want me."

"Want you? I was half out of my mind with wanting you. I am not accustomed to denying myself, I am ashamed to confess, and it is not an experience I care to repeat again."

"You expect me to be a complaisant wife?" She bristled with feigned indignation.

"No, no," he interjected hastily. "I know it sounds false,

coming from such an unscrupulous rake as myself, but I swear I will be the most faithful husband.'' He leered wickedly. ''I only meant I plan to say 'damn convention' and marry you in unseemly haste.''

''Oh,'' she replied with a delighted smile. ''I should like that.''

''I thought a spcial license would be best.'' At her agreement, he continued, ''Where do you wish to wed?''

She pondered. ''Harcourt, I think. If Frederick does not object.''

''He doesn't.''

''You told him you wanted to marry me?''

''It is the proper thing to do. He is the head of the family.''

''You are the last person in the world I would expect to observe the strict proprieties.''

''I warned you, I am a stickler for the proprieties. Is it not said that the strictest papa is a reformed rake?''

''And will you be a strict papa?''

''I promise you, our daughter will hate me.''

She sighed at the thought of children.

He looked at her with passion-filled eyes. ''And even if we are not so blessed,'' he whispered as he lowered his head for another kiss, ''it will not be for want of trying.''

When they had restored themselves to some semblance of order, they sat in each other's arms again, Elizabeth's head resting comfortably against his shoulder.

''Elizabeth?''

''Hmm?''

''There is something I must ask you.''

His serious tone startled her.

''What?''

''Do you snore?''

''What?''

''Do you snore? I wish to know, for it will decide whether we can share a bedroom or not. I cannot abide sleeping with a lady who snores.''

''You are a horrible person,'' she shrieked in laughter as she beat him about the head with a pillow. He quickly pinioned her arms and drew her to him, and Elizabeth lost all desire for anything but his kisses.

The Countess of Wentworth silently closed the library door she had just opened. Somers and Elizabeth were far too involved with each other to have even noticed her. A broad smile lit her face as she proceeded down the hallway, her mind already filled with thoughts of the grandchildren to come.

Epilogue

As the sun's rays marched across the grounds of Kempton with their welcoming warmth, the knots of people crowding the terrace slowly spread down the steps and out onto the lawn. Lords and ladies, relatives and friends, relaxed in the brilliant August sunshine. The excellent food from the earl's kitchen and the ample wine and spirits from his cellar pleased the crowd, already in a mellow mood from the happiness of the occasion.

Elizabeth sat to one side of the terrace, carefully rocking the sleeping babe in her arms. A smile tugged at the corners of her mouth as she looked at the miniature human she held, so resplendent in the frothy christening gown of imported Belgian lace.

How tiny babies were! How small they were, yet at the same time how perfect, with their tiny hands and fingers, feet and toes. The ideal size for cuddling and holding.

"Are you playing with dolls again?" Somers whispered teasingly in her ear.

She motioned for him to sit at her side.

"I cannot help it. She is such an angel."

"She is the oddest-looking angel I have ever seen. All small and wrinkled. At least she is asleep and not screaming her head off. I cannot abide screaming babies."

"That is the beauty of being a grandparent," she told him archly. "When she begins to scream, you simply hand her back to her mother."

"I do not remember that happening when her mother was

that age," he protested. "Seems like you always handed her to me."

She fixed him with a withering stare.

"Well, perhaps once or twice."

"It was a lovely christening, wasn't it? I am so glad your mother was feeling well enough to attend."

"Wild horses could not have kept her away." He grinned. "She will outlive us all."

"Do you think she looks more like Stephen or Caroline?"

"My mother?"

"The baby, you idiot."

Somers critically examined his granddaughter. "She looks like a baby to me."

"She has Stephen's chin, I think. But the rest is all Caroline. And she definitely has your ears."

"My ears? How can you tell?"

"She has those little dents right at the top . . . see?" She pointed out the tiny creases in the baby's ears. "Just like the ones here." She brushed back the graying hair, touching the identical feature on his left ear.

"I like it when you do that."

"What?"

"Touch my ear." He bent close and whispered something in hers.

"Somers!"

"It's our party, isn't it?" he grumbled. "We can leave when we wish."

"Grandparents do not behave in such an unseemly manner. Particularly in the middle of the afternoon."

"No one asked me if I wanted to be a grandparent."

"Yes, I noticed how displeased you were when you escorted your daughter down the aisle last year. I am sorry to say, it is a hazard of marriage."

"You mean we are going to be plagued with more of these if they all wed?" Somers face showed mock dismay. "That does it. No more weddings in this family. Court and Frederick will remain lifelong bachlors."

She laughed. "Frederick perhaps, since he is more interested in horses and dogs and those detestable snakes he keeps finding.

But Court? I am afraid he is already a shocking flirt at seventeen. He is most thoroughly your son.''

He rolled his eyes heavenward. "Haven't I noticed. Trained him well, I do say.''

Elizabeth gave him a light slap on the leg. "Don't encourage him, or you will end up stuck with some inspidid creature like Cynthia Wells for a daughter-in-law. He was making sheep's eyes at her all the time at church. I think I would as lief die as have to face that.''

"All right, I will speak to him and tell him to flirt as much as he likes but not to throw his heart over the fence until he meets a woman as beautiful and sensible and exciting as his mama.''

"Better.'' The fondness in her eyes spoke words.

"Do not look at me like that, or I will drag you away from the party.'' He leaned back with a sigh of regret, crossing his trousered legs. "I talked with Penhurst earlier; he thinks there is a very good chance he can get William a post.''

Elizabeth gazed past her husband to the tall, slim young man engaged in earnest conversation with the under secretary.

"That would be marvelous news,'' she said. "Not that Penhurst doesn't owe you a few favors.''

"Now he owes me one less.''

"I am glad we have been able to help William. It has made it less . . . less painful having to keep the secret.''

"It will be a good position, one with the potential for much more. An auspicious opportunity for a country vicar's son. If he has half of his mother's determination, he shall go far.''

Elizabeth gave a deep sigh of contentment as Somers' arm went around her shoulder and she settled back against him. "We have all been so very blessed,'' she said.

"None more than I,'' Somers replied. Stealing a kiss from his wife, he marveled at how she still had the power to turn his blood to fire after twenty-two years of marriage.

"Somers,'' Elizabeth protested weakly. "Our guests.''

"Damn the guests.'' Mindful of the sleeping child, he pulled Elizabeth closer. "Grandmother or no, you are the most

desirable woman on earth, and I do not care who knows it.''
Then to the mingled amusement and astonishment of the
assembled guests, he kissed Elizabeth in a most shocking
manner.